From Devon With Death

By Stephanie Austin

Dead in Devon

Dead on Dartmoor

From Devon With Death

The Dartmoor Murders

A Devon Night's Death

a&b

From Devon With Death

STEPHANIE AUSTIN

Allison & Busby Limited
11 Wardour Mews
London W1F 8AN
allisonandbusby.com

First published in Great Britain by Allison & Busby in 2020.
This paperback edition published by Allison & Busby in 2020.

A CIP catalogue record for this book is available from
the British Library.

10 9 8 7 6 5 4 3 2

ISBN 978-0-7490-2504-5

Typeset in 11/16 pt Sabon LT Pro by
Allison & Busby Ltd.

The paper used for this Allison & Busby publication
has been produced from trees that have been legally sourced
from well-managed and credibly certified forests.

Printed and bound by
CPI Group (UK) Ltd, Croydon, CR0 4YY

For Mum

CHAPTER ONE

The corpse under the bridge had been waiting a long time. You might say it had been waiting for me since I was the one who found it. It's become a habit of mine lately, discovering dead bodies. According to certain members of the local police force it's a nasty habit and I admit it's not something I'm proud of. I had stopped at the Old Mill Brewery, a stone building that stands alone on the ragged fringe of Ashburton, at a place where river and extinct railway come together, where muddy lanes take over from tarmac and a tangle of overgrown bushes hang over the water. Currently, the building is neither mill, nor brewery, but houses Rendells, the auctioneers. I'd come to eye up lots in their forthcoming auction, see if I could spot anything I might want to buy for my antique shop, *Old Nick's*.

I was reminded, as I parked White Van, that this area was about to lose its ramshackle charm: where a farm shop and agricultural suppliers once stood was now a muddy landscape patrolled by diggers, the site cleared to make way for a development of smart new houses. Lord knows the little town of Ashburton needs affordable housing, but I don't think I'm going to like it, and judging by the prices advertised on the hoarding, some people's idea of affordable is not quite the same as mine.

I watched men and machines at work beyond the wire fence. A few weeks before, a freakish blizzard swept across Dartmoor, forcing isolated hostelries to open their doors at midnight to trapped motorists, but the snow had cleared in hours and Christmas had been as mild and gentle as the baby in the manger. So far, January had been calm. Beyond a sugary dusting on the high tors we had seen no snow, only an occasional frost, and no rain to speak of. The men behind the wire could work unhindered. The trees were winter-bare but yellow catkins hung like lambs' tails on the riverside alders and people talked hopefully of an early spring.

I don't like mild weather in January. I don't trust it. Winter could lie in wait through the snowdrops, stay hidden until the primroses flower in the hedgerows, then sweep in like an icy blade and scythe the lot. Call me a cynic, but it's happened before.

I decided I would leave White Van parked where it was for a few minutes and nip up the lane behind St Andrew's churchyard to the church hall. A community market was held there weekly, which sometimes proved a source of interesting finds. I'd picked up a three-tier cake stand there last time, and I don't often get the opportunity to look around it. I'm usually busy with errands for Maisie on a Tuesday morning, but her return from a Christmas visit to her daughter up north had been delayed by a chest infection, so she didn't require my services.

I stopped to look over a low wall at the clear, fast-rushing water of the Ashburn. With no rain or icy meltwater to swell it, it was little more than a brook. It rose no higher than the pink wellies of two little girls who splashed about, giggling with delight, while their mother leant on an empty buggy and chatted to a friend on the little bridge above them.

I was lucky at the market, finding a small corner cupboard in pine not too heavy for me to lug back along the path without the bother of having to move the van. The deal was quickly struck and it was only a few minutes later that I was retracing my steps to the Old Mill Brewery.

I could still hear the toddlers playing in the water, but something seemed to be the matter. I could see them up ahead, the smaller girl clinging to her sister who was stretching her arms towards her mother on the bank, her pink wellies kicking up the water as she stamped up and down in panic. 'Get me out, Mummy!' she was screaming. 'Get me out!'

There were no piranhas in the Ashburn that I was aware of. The little girls didn't appear to be in any danger, but they were frightened. The bank was a steep drop and their mother, whose friend was no longer in sight, was pregnant and in no condition to rescue them. I lowered the pine cupboard to the ground for a moment to rest my arms and watched.

'How did you get down there?' she cried angrily, as if she'd only just noticed where they were. Tentatively, she began to edge down the bank towards the stepping stone that must have been their way down to the stream.

'Wait!' I called out. 'You'll hurt yourself if you slip. I'll get the children out.' I hoisted up the cupboard once again. 'Just let me put this in my van. I've got wellies in the back.' I nodded towards the car park. 'It'll only take me a moment.'

As I trotted off I heard her say, 'You'll just have to hang on, Hayley. The nice lady's going to help you.'

I returned, booted up, and easily dropped down to the stepping stone and into the water. 'What's the matter?' I asked the little girls who were now sobbing piteously.

I picked up the smaller one. She weighed no more than thistledown and I swung her easily onto the bank and held her up to the outstretched arms of her mother. Beneath her blue knitted jacket I could feel her heart racing in her little chest.

'Come here, baby!' her mother cooed. 'What are you keeping on about, Hayley?' she added more sharply to her sister in the water.

'There's a man,' she sobbed.

'What man?'

'A dead man,' she hiccupped breathily, 'in the water.'

'Don't be silly,' her mother told her. 'Course there isn't!'

I dropped back down into the stream and picked her up. She was heavier, more solid than her sister and she clung to me in fright, burying her face in my curls. 'Where?' I asked her softly. 'Where did you see this man?'

She pointed downstream to the low stone bridge, her face turned away. I carried her up the bank and set her down by her mother. 'Shall I look?' I asked. The little girl nodded silently, eyes shiny with tears.

'It's probably nothing,' I told her mother, who by this time was ruthlessly buckling the younger child into the buggy, 'but I'll check it out.'

'Oh, it's OK,' she told me. 'Don't bother!'

'We don't want them having nightmares, do we?'

She hesitated. I could tell she wanted to be off pushing the buggy and forget all about it. She sighed and shook her head, rolling her eyes towards heaven as if it was all too much.

I sloshed my way downstream towards the bridge. The water barely covered my ankles, yet I could feel its rushing force against my boots. It might be no more than a stream now, but the Ashburn had burst its banks and roared through the town like a lion in times gone by. I heard the mother speak again. 'You'd better not be making this up, Hayley!'

I rather hoped she was. For there was something in the dark water beneath the bridge, something caught. I could make out the roundness of a head, the long fork of a body. Fear knotted my stomach but as I stooped, forced to bend almost double beneath the low stone arch, something about this body struck me as wrong. It was floating. There was no weight, no substance to it.

It was a dummy, the body fashioned from a pair of workman's overalls, the face a mask. One arm had become stuck between two pointed stones, holding the body still, so that it bobbed obscenely on the surface of the shallow water. I prodded its free arm and something within it rustled. Cautiously, I squeezed. The sleeve was stuffed with packaging, with air-filled plastic bags. The whole corpse seemed to be stuffed with the same material; the head too round to be human, the hands crude balls bandaged into mittens.

I ducked out from under the bridge and stood up. 'It's all right!' I called out to the mother and her girls. 'It's not real.' I smiled up at Hayley, standing nervously on the bank. 'It's just a big doll,' I told her. 'You know, like the one they make for the bonfire on Fireworks Night? Like a scarecrow.'

Hayley stared at me, her fist to her mouth. 'It's not real?' she asked in a tiny voice.

'No. I expect some naughty children threw it in the river.'

'There you are, Hayley, what did I tell you?' her mother said. 'Now, thank the lady.'

'Thank you,' Hayley mumbled obediently as she was grabbed by the hand and dragged away.

I watched her mother as she trundled the buggy in front of her. 'I'm fine down here in the water,' I muttered. 'I can get out without any help, thanks for asking.'

Hayley turned around to look at me and I waved.

I waited until they were out of sight, then ducked back under the bridge. There were things about this dummy that were disturbing. I reached in my pocket for the small torch attached to my key ring and I shone it around. Its slender beam lit the wetly glistening stones above my head, the tiny ferns sprouting between them, and danced like silver glitter on the dark surface of the water.

I shone the light over the dummy, over the face. This was not some cheap Halloween mask bought in a joke shop, but fashioned from papier mâché, carefully painted and varnished to preserve it, the eyes wide and staring, the mouth gaping and ghastly. It was a face frozen in a scream. Where the head was joined to the body a bandage had been wound around to form a neck, and this was stained blood-red as if the throat had been cut. Pinned to the chest was a postcard protected by a clear plastic envelope. On the front was a coloured picture of some thatched cottages with *From Devon With Love* printed in red. I turned the envelope over. Scrawled on the back of the card in crude letters were the words: *Cutty Dyer Dun This.*

I crouched, the river swirling around my ankles, drips from the wet stones above me falling into my hair. Who would make such a grotesque object and put it into the water? Kids would seem to be the obvious culprits. But there was a strange sophistication about the way it had been put together, about the painting of the face, and despite the clumsy spelling of the note, the crudely scrawled letters, it looked like the work of an adult hand to me.

As I eased myself out from under the bridge, grateful to stand up straight, a familiar voice yelled my name. I nearly bashed my skull on the stone arch.

Two men were staring at me from the bank: one tall and silver-haired, a long pale blue scarf draped with artful carelessness around his shoulders; the other short and round, wearing spectacles and a fedora. Ricky and Morris must have come to take a look at the auction lots. They possessed a magpie's eye for beautiful things and Morris was always hoping to add to his teapot collection.

'What the bleedin' hell are you doing down there?' Ricky demanded.

'Are you all right, Juno?' Morris blinked anxiously over his gold-rimmed specs. 'Do you need a hand up?'

I could have got out by myself, but I accepted Ricky's proffered arm and let him haul me up the bank. 'Jesus, Juno!' he moaned.

'It's all muscle,' I told him.

'It's all cake!'

'Take no notice of him.' Morris stood on tiptoe to give me a kiss on the cheek. 'You're beautiful.'

'How did you know where I was?' I asked.

'We parked next to the old Van Blanc so we knew you were around here somewhere,' Ricky waved his fag hand at me, his fingers trailing smoke. 'We went inside Rendells and I shouted, "Has anyone here seen that tall bint with all the red hair . . . you know, looks like a Boudicca who's lost her chariot . . . ?"'

'He did no such thing,' Morris assured me, suppressing a little smile. He needn't have worried. Ricky would have to work harder than that to wind me up.

'What were you doing down there in the water, anyway?'

'Finding a dead body.'

Ricky raised his eyebrows. 'Again?'

'Don't you start. You sound like Inspector Ford!' I told them about the unpleasant effigy under the bridge and we agreed it was almost certainly the work of kids. 'Cutty Dyer!' Ricky shook his head and threw his cigarette butt on the ground causing Morris to tut and mutter beneath his breath. 'Kids!' he went on. 'They probably lobbed the thing over the fence by the skate park.'

'The fence is quite high there,' I pointed out. 'They must be good at lobbing.'

'They are. Haven't you seen that big tree in the park?' he asked. 'Festooned it is, hanging in trainers.'

Morris turned to more practical subjects. 'You haven't got a day free this week, have you, Juno? All the panto stuff has started to come back.'

'That's right,' Ricky nodded. 'We've got *Aladdin* and *Puss in Boots* piled up in the hall. We can hardly get in the kitchen.'

Before Christmas they'd supplied costumes for pantomimes all around the country. Now the costumes were coming back and they could use my help to unpack.

Before I inherited *Old Nick's* I used to give a lot more of my time to their costume hire business. Now time was something I didn't have so much of.

I agreed to go and help them out on Sunday. It was the only day I had free. Then they went into the auctioneers and I realised I'd better get a move on if I wasn't going to be late for my next job. But I still wasn't happy about the dummy in the water and wondered what to do about it. I wasn't convinced this was a childish prank. But if kids weren't responsible, then what kind of nutter would make such a thing? It was obviously intended to be seen, to disturb people, cause upset. That postcard was meant to be read by someone.

CHAPTER TWO

'And who, or what, is Cutty Dyer?' Elizabeth enquired when I finally made it back to the shop and told her the tale. She hasn't lived in Ashburton long and couldn't be expected to know. Cutty Dyer was a Dartmoor myth like Lady Howard's phantom coach, the Hairy Hands at Postbridge and superfast broadband. Since arriving a few months ago, she had obtained a part-time job as a receptionist at a doctor's surgery, but volunteered to look after *Old Nick's* on whatever afternoons she could manage. This was a great help to me, freed me up to carry on with what I still considered my real business as a Domestic Goddess. Inheriting an antique shop had never been part of my plan.

My return to the shop had been delayed. Chatting with Morris and Ricky had made me late arriving for my cleaning job. Then I made a visit to the local police station. To be honest, I wished I hadn't bothered.

'Depending on what you read,' I answered, leaning on

the counter, 'Cutty Dyer is a spirit or an ogre who lurks under the bridges of Ashburton, in particular King's Bridge, grabs children who stray near the water, cuts their throats and drinks their blood. He's also inclined to do the same thing to wandering drunks.'

Elizabeth raised a delicate eyebrow. 'Nasty!'

'And he's local. He only operates in Ashburton. You don't find tales of him anywhere else on Dartmoor.'

'Presumably, this tale was invented to deter children from straying too near the river?'

'Or deter people from getting drunk,' I suggested. 'There were a lot more pubs in Ashburton back in the day.'

'So what did the police have to say?'

I groaned. I regretted ever having reported finding the wretched dummy. I was curious about where it had been put into the water. The River Ashburn rises on Rippon Tor, comes down off the moor at Horridge Common and flows through the town, playing hide-and-seek as it slides sneakily under streets and behind buildings. In fact, it's perfectly possible to walk around the streets of Ashburton and not realise a river flows through the town at all. Many tourists do just that.

I grabbed a copy of the town guide, which, like a lot of shops, we keep on the counter for visitors, and opened it at the map, spreading it out so that Elizabeth could see. I placed my finger on a thin blue line. 'The river comes into the town here, at Great Bridge, flows past Crockerton Cottages, then slides around the back of the Victoria pub. It flows along Cleder Place—'

Elizabeth tapped an elegantly manicured nail on the map. 'That's the little green where there are picnic tables . . .'

'Yes, right on the bank . . . As I pointed out to the desk sergeant at the station this morning, it would be lovely for the visitors and holidaymakers if that thing had floated past while they were sat scoffing their sandwiches.'

'What did he say?'

'That we don't get picnickers in January.'

Elizabeth frowned, tracing the blue line with her finger. 'But you found this dummy at the other end of town. Do you really think it could have floated that far? It would have to have gone under this building here . . .'

I nodded. 'That's the town hall. The river flows right underneath. You can see it come out again if you stand on King's Bridge. It passes between the backs of these cottages and then it disappears again under West Street . . .' I sighed. 'You're right, that dummy would probably have got stuck underground. Ricky reckons someone threw it into the river as it passes the skate park, which means it would only have been carried a few yards downstream before it got stuck where I found it.'

'And it's still there?'

'The Laughing Policeman didn't seem to think anyone needed to remove it.' I had told him that a shower of rain could raise the water level enough to free this thing, float it downstream and cause a heart attack to some passing dog walker, but he didn't take me seriously. But then, he hadn't seen it. Quite obviously the work of kids, he'd said, but he'd make a note of the fact I'd reported it.

'Of course,' Elizabeth went on. '*Where* is not as important as *why* . . .'

'The postcard's the puzzling thing . . .'

The bell on the shop door jingled at that moment and a skinny schoolboy strolled in lugging a large schoolbag, which he immediately let slip from his shoulder to the floor.

He grinned at us, his fair hair sticking up in spikes.

'Hello, Olly!' I said.

He raised both arms above his head like a victorious boxer at the end of a bout and grinned. 'Guess who came top in the geography test?'

'Well done!'

'I'm glad all that work I forced you to do was worthwhile.' Elizabeth seemed determined to be unimpressed. She looked at her watch. 'I suppose you've come in for a lift home. It's not time to go yet,' she warned him. 'I'm not cashing up for another hour.'

'S'alright,' he shrugged, 'I got homework.'

'You heard of Cutty Dyer, Ol?' I asked.

'Yeh. Kids' stuff,' he sniffed dismissively. 'Nan used to believe in him though. Why?'

I told him about the effigy under the bridge and his nonchalance evaporated, his blue eyes growing round with excitement. 'Where is it? Can we go and have a look?'

Elizabeth smiled. 'Didn't you mention something about homework?'

He groaned but picked up his schoolbag. 'Can I use your kitchen table?' he asked.

As he passed Elizabeth's chair, he gave her a little pat on the shoulder. I was pleased to see this tiny gesture of affection. When I first met her, a few months before, Elizabeth was homeless and Olly, alone at fourteen, needed an adult to take care of him. I'd put the two of them together and felt responsible for their happiness. As he headed through the back door of the shop and up the stairs towards the kitchen, I called out to him, 'There's milk in the fridge and biscuits in the cupboard. Help yourself.'

'Ta!' he called back.

'Is everything working out?' I murmured as soon as he was out of earshot.

'Fine,' she assured me.

'No more trouble with bullying?' Olly was small for his age and had suffered quite a lot at school.

She smiled. 'I think we've put a stop to that.'

'You talked to his teachers?'

'Well, I did,' she said, looking a little evasive. 'But I also taught Olly some useful moves, if you know what I mean.'

I didn't quite. Elizabeth had been retired for years, a music teacher, or so she claimed. But I had the distinct impression that for some period in her youth she might have served in the armed services. As what, I wasn't sure. I know many women of her age but she's the only one who carries a pistol in her handbag. Or I assume she still does, I don't like to ask.

She deliberately changed the subject. 'We've had quite a profitable afternoon.'

Old Nick's always did well when she was on duty.

Sophie and Pat, who shared the manning of the shop with me in return for free selling space, did their best, but we'd all noticed that profits increased when Elizabeth was in charge. This might have been something to do with her elegant charm, the same charm with which she handled difficult patients in her job at the surgery, but I suspect had more to do with the steely determination that lurks in her grey eyes. Whatever her secret was, she'd sold a painting for Sophie and toys for Pat. She'd even sold a brooch and some paperbacks for me.

'You know, my dear, it's not my business,' she admonished softly, 'but you really ought to be charging those two girls some rent.'

'I know, but Pat's trying to raise money for the animal sanctuary and Sophie's as poor as a church rat.' I swept an arm around the bare shelves at the back of the shop. 'If only I had some takers for these empty units—'

'Well, you haven't at the moment, and those two should be paying you something.'

'I don't want to add to their troubles.'

'And what about your own troubles?' She indicated the pile of nasty brown envelopes, which lay unopened on the counter. 'When the new financial year starts, you're going to get a big demand for business rates.'

There are times, usually about three a week, when I wish Nick had never left me his shop.

'I know Sophie and Pat feel awkward about it,' she went on. 'At least charge them some commission on sales. They'd be quite happy, you know.'

'You've talked about it?' I was surprised and a little put out. They hadn't discussed it with me. Not yet. We had agreed last year that we'd review the situation at Christmas, but somehow, I had let the subject slide.

'They'd feel a lot more comfortable, and at least you'd be getting something.'

'I'll think about it,' I promised reluctantly. I got a similar lecture from Ricky and Morris almost every time I saw them. But I genuinely wanted to help Pat and Sophie. Without their support, and now Elizabeth's, I wouldn't be able to carry on the business I'd been engaged in before I met Nick. All right, I was only cleaning, and looking after dogs and grannies, but it had taken several years for me to build the business up and I was reluctant to let it go. I couldn't afford to, anyway. I couldn't live on the shop's paltry takings.

It was almost dark when I got home, the sun just dipping behind the hill I can see from my living-room window, the quirky huddled rooftops of the town below already lost in shadow. I opened the front door and breathed in deeply. Whatever was cooking in the kitchen of the flat downstairs smelt of garlic and chilli. Adam and Kate run a cafe and test out recipes at home. I am a very willing guinea pig, happy to put up with rattling windows, rumbling pipes and all the creaks and groans of the old ruin I rent from them in exchange for leftovers and free samples.

I climbed the stairs in happy expectation and sure enough, on the table outside my flat door lay some objects wrapped in foil and a large plastic container. The foil objects I quickly identified as vegetable samosas, but whatever was in the container sloshed about. I took the lid off. It looked like something scraped from the depths of a primeval lagoon, a deep muddy green. It smelt a bit that way too. I replaced the lid and trotted downstairs.

Kate answered to my knock and stood in the doorway, her dark plait hanging over one shoulder, a spatula in her hand. Her cheeks flushed from a hot stove, she looked particularly pretty.

'Thanks for the stuff,' I said.

'You're welcome,' she answered brightly.

'That . . . um . . . soup . . . is it?'

'Swamp,' she nodded. 'We call it swamp soup. It's delicious.'

'What's in it?' I asked, failing to keep the note of suspicion out of my voice.

'Sweet potato and kale, it's delicious,' she repeated, 'but for some reason, it doesn't sell well.'

When you think about some of the things that can be found lurking in a swamp, perhaps that's not surprising, but I decided it would be churlish not to give it a go.

'Sweet potato and kale,' I repeated. 'Thanks. Right.'

'And onion, of course,' she called out as I climbed the stairs, 'and garlic and chilli.'

'Of course,' I called back.

'Let me know what you think!'

'I will,' I promised, as I closed the door.

Kate is not usually wrong about food, and she wasn't

on this occasion. The swamp soup tasted delicious; unusual but delicious.

After I'd downed a bowlful and a couple of samosas, I looked on the Internet to see what else I could discover about Cutty Dyer. He's not as widely known as some other Dartmoor legends, although stories of his bloodthirsty activities in Ashburton date back to the seventeenth century. I found information about him on several websites, although there are no stories of his being active recently. I doubt if many kids in the town have ever heard of him, which made the message on the postcard attached to the effigy even weirder. But the old people, like Maisie and Olly's Nan were brought up on scare stories about what might happen to them if they strayed too near the river at night.

I didn't really find out anything I didn't already know, so after a while I sat down on the sofa with my diary, making sure I had cleared it completely for the end of the week. Mrs Berkeley-Smythe was coming home from her latest cruise and would need all of my attention. She was the client I have worked for the longest and who I've seen the least, due to her determination to avoid living on dry land as much as possible. She spent most of her life on cruise ships and paid me to look after her house while she was away. Most of the time this meant clearing the junk mail, watering her house plants and keeping her garden tidy, but before she came home from a cruise, I always gave the whole place a proper spring clean. I'd already vacuumed, dusted, made up the bed and polished the hundred wretched horse-brasses surrounding her inglenook fireplace. Tomorrow I would put the heating on to warm the house through, reinstate the fridge and freezer and get in essential supplies – coffee, ice cream and several bottles of sherry. Mrs B-S was a living testament to what can be achieved on a diet of sugar, caffeine and alcohol. I always looked forward to her coming home and just as much to her going away again, which was usually after a few weeks. The longest period I have known her stay ashore was three months when she underwent surgery for a hip replacement. When she arrived home she would need me to help her unpack her cases and drive her to various appointments with her accountants and doctors. I always tried to clear the diary of everything else and give her two complete days. All other things went on hold except for my morning dog walking. This was not affected by Mrs Berkeley-Smythe: she was not an early riser.

This time the task of diary clearing had been made easier by Maisie's continued absence and Elizabeth's help in the shop. I thought about our conversation earlier and was just beginning to ponder gloomily how I was going to manage to pay the bills when I was distracted by the phone ringing. The caller didn't bother to identify himself, but I could tell from the flat, northern vowels who the voice belonged to. 'The rumour is that now you've run out of dead bodies to find, you've started making your own.'

'I'm going to kill that bloody desk sergeant.'

Detective Constable Dean Collins chuckled down the phone.

My cheeks flamed with a mixture of anger and embarrassment. 'Now I suppose I'm a laughing stock at Ashburton police station.'

'Only amongst the uniforms,' he assured me. 'Here at Serious Crimes, you're a legend.'

I decided to change the subject. 'How is baby Alice?'

'Beautiful.'

'And Gemma?'

'Well. Actually . . .' he cleared his throat self-consciously, 'she's expecting again.'

'Blimey! You don't mess about, do you?' I said. 'It was only a few months ago you were lying at death's door.'

'Yeah, and I'd have been through the bloody door if it hadn't been for you.'

I felt my cheeks reigniting. 'Did you actually call about something?' I demanded.

'Yes. This effigy thing. Tell me about it.'

I gave him all the details and he said he'd go down to the bridge next morning and take a look. 'Someone's got a peculiar sense of humour. Probably best not to let the thing float around. I'll get it put away somewhere.'

I was glad someone in the police force was prepared to take it even slightly seriously. We chatted for a little longer and then he rang off. I lay back and closed my eyes, shrieking as Bill landed with all four paws on my stomach. 'Foul cat!'

He interpreted this as a form of endearment and began treading up and down on my ribcage, purring loudly. 'Why don't you go downstairs and live in your own flat?' I demanded, unable to resist stroking his black velvet head. He gazed at me in rapture from his one green eye and nuzzled his cheek against my hand. 'My landlords do not approve of our affair,' I reproved him as his purr changed down to a more passionate gear. 'Truth is, they're jealous.'

The phone rang again then, disobliging Bill as I had to lean forward to pick it up.

'Juno Browne?' The voice that asked was bright, breathy and Welsh. 'This is Sandy Thomas, *Dartmoor Gazette*.'

'And what can I do for you?' I asked, with all the enthusiasm of someone who has been misquoted and inaccurately reported before.

'We'd just like a few words from you about the Cutty Dyer incident before we go to press.'

'How do you know about that?'

'Oh, we can't reveal our sources,' she answered piously.

Surely that sergeant at the police station wouldn't have told the local newspaper about what I'd found? But of course, I'd told Ricky and Morris. They'd probably repeated my story to everyone they met in the auction house. Any one of them could have phoned the local rag. 'It wasn't an incident,' I told her crossly. 'It was just a dummy, probably a leftover from Hallowe'en or Fireworks Night and thrown in the river by children.'

'But you reported it to the police.'

'It was quite . . . realistic,' I admitted reluctantly, 'gruesome, and plausible enough to give someone a shock if they saw it in the water.'

I could hear her tapping away on her keyboard at the end of the phone, her fingertips on fire. The *Dartmoor Gazette* was a weekly paper and usually there was more than enough drama in the everyday lives of folk on Dartmoor to keep its pages filled. It must be a thin week for news if my finding a Guy Fawkes dummy in a stream was needed to make headlines.

'So, how many dead bodies is that you've discovered now?' she asked.

I gritted my teeth. 'It wasn't a dead body!' I insisted.

'No, no, nooo . . .' she agreed soothingly, 'but how many is it?'

'Look, each one of those bodies belonged to a person who was murdered,' I said angrily. 'Have you any idea how it feels to discover someone—?'

'No,' she interrupted, breathy with excitement, 'but I'm sure our readers would love to know.'

The only reason I didn't fling the phone down at that moment was because I was gripping it so hard I couldn't let go. I sighed loudly.

'So, how many is it?' she asked again.

'Just the three,' I muttered.

'Well, that's three more than most people, isn't it?' she trilled brightly, and rang off.

I wished at that moment I could have made it four.

CHAPTER THREE

At least I hadn't made the front page. That dubious honour was reserved for sheep rustlers and a nasty pile-up on the A30 outside Bodmin. But as I opened up the dratted rag I had purchased in the newsagent next morning, I found a headline blaring at me on page two: *Jinxed Juno Discovers Fourth Corpse*. There was even a photograph of me, looking dishevelled and dreadful and clearly startled by the flash from a camera shoved in my face. I had no memory of it being taken but there was a police officer in the background, so I imagine it was following an arrest. I read the first few words of the article before I could take no more, screwed the entire paper into a ball and lobbed it into the nearest bin.

I strode up North Street, simmering. I was vaguely aware of someone on the opposite pavement scurrying along, trying to catch up with me, calling my name, but didn't pay enough attention to the eager, bobbing figure in the flapping blue coat until she had crossed the road and it was too late to take evasive action. Jessie Mole was standing on the pavement in front of me, effectively blocking my way, her face peering up into mine. Her pale blue eyes were staring and she was close, much too close.

'You're that Juno Browne,' she breathed, grinning. 'I've seen you in the paper!'

On a good day, Jessie Mole is a menace. She's the sort of person that makes you duck into shops when you see her coming and hope to God she doesn't follow you inside. It's not just that she has no concept of personal space or other people's boundaries, and no idea when a conversation has ended and anyone with half a brain would realise it's time to say goodbye, she has a voracious greed for gossip about other people's lives that is genuinely off-putting. It's something to do with the way she tries to lock eye contact with you, as if she's trying to drain your brain through your eyeballs and suck out your soul. And she's odd: she wears ankle socks and a bow in her hair, although she must be every day of fifty. Right now she seemed in the grip of a feeding frenzy. 'What did it look like, that body?' She had clutched my arm and was not the slightest bit abashed when I very deliberately removed her hand from my sleeve. 'Did it look like a real one?' she carried on excitedly. 'You know what they look like, don't you? You're always finding bodies.'

Her face was so close to mine it was almost out of focus. I stepped back and she took another pace towards me. 'I don't want to talk about it, Jessie,' I said firmly, sidestepping around her. 'Goodbye.'

She struggled to keep up with me as I quickened my pace. 'It says in the paper Cutty Dyer did it,' she carried on remorselessly. 'Did it have its throat cut?' I knew she couldn't keep up for long. She had been lame since childhood and repeated operations had failed to correct the fault. 'Was there a lot of blood?' she called after me as I swung around the corner and out of sight.

By the time I reached *Old Nick's*, steam must have been rising from my hair. One look at my face as I kicked open the door of the shop was enough to convince Sophie, sitting quietly at her worktable, not to mention the newspaper I could see lying on the counter. She gazed at me, her dark eyes huge, a paintbrush poised in one hand. 'Hell's teeth!' she swore softly.

'No, just Jessie Mole. If she follows me in here, I'll kill her.'

Sophie laid her paintbrush down. 'I don't think she'll dare.'

Jessie is a particular nuisance in shops. She tries to lock shopkeepers in a stranglehold of gossip, oblivious of the customers they might be trying to serve. As Ashburton is a small place and the number of shops is limited, it hasn't taken her long to exhaust the patience of the entire shopkeeping community.

'She came in here the other day,' Sophie said,

'hanging around, looking over my shoulder when I was trying to paint—'

'When was this?' I asked.

She shrugged. 'One day last week,' she responded vaguely. 'You weren't here. Anyway, I was longing for her to leave when Pat came in and got rid of her. She just ordered her out, said she wasn't prepared to put up with her nonsense.'

'Good for Pat.'

'I don't think she means any harm – Jessie, I mean,' Sophie added, picking up her brush and surveying the painting in progress.

'Maybe not,' I conceded, 'but she puts customers off.' I'd seen many people execute a last-minute swerve and change course when they'd spotted Jessie through a shop window.

'She is creepy,' Sophie admitted.

I sat down heavily on a stool and sighed. 'I wish I'd never mentioned that effing dummy to the police.'

'You did the right thing,' she said, gazing at me solemnly. She laid down her paintbrush for a second time. 'Tea?' she volunteered sympathetically. 'Coffee?'

I glanced at my watch. 'I'll make it. I just popped in to check all was well. I'm going up to Mrs Berkeley-Smythe's place to switch on her heating, and then I'm off up to the Brownlows' house. They've got visitors coming to stay and their spare bedroom needs a good going-over. But I've got time for coffee.'

I climbed the stairs to the kitchen above, in what used

to be Old Nick's flat, and flipped the switch on the kettle. I got an unflattering view of my reflection in its shiny surface and detoured to the bathroom to see if things were as bad as they looked. Raking my fingers through a tangled mass of red curls did not make the frowning apparition in the mirror look any tidier. I had taken five dogs for a walk on the moor that morning, I reminded myself, and more or less sprinted to get away from Jessie Mole, so no wonder I looked a mess. Not that I would look much different if I hadn't.

On my way back to the kitchen I paused on the landing. There was a tiny framed photograph on the wall, a picture that probably no one but me ever stopped to look at. Old Nick stared at me from twinkling eyes. Old Nick, for whom I had worked just a few months and who had rewarded me on his death by leaving me the building in which I now stood.

'Bastard,' I whispered softly, and swore I heard him chuckle.

On my way back from the Brownlows' house, I called in at the information centre behind the town hall. I wanted to send a card to an old college friend. I prefer cards with original photos of Dartmoor and knew there was a rack full of them there, together with local maps and books. I found postcards identical to the one attached to the dummy: *From Devon With Love* written in red and a picture of thatched cottages. There was a range of cards with the same wording but different pictures: Widecombe Fair, Dartmoor ponies, or a cream tea laid out on a lacy tablecloth – all a bit naff, if you ask me. I selected a card with a picture of a twisted thorn tree standing alone in the bleak landscape of the moor, almost bent double by a cruel wind, dark clouds piling up for a storm in the sky behind it – much more my sort of thing.

I walked the dogs by the river next morning, through misty woods. The winter trees were leafless, their branches bare, the forest floor like old owl feathers speckled with greys and browns as autumn leaves decayed. Yet there was the green on the ivy-tangled trunks and every branch wore a velvet coat of emerald moss. The sun broke through the mist for a moment and the water in the river flashed silver, pouring like a layer of glass between stepping stones. The Tribe – the five dogs that I walked on weekday mornings – splashed happily in the shallows, snapping at the shadows of little fish, all except for Sally the ancient black Labrador who never left my side, happy to watch the younger dogs, her tail slowly wagging, and barking occasionally.

I couldn't look at the water without remembering that damned dummy. Such an odd, strange thing. Just thinking about it filled me with a sense of unease, like this quiet, still January waiting for winter to come. I felt as if I was holding my breath, waiting for an axe to fall.

After a long circular walk, I deposited the canines in their respective homes and popped back to the flat to change my muddy boots. Then I drove up to Stapledon Lane to await the arrival of Mrs Chloe Berkeley-Smythe. As it turned out, she got there before me.

Stapledon Lane is where the police station and old courthouse used to stand. Now, these buildings are desirable residences. No less desirable is the handsome stone cottage belonging to Mrs Berkeley-Smythe, situated at the turn of the lane, commanding a fine view of the town below and the hills above. But its narrow front door and the two steep steps leading up to it make it less than ideal for anyone attempting to lug large suitcases into its cramped hall. A limousine from Southampton and its driver come as part of Mrs B-S's cruising package and as I arrived the poor man was trying to drag a suitcase the size of a sofa up the steps without getting it wedged in the front door. There's an art to it, as I know.

Mrs B-S was standing by the car, her refined foghorn voice blasting down the lane.

'I'm so sorry, I can't possibly help you, I've got a bad back. I'm so sorry.'

I called out to her and waved.

'Juno, my dear!' she cried as I approached, and enveloped me in an embrace that smelt of hairspray, face powder and high-powered perfume. 'I can't wait to get inside. I'm exhausted, utterly exhausted.' I agreed that being driven from Southampton in the back of a limousine must be an exhausting experience. 'Could you help poor Charles here?' she asked. 'Would you mind?'

Charles and I had met before. He was Chloe's favourite driver and she always requested him, the poor sod. Between the two of us we managed to squeeze four large suitcases and three vanity cases into the cottage, allowing Chloe to flutter through into the living room, declaring, 'I must lie down. I really must lie down.'

I paid Charles a handsome tip from her weighty leather purse and allowed the poor man to escape. He probably needed a lie down himself after driving her all the way to Ashburton, although he assured me, with a broad wink, that Chloe usually slept all the way after the first few miles. No wonder she was so exhausted. I noticed that she had managed to totter as far as the sherry before sinking into the cushions of the sofa. She lay there now, still wearing her coat, eyes closed, one heavily ringed hand hanging over the edge as if she were lying in a punt and trailing her fingers in the water.

'Good trip?' I asked.

'Wonderful!' she sighed. 'But whenever I come back here and look around my darling little cottage, I wonder why I leave.'

I smiled. 'You say that every time. You usually last about three days before you're planning your next trip . . . or have you got something planned already?'

'Nothing . . . well, only Cyprus . . . but that's weeks away.' She opened her eyes. 'Come with me!' she begged.

'No, thanks.'

'I'd pay.'

'You'd have to, and it's very kind of you to keep offering, but I can't – really.'

'Well, I'm going to have to stop cruising soon,' she moaned. 'I shall run out of money.'

'You say that every time too.'

'Do I?' She surveyed me from beneath heavy eyelids shaded a delicate mauve. 'Why aren't you married? Or living in glorious sin with some sexy man somewhere? It's such a waste . . . You're not gay, are you, dear? You've never struck me that way.'

'No, I'm not gay,' I assured her. 'Now, I've done your shopping. There's milk, cream, prawns and pâté in the fridge, and your favourite coffee ice cream in the freezer.'

'You are wonderful,' she sighed.

I pointed out three piles of post on her coffee table. 'Hospital appointments in the first pile . . . you need to look at those . . . bills in the middle pile . . . and in this one' – I pointed to the largest pile, more of a stack, really – 'is the brochures you've ordered.' There were also several parcels under the table, items ordered by Mrs B-S before she went afloat and taken in during her absence by her long-suffering neighbour.

Chloe barely glanced at them. 'I shall need to go to the bank.'

'That's fine. It's a bank day tomorrow.' Ashburton no longer has a bank of its own, but two of the high street banks provide a mobile service, each visiting once a week, their immense wagons taking up three spaces in the town hall car park. 'I'll take you there in the morning,' I promised. 'Now I'll make a start on the unpacking.'

'Oh, it's too exhausting!' she complained. 'Sit and have a sherry.'

'I'll have one later.'

'Well, you wouldn't pour me another, would you?' She looked around vaguely as if she couldn't remember where the bottle was. 'And pass me the remote. Oh, you are an angel!'

As I left the room, the television blared into life and I heard her flicking through the channels until she found the one she wanted: the shopping channel. 'There's a present for you in one of the cases,' she called out. 'I can't remember which one, but you'll find it.'

'It would help if I knew what I was looking for,' I called back.

Chloe laughed. 'I can't remember that, either. What on earth did I get you? Oh, I expect you'll know it when you see it.'

Her cases were beautifully packed, each garment carefully folded, not by Chloe but by some member of cabin staff, the most delicate items wrapped in tissue paper. I began unpacking, sorting and selecting clothes for the washing machine and the dry-cleaners, and hanging up those that could be returned to the wardrobes. This was a process that would take the rest of the day and most of the next as well. All this unpacking had to be done in the hallway as the cases were too heavy to lug upstairs. Once unpacked, and I managed to empty two that day, they could be stored in a spare bedroom, a room devoted entirely to shoe racks and sets of matching luggage. During the unpacking I came across a silk pashmina in mint green, which I decided wasn't Mrs B-S's shade at all.

Hoping that this might be mine I went into the living room to check. But Chloe was snoring gently in front of the shopping channel, a clutch of partly opened envelopes scattered on her ample bosom and spilling onto the floor. I decided not to disturb her.

CHAPTER FOUR

'I am doing a wonderful job of spending the children's inheritance,' she announced to the world in general next morning as she descended the steps from the mobile bank where she had spent the last half hour. 'It serves them right. I don't know what I've done to deserve such beastly children . . . well, yes, I do,' she added, laughing, 'I've always done precisely as I chose. I don't see why one should put one's children first, do you? I always brought them up exactly as I did the dogs. But I shall have to slow down soon, start downgrading to a cheaper cabin . . .'

'Where do want to go next?' I slipped in as Chloe drew breath.

'Well, I thought the Adriatic . . . the Croatian Islands . . . Oh, you mean *now*?'

I laughed. 'Yes, I mean, where do you want to go *now*?'

'Well, you know, I'm absolutely exhausted. I shall die soon if I don't have a coffee. But I thought first we might visit that nice little boutique around the corner. You know, you must stop me spending money. And there's that pretty little place that sells the handmade soaps and bath things, so convenient, it being next door.'

I was only half listening to her. We were standing on the bridge outside the town hall: King's Bridge, the very bridge where, according to legend, Cutty Dyer was most likely to be found lurking. By leaning over the wall, I could watch the river rushing out from under the civic building, a brief glimpse before it disappeared beneath the bridge we were standing on. I couldn't help wondering about that damned dummy being swept along.

An hour later, I managed to steer Chloe and several large carrier bags through the door of the Old Library Cafe.

'I wish you'd let me buy you those lovely silk culottes,' she was announcing as I forced her through the door, her foghorn voice drawing the attention of everyone in the place. It was packed, there were no free tables.

'It doesn't look as if there's anywhere to sit,' I murmured.

'No, here's a place!' she cried. There was a man sitting alone at a table for four, making use of the free Wi-Fi, tapping away at a laptop, the table spread with papers. 'He really can't expect to occupy a table for four,' she whispered loudly, sliding behind the table and effectively trapping him in his seat as she placed all her shopping on top of his paperwork and sat down heavily on the bench next to him. He glowered at her from behind heavily framed spectacles and then flicked an irritated glance at me as I took the seat opposite.

'I'm sorry,' I said, picking the offending shopping bags off the table and sliding them onto the floor beneath.

He stopped working and for a moment closed his eyes, pinching the bridge of his nose and suppressing a sigh, like a man at the end of his tether. I got the feeling that he'd been tapping away for hours and that the cafe had gradually filled up around him. Then he snapped the laptop shut and began gathering up his notes from the table. Chloe deliberately ignored him and carried on talking to me. 'Do let me give you one of these bath bombs I've just bought,' she prattled on gaily, rummaging in one of the bags and producing a scented ball wrapped in a net bag. 'You just pop it in the bathwater and it whizzes about all over the place. Such fun!'

The man, meanwhile, had stood up – he was very tall – and was trying to extricate himself from the corner by squeezing his body between the table and the wall. He dropped half his papers and I scrabbled to help him pick them up. I felt torn, sorry for a poor man minding his own business and being swept up by Hurricane Chloe, and cross at his unsmiling irritation. After all, he couldn't expect to hog the entire table when there was nowhere else for us to sit. He snatched a piece of paper I was offering him. 'Thank you,' he muttered savagely, and stomped out.

'Well, what a horribly rude man!' Chloe exclaimed. I'm sure he heard. She has a very poor grasp of when a person is out of earshot and unwittingly offends people all the time. I still cringe at the memory of '*What a very plain baby!*'

'Oh look, look!' she cried, pointing at the floor under the table. 'There's another of his bits of paper! You'd better run after him, Juno, and give it back to him.'

'Mine's a cappuccino,' I told her as I scraped my chair back from the table and hurried after him. I could see him across the road, already at his car, the tailgate up, putting his things away. 'Excuse me,' I yelled at his back. 'Hello? You dropped this.'

He turned around, scowling. He had taken off the heavily framed specs and I realised he was younger than I thought. He had a lean, hawk-like face beneath untidy dark hair. He wasn't bad-looking in a sort of angry bird-of-prey way.

I held out the piece of paper. 'You dropped this.'

He took it from me and glanced at it. 'I would have been lost without this,' he admitted and for a moment he smiled. 'Thank you.' He looked at me and put his head on one side, considering. 'I've seen you before somewhere, haven't I?'

Dratted bloody Gazette. 'I don't think so. Anyway,' I added as I turned away, 'my coffee's getting cold.'

'I could buy you another.'

I stopped, turned back to him. 'No, thanks, I'm with a client.'

He raised a dark eyebrow. 'Client?' he repeated. 'I thought she was your mother.'

'My mother?'

He smiled. 'Well, what kind of client offers to buy you silk culottes?'

'Smartass,' I muttered as I strode back down the car park towards the cafe door.

Mrs Berkeley-Smythe insisted on lunch after she had perused the cafe menu and so it was afternoon by the time we got back to Stapledon Lane. I returned to unpacking her luggage while she sorted through her morning's shopping, trying to remember what she'd bought and, in some cases, why. Suddenly she called out to me from the living room in a tone urgent enough to bring me in from the hall.

'Where did this come from?' She held up a torn envelope, thickly stuffed with papers.

'Who on earth is Daniel Thorncroft?' she asked, reading the name scrawled in black letters on the front.

'Where did you find it?'

'In one of my shopping bags,' she responded. 'It must belong to that objectionable man in the cafe this morning. It must have slid in there when he dropped his papers.' Before I could stop her, she had picked out a letter and unfolded it.

'That might be private . . .' I began, but it was too late.

'Dear Mr Thorncroft,' she read aloud, 'first may I express my condolences on the death of your aunt,

Mrs Selena Harrington. Mrs Harrington was a valued client of Langley Brown . . . oh, it's from his solicitor.' Interest lost, she folded the letter and began trying to stuff it back in the envelope. 'You'll have to take it back to him.'

'Is there an address?'

She glanced at the envelope. 'Moorview Farm.'

'Well, I haven't a clue where that is. I'll take it back to the cafe and leave it there. He'll probably realise that's where he lost it and go back for it.'

But by the time I got back to the cafe it had closed for the afternoon. I didn't feel I could just shove the envelope under the door without explanation, and anyway, it was too thick.

Grumbling, I got back into White Van and flung the envelope on the seat beside me. Then, curious, I picked it up to see what else might be inside. I shook out the contents and groaned. Amongst other papers was a thick wad of fifty-pound notes held in a rubber band. I counted. It was a lot of money.

I phoned Chloe, asked her to check in all her carrier bags that there were no loose fifty-pound notes floating around. I wanted to be sure that none of this money was missing before I returned it. I couldn't expect anyone else to assume responsibility for it. I was going to have to take it back to him myself.

Before I went home, I decided to check in at the shop. Sophie was on duty, still working on her painting, primroses in a winter woodland, and Pat was there too, arranging some new stock she had just brought in. I sensed a bit of an atmosphere.

'Busy day?' I asked.

'If you mean customers, I'm afraid not,' Sophie said sadly. 'We've had a few people in through the door but none of them bought anything . . . Oh, and Jessie Mole came in.'

I looked at Pat. 'I thought you'd seen her off.'

'Well, I have now,' she muttered angrily. 'I'm not putting up with any nonsense from the likes of her.' Pat was a good, kind-hearted woman who ran an animal sanctuary, Honeysuckle Farm, with her sister and brother-in-law, but she was blunt and plain-speaking and not a person I'd have wanted to cross. She was clearly angry and upset.

'What happened?' I asked. 'What did she say?' Sophie was shaking her head, flashing her dark eyes at me. She laid a warning finger against her lips.

'Nothing.' A hectic blush had risen up Pat's neck and her eyes shone with tears. 'Nothing!' she repeated, stomped to the door and went out. I gazed after her in surprise and then at Sophie, who was puffing out her cheeks in a sigh.

I'd never known Pat behave like that before. 'I'd better go after her.'

'No, I wouldn't, honestly,' she said earnestly. 'I think she's best left.'

'What happened?'

Sophie frowned. 'Jessie must have followed Pat here. She went straight up to her and started whispering. I don't know what she said but Pat got really angry, grabbed her by the arm and marched her out of the shop. Then they were outside in the lane, arguing.'

'And you couldn't hear what they were saying?'

'Well, I heard something,' she admitted reluctantly, 'but I'm not sure if I got it right.' She hesitated. 'Jailbird. I'm sure Jessie said the word "jailbird". Well, Pat really lost it and started slapping her. Jessie ran off. Pat came back in and has hardly said a word since. I asked her if she was all right, obviously, but she said she didn't want to talk about it.'

'Perhaps when she's calmed down a bit . . .' I mused. 'She's opening up tomorrow morning, isn't she? It's Saturday, so I won't have to walk the dogs. I'll pop in here and see her first thing.'

'Do you fancy coming down to the arts centre this evening?' Sophie asked. 'I'm going with Mum. There's a folk group on tonight: Vixen Tor, they play music inspired by the moor.'

I had a horrible vision of bearded men in hairy jumpers, their fingers jammed in their ears, intoning dirges about tin mines, but Sophie assured me the group contained an old schoolgirl friend of hers who was a demon fiddler, and it should be well worth a visit. I still hesitated. My priority ought to be to locate Mr Daniel Thorncroft and give him back his money. I could take the envelope to the police station and leave it there, but for some reason I felt compelled to return it personally. But first I would need to consult a map to find out where Moorview Farm was, and the place might not be easy to find in the dark. The demon fiddler won out. Mr Thorncroft would have to wait.

CHAPTER FIVE

I was late getting up in the morning, partly because I knew I didn't have to walk the Tribe, but also because the cider I'd consumed along with the diddly-diddly fiddly music at the folk concert the night before meant that I awoke a little muzzy-headed.

Pat had already opened up when I arrived at *Old Nick's* and was posting up pictures of the latest arrivals at Honeysuckle Farm in need of loving homes. She was always adding pictures of needy waifs to the wall behind her unit. Sadly, she very rarely took any pictures down. I couldn't help noticing she was wearing a particularly hideous crocheted cardigan this morning. She knitted the most beautiful things for the shop, but the clothes she made for herself were ghastly, all colours, as if she was using up her odd bits of wool.

I thought I might as well get straight to the point. 'I was worried about you yesterday, Pat. You seemed upset.'

'I shouldn't have lost my temper,' she responded, looking uncomfortable, 'not with the likes of Jessie Mole. She ain't worth it.'

'Do you want to tell me what it was about?'

'Well . . .' she began reluctantly. 'It's Luke, our Ken's boy.'

Ken was married to Pat's sister. I knew Sue didn't have any children but was vaguely aware that Ken had been married before. 'I didn't know Ken had a son.'

'No, Luke's his nephew. Well, we tell people he's been working away, but truth is, he's not long out of prison.' Pat flicked me a glance, as if she was checking on my reaction to this before she went any further. 'It was manslaughter. He got in a fight in a pub . . . he was just unlucky. He's a shy lad,' she went on, 'not the sort to pick a fight – he wouldn't ever mean to hurt anyone. He had a terrible time in that prison, got beaten up . . . Anyway, somehow that Jessie Mole got wind of the fact he's been inside. Well, the lad's trying to make a fresh start. The last thing he needs is her gossiping about him all over Ashburton. She's got nothing but a mouth full of spite—'

'Is he living here now?' I asked.

'He's staying with us at the farm. He's got no one else. Since he's come out he's been working for a firm hedge-laying up on the moor. Course, he helps out with the animals, but he wants to start his own gardening business. That's what he used to do before he went inside. Trouble is, he's got no confidence now. We got him these business cards made.' She dug one out of her cardigan pocket and handed it to me. *Luke Rowlands*, it said, *Gardening Services*.

'Tell you what,' I said, after I'd studied it for a moment, 'I'll pass this on to Ricky and Morris. They need some work done in their garden.'

'Don't you usually do their gardening?' she asked uncertainly.

'I tidy a few flower borders for them occasionally. All Ricky and Morris do is ride around the lawns on their fancy mower. There's a lake at the bottom of their lawn, and a little woodland. All the paths are completely overgrown. You can't walk around the lake at all. The shrubs need hacking back and the trees want crown-lifting – I've been telling them about it for ages – it's a job for someone heftier than me, preferably someone with a chainsaw.'

'It sounds right up Luke's street.' Pat began to look a bit happier. 'He's got references.'

'Has he got a chainsaw?'

'I'm not sure what tools he's got,' she admitted, her brow wrinkling, 'but it don't matter, because Ken will loan him anything.'

I waggled the business card at her before I popped it into my bag. 'I'll ask them tomorrow.'

'Thanks, Juno.'

'And don't go slapping Jessie Mole again,' I advised her. 'She could have you up for assault.'

'She'd better learn to keep her mouth shut,' Pat

answered, eyes narrowing. 'Bloody murder her, I will!'

Unfortunate remark as it turned out.

When I left the shop I drove up the hill from Ashburton, past the old disused rifle range, until I reached Cold East Cross, where the road forks left for Ponsworthy. Here, on the right, is Halsanger Common, an area of wide-open grassland where I often bring the Tribe for a run. It was here, set back from the road up a steep track, and almost out of sight, that I found Moorview Farm, just as it was marked on the map.

It turned out to be a large stone house with views over a patchwork of green fields and distant dark woods, the high tops of the moor breaking the skyline. Down in the valley below, a glittering loop of river could be glimpsed between the trees. It's the sort of place I have always dreamt of owning and I was practically salivating by the time I drew to a halt by its granite gatepost and clambered out of White Van. An untidily chained gate blocked the path. I didn't want to wrestle with it and decided to walk up the track to the house. The day was grey and dull, threatening rain, sabres of sunlight thrusting through the blanket of cloud, lighting up patches of green in the wide winter landscape. Colder up here than in the shelter of the town, the place was exposed to roaming winds and I shivered.

The farmhouse, which had probably stood for more than two hundred years, was in need of a little refurbishment. The roof sagged wearily as if it was considering collapse; a large portion of what must have been missing slates was covered by rusty corrugated sheeting. There was a straggly plant growing from a crack in the chimney, and an upstairs window, presumably without glass, was shielded by a blue plastic tarpaulin. Any paint that had once coated the door and window frames had been scoured off by unforgiving winds, and it was only the presence of the same car I had seen in the town, and a wisp of smoke from the chimney, that convinced me that Mr Daniel Thorncroft must be at home and I had not arrived at an empty derelict.

My arrival had been spotted. Before I reached the front door, it swung open and the lean figure of Mr Thorncroft blocked the doorway, reminding me once again of a scruffy hawk. It was something to do with the way his hair stuck out behind his ears. He needed a good haircut. He was wearing a stained, pea-green jumper, the knitting laddered with holes, but at least he wasn't sporting the severe specs.

'Ah, Miss Browne with an "e",' he declared, his gaze sweeping me up and down. 'I've been reading about you . . .'

Effing Gazette. He must have read about me in their pages. He wouldn't have known the correct spelling of my name otherwise.

'You're quite a girl. You'd better come in.' He stepped aside to let me enter. I hesitated.

'I promise you, there are no corpses in here,' he added as I stepped across the threshold, 'other than myself.'

I looked around a large kitchen, dim and shadowy, lit only by battery-powered storm lanterns hanging from an overhead beam. The beam itself, cracked, was held up by an acrow prop.

'I'm sorry about the conditions in here,' he went on as I stared about me, 'but this is the warmest spot in the house, the only warm spot, in fact.' He nodded in the direction of the old kitchen range. 'At least I've managed to get that thing going.'

A threadbare rug covered the stone flags, an old sofa took up one wall, with stacked pillows and bedding rolled up on it. It seemed Mr Thorncroft was camping in his kitchen. Beyond an old leather armchair, the only other furniture was a scrubbed table, covered in paperwork, and two bentwood chairs. He flicked a tea towel over the seat of one of them. 'Sit down.'

'I really only came to give you this.' I handed him the envelope and he frowned. 'It must have slipped into Mrs Berkeley-Smythe's shopping bag,' I explained as he peered inside. 'We didn't discover it until we got home. And then there was no real address.' I don't know why I was speaking in such a rush, but I felt nervous. 'You can count it, if you like,' I added, with what sounded in my own ears like unnecessary defensiveness.

'I didn't realise I had lost it.' He tossed the envelope onto the table, its contents uncounted. 'Thank you.'

'Well, that's what I came for,' I added, feeling suddenly awkward and anxious to make an exit.

'Let me make you a coffee after you've come all

this way. I'm afraid it'll take a while.' He picked up an old-fashioned percolator from the stove. 'We've no electricity, I'm afraid.'

'Well, I really must—' I began.

'I'm not going to bite you. And Lottie and I don't get many visitors, do we, Lottie?'

Lottie turned out to be a little whippet who'd been curled up in the armchair all this while, watching me apprehensively from soulful dark eyes. I hunkered down and held out a hand to her. Whippets are shy of strangers and startle easily. 'Hello, Lottie.' Tentatively, she sniffed my fingers.

'She was Claire's dog,' Mr Thorncroft went on as he spooned coffee into the percolator, 'a rescue, terrified of everyone, especially men. Claire was the only one who could get close to her . . .' He stopped.

'Claire?' I asked.

'My wife.' I could sense him drawing breath. 'She died. I'm afraid Lottie's still pining,' he added after a moment. His voice was suddenly husky and he cleared his throat.

'I'm sorry.' I stroked Lottie's smooth head and the tip of her tail began to wag. She licked my hand.

'She must like you.' Mr Thorncroft sounded surprised. 'She's usually run away and hidden under the bed by this point.'

I straightened up, and as I did I caught sight of a photograph propped on the mantelpiece: a young woman with dark hair, face made radiant by a loving smile. This, surely, must be Claire. By now my host had regained his composure and was watching me, arms folded, leaning against the range. Even in the dimness of the kitchen I could see that his eyes were unnaturally bright. I wondered if he might be high on something. I thought I'd better make conversation. 'Have you lived here long?'

'I don't really live here. My aunt left me this place. It's wonderful,' he said with a sour smile. 'I love it. Most of it is falling down.'

I gazed out of the kitchen window at the breathtaking view. 'It is wonderful,' I agreed. 'At least, it could be made wonderful.'

'If I spend every penny I'm ever likely to earn between now and the day I die on it, it might be made habitable.' He gazed about him. 'I'm wondering whether I could move my life here.' He shrugged. 'The sensible thing would be to sell the place and forget all about it, but for some reason I'm reluctant to do that.'

'Did your aunt live here?' I couldn't imagine an elderly lady living in this cold, crumbling ruin on her own. It was as if a chill had crept into its stones. The house needed to be lived in. It needed warming through.

'Until a few years before she died. She moved into a retirement flat in Torquay. Unfortunately, she left me that as well.'

'Unfortunately?'

'It's a retirement flat, which means that even if I wanted to live in it – which I don't – I can't because

I'm too young. I can't even use it for holidays. But, as the owner, I am liable for all the bloody extortionate maintenance fees. I'm trying to sell it. At least then I'd have some money to start doing up this place.' He swept a long arm in the direction of the paperwork on the table. 'My aunt's affairs are in a hell of a mess. Believe me, inheriting property is not all it's cracked up to be.'

'I know,' I agreed, without thinking. 'Last year one of my clients died and left me his shop, and now I have business rates and—'

'What sort of client,' he interrupted, frowning, 'leaves you a shop?' I saw by the merest twitch at the corner of his mouth that he was joking. 'What *do* you do for them, Miss Browne with an "e"?' he asked, raising his brows at me.

'I don't know,' I confessed. 'I have no idea why Nick left his shop to me. I think it was part of a plot to take revenge on the children who'd ignored him for years . . . But I really don't know . . . Anyway,' I added, looking at my watch, 'it's time I went.'

'Without your vile coffee? I won't hear of it. Don't worry,' he went on as he began to pour, 'this mug is clean.'

I don't really like my coffee black but there didn't seem to be any milk on offer so I took the mug of dark liquid and sipped it cautiously.

'How is it?' he asked.

'Like something rinsed from an ashtray,' I told him truthfully.

'It's improving, then.' He grinned as he took the mug from my hand. 'I still owe you a proper one, next time you're in Ashburton. I'm usually to be found lurking in one cafe or another, anywhere where there's warmth and free Wi-Fi – none up here, of course.'

I smiled weakly and headed for the door.

'Goodbye, Miss Browne . . .' he began.

'Juno,' I said. 'Call me Juno.'

'Oh, I think I prefer Miss Browne with an "e".'

I shrugged. 'Suit yourself, Mr Thorncroft.'

As I walked back down the track, large heavy sploshes of rain fell sudden and fast, forcing me to break into a run. Before I reached the gate and the shelter of the van, it had turned to hail, frozen white balls that pelted painfully on my scalp. Another host might have called me back, invited me to shelter until the shower had passed. But the door of the farmhouse had shut. I had already been forgotten.

CHAPTER SIX

'Well, I think he's odd,' I told Chloe Berkeley-Smythe that afternoon. I'd gone to her house to finish unpacking but she'd decided she wanted to go shopping, which really meant returning the items she'd bought the day before. Fortunately, the dress shops in Ashburton are well used to her.

'Who, dear?' Chloe asked, pouring tea. She had been to the hairdresser in the morning and her hair was restored to its usual silvery beige, her nails a glossy plum colour. She found all this pampering terminally exhausting, so we were getting our strength back in Taylor's tea room.

'Mr Thorncroft,' I reminded her. I hadn't been able to put my finger on what it was I didn't like about him. He'd been hospitable, after a fashion, and amusing in a slightly desperate, manic way, but still managed to be irritating.

'Well, we've done our duty in returning his money, so we can forget all about him,' she said, hunting in her handbag for her sweeteners. I loved the use of *we*. 'That's a new art gallery that's opened, just up the road,' she went on, pulling out a purse, a lipstick and a handful of wrapped toffees. 'It wasn't there the last time I was here, was it?'

'I'm not sure. It opened just after I opened *Old Nick's*.' To be honest, I hadn't been too pleased about it. *Old Nick's* had enough competition in Ashburton as it was, with fifteen other antique traders and a scattering of gift shops, and we were already disadvantaged by being stuck up a lonely side street, the aptly named Shadow Lane.

But the new gallery, *Swann's*, was in a different league from *Old Nick's*: smart and expensive, concentrating on paintings and sculpture by feted artists, far superior to the odd collection of stuff we try to peddle in *Old Nick's*. The owner, Meredith Swann, crafted the original jewellery she sold: original twists of chunky silver, settings for sea glass, quartz and semi-precious stones. The silver swan she wore around her slender neck was an example of her own work. She had come around to see *Old Nick's* shortly after she'd opened, ostensibly to introduce herself. But her real motive was soon apparent. She wanted Sophie's paintings for her gallery. Sophie is really talented, has work on display in shops and galleries all over Devon and I've no problem with her spreading her wares, but somehow, Ms Swann's blatant interest in poaching her works rankled with me.

Sophie must have felt awkward about it too, because she turned her down.

'She's a lovely-looking creature, the owner,' Chloe went on, finally finding what she was searching for under a bundle of tissues. 'She reminds me of someone, some actress, I expect.'

Meredith was certainly glamorous enough to be in films. I envied her straight, conker-brown hair. She had that smooth, glossy look: hair, skin and lips all possessed of the same glowing sheen. It was a healthy radiance that I suspected was born out of iron discipline – a stringent diet and rigorous exercise routine, also resulting in the unhurried feline grace with which she moved. She probably meditated as well.

Chloe had insisted on going into her gallery for a wander around and I gazed with envy at hand-blown glass in jewelled colours, sophisticated, modern pottery, woven alpaca shawls, original silver jewellery and delicately painted silk scarves. I had to admit Sophie's exquisitely detailed watercolours would sit well on these walls. For her own sake, I decided, I must talk her into it. Business is business, after all. Meanwhile, Chloe had fallen for a sculpture of an otter, although she had a tough time deciding whether she liked it more than a hare by the same sculptor. The cost of it made my eyes water.

Just as we were leaving, Verbena Clarke had walked in. Relations between Verbena and me are always strained. She is the only one of my employers to have sacked me. It's true, she later felt forced to offer me my job back, but by then the damage was done. She had never been pleasant to work for and I cheerfully told her to get stuffed. Standing back to let her through the gallery, the most she could summon in thanks was a stiff nod of acknowledgement. I could feel her glowering at me as Chloe and I passed the window, and I had turned to give her a smile and an annoying little wave.

Tea and *tartes citrons* later, we emerged from Taylor's and headed back towards the car park. I was trying to steer Chloe firmly, to discourage her from more shopping. I wanted to get back to her house and finish her wretched unpacking. But after a few steps, she suddenly grabbed my arm, hissed, 'Quick! Hide!' and pulled me through an open door into the grocer's.

'What's the matter?' I asked, gaping at her.

'Those two people over there,' she was trying to peer out of the door without being seen, 'on the corner, outside the estate agents, do you see them?'

'That couple?' I could see a man and woman, probably in late middle age, the woman willowy and slightly taller than her male companion.

'They're looking very smug and pleased with themselves,' Chloe went on, her plucked brows puckered in a frown. 'You don't think they've bought a property here, do you? Of all the cheek!'

She was so indignant I began laughing. 'Who are they?'

Chloe didn't answer, still concentrating furiously on the couple outside. She drew back hastily as they strolled past on the opposite pavement. 'See where they're going!' she commanded imperiously, prodding me between the shoulder blades.

I looked out in time to see them disappear into the tea room. 'They've gone into Taylor's,' I told her.

'Thank goodness, we can escape!' She hurried off, leaving me to give an apologetic shrug to the girl behind the counter, who was staring, open-mouthed.

'Who on earth are they?' I asked when I'd got Chloe and all her shopping safely stowed back in the van.

'I met them on a cruise – don't remember which one – they're retired actors, perfectly charming couple, of course!'

'Well, if they're perfectly charming, why do you take such exception to their being here?'

She began shaking her head distractedly. 'I suppose it's my fault.'

'What is?'

'That they're here. You see, they were talking about Devon and how much they would love to move here, and you know when I go away I always take my thingy with me . . . you know, the thing I keep all my photographs on . . .'

'Your tablet?'

'That's it. Well, I was showing them pictures of Ashburton and Dartmoor and telling them how lovely it was . . . but I didn't mean them to come here! I mean, when you exchange addresses with people you meet on holiday and tell them to visit you anytime, you don't actually expect them to turn up. It's just not done! The most you expect is a Christmas card.'

'Well,' I ventured when I could stop laughing, 'perhaps they're not living here. They may only be visiting.'

Chloe was shaking her head with conviction. 'No, they're here to stay,' she moaned in the voice of a doomed prophetess, 'I can feel it in my bones.'

If Chloe's bones were reliable, they were the only part of her anatomy that was.

'Did you actually give them your address?' I asked.

She blinked uncertainly. 'I don't think so.'

'Then you haven't got much to worry about. You're hardly here, anyway. You're on the high seas most of the time. Do you remember their names?'

'Oh. Derek? No, that's not right. Something beginning with a "D" . . . I don't remember . . . Amanda!' She held up a finger in triumph. 'I'm sure *her* name was Amanda.' She closed her eyes and shuddered. 'As long as they don't want to visit me. Visitors are too exhausting.'

So exhausting was the prospect that on our return to the cottage, she had to lie down.

I carried on with the task of unpacking. I was determined to get it finished. I didn't have any more free days to offer her, and wouldn't see her again until midweek when I was driving her to see her consultant at a private hospital in Torquay.

When I'd finally hung everything on hangers and got all the suitcases squared away, I popped my head around her living-room door. She was lying on the sofa, watching the shopping channel, her feet up and a glass of sherry at her elbow.

'Do have a little drinkie before you go,' she said, waving the television remote in the direction of the decanter. 'Now, you mustn't let me spend any money,' she added as I poured. 'What do you think of that ring with the yellow zircon?'

'Not a lot,' I said frankly.

She heaved a sigh. 'You're right,' she added sadly, switching it off.

'You know, when you dragged me into the grocer's to hide,' I told her, taking a seat, 'I thought you'd spotted Jessie Mole.'

Chloe shuddered. 'That creature!'

I grinned. 'You know her, then?'

'I used to employ her. Years ago, when Howard was still alive, before I took up seafaring.'

'Employ her?'

'She was my cleaning woman. I had to let her go.'

'Why?'

'She was . . .' Chloe hesitated, frowning, trying to find the right word '. . . *intrusive*. I don't think she ever stole anything – other than sprays of my perfume – but she used to snoop. She'd disturb things she had no business touching. She'd go through all my pots and potions. I could always tell because she never screwed the tops back on the bottles properly. She wasn't very good at covering her tracks. I caught her once reading my mail.' She took a sip of sherry. 'You know, for months I wondered why the milkman disregarded all the notes I left for him . . . I never got what I ordered. So, one morning I got up early to see if I could catch him . . . I was going to ask him why he kept ignoring my instructions, give him what for . . . I stationed myself by the window there, where I could see the front step. There was my empty milk bottle with the note rolled up in the neck of it. Then Jessie came walking up the road – she couldn't see me, I was behind the net curtain – I saw her stop, look about her, take the note from the bottle, read it, then put it in her pocket and walk on.'

'She stole your note for the milkman?' I laughed. 'What on earth for?'

'Well, precisely! What sort of person steals notes from milk bottles?' she demanded. 'What's the point?'

'Didn't you tackle her about it? Ask her what she thought she was doing?'

'No,' she chuckled, 'but next day I put out a rather different sort of note. I never saw her again.'

Before I left Chloe, we went through my diary, making sure I had all her hospital appointments noted down. She liked to get a full MOT when she came home, to ensure she was fit enough for her next cruise.

I was later leaving her than I'd hoped. It was gone six, the shop would be shut and Pat would have gone home. I decided I'd pop in anyway, in the faint hope that I might have sold something during the day. There was no sign of Pat, but I discovered she'd left a note for me on the counter. *Someone brought in parcel for you. I didn't catch his name. I've put it in your unit.*

The place where I displayed my wares had once been the old storeroom. Here I kept the bric-a-brac and oddments of furniture that made up my stock, and also the vintage clothes I sold on commission for Ricky and Morris. I looked around and found the parcel, wrapped in brown paper, propped up against the wall. It was oblong and flattish and quite heavy. My name was scrawled on it in handwriting I didn't recognise, and there was no indication where it had come from. I certainly hadn't ordered anything.

I wondered, as I tore the paper off, if it might be a birthday present from someone, but my birthday was something I tended to keep quiet about and very few people knew when it was. Inside was a picture in a simple black frame. I found I was looking at the back of it and turned it over to see a print – *Ophelia* by John Everett Millais. I gazed through grimy glass at the poor drowning mad girl floating downstream amongst the flowers, her eyes open, her hair rippling on the water, the weight of her long, pale dress gradually dragging her down, singing as she died.

I searched around but there was no explanatory note – nothing.

I looked at the picture again. I remembered reading how the model, Lizzie Siddal, spent days lying in a bath of cold water while Millais painted her. She caught a terrible cold, apparently. But this time the picture made me think of something else, of a grotesque effigy under the bridge, bobbing obscenely on the surface of the water.

* * *

I phoned Pat when I got home and asked her if she could tell me anything about the man who'd delivered the picture. 'He didn't say who it was from?' I asked.

'No,' she said. 'Sorry. He spoke as if you'd know all about it. And I barely got a look at him. He was wearing one of those baseball caps. I was busy serving a customer at the time and he was in and out in seconds, just dumped the thing on the counter and left.'

'OK. Thanks.' I put the phone down, still with no idea where the picture had come from or why it had been left for me at the shop. Had it been brought in for me to sell for someone? I didn't remember making any such arrangement. I'd just hang it on the wall and hope an explanation for its presence would come to light.

I sat down on the sofa and leafed through the mail I'd picked up from the hall table, which mostly consisted of credit card statements and begging letters from charities. There were three envelopes that obviously contained birthday cards, but I decided I'd be good and wait until the morning to open them. I propped them on the mantelpiece, kicked off my shoes, and was pondering what to have for supper when Bill strolled in from the kitchen and leapt up on my lap. As usual, doors and windows were all shut, and how he'd got in was a mystery.

'Do you know *Hamlet*?' I asked him. 'Ophelia was Hamlet's girlfriend. She went mad because he was so rotten to her and killed her dad, stabbed him behind the arras. She fell in the river and drowned.'

Bill was too busy purring and treading up and down on my lap to answer. I lay back and let him tread away. I'd had to learn the speech about Ophelia drowning for my English A-level. I still remembered bits of it.

'*There is a willow stands aslant a brook*,' I began, '*That shows his hoar leaves in the glassy stream; there with fantastic garlands did she come* . . . Blah-di-blah, lots of stuff about flowers . . . *Fell in the weeping brook. Her clothes spread wide; and, mermaid-like, awhile they bore her up* . . . something, something, something . . .' Bill had closed his eye and stopped purring but I could tell he was impressed. '*But long it could not be*,' I went on, '*till that her garments, heavy with their drink* . . . *pull'd the poor wretch from* . . . something . . . *to muddy death*. There!' I felt triumphant. Well, I'd remembered most of it.

CHAPTER SEVEN

I reckon January is a rotten month to get born in. I could hear the rain before I opened my eyes, pattering on the glass of Kate and Adam's conservatory, if that's what you can call the structure of rotting wood and cracked glass that is gradually peeling itself away from the back of the building. The roof is just a few feet below my bedroom window and even a light shower makes a hell of a racket. This didn't sound like a light shower, though; it had a relentless, monotonous rhythm to it as if it had set in for the day.

It wasn't just the weather. Christmas might seem like a distant memory, but it's not really, not in financial terms. I don't mean to sound mercenary, but generally January is not a time when people splash out on birthday presents. And you can't go anywhere interesting either because all the attractions have closed for the winter and restaurant owners have grabbed the opportunity to go away on holiday.

Bill had brought me a present: half a vole lying on my duvet cover. I struggled out of bed, picked the poor thing up by the tail and flushed it down the loo. Just as I was washing my hands I heard a buzzing noise from the laptop. I groaned, shrugging on my dressing gown. It was still ridiculously early, the light outside just a dull greyness struggling through the curtains. But Seoul is seven hours ahead of us and in South Korea my one remaining relative, Brian, was up and eager to wish me a happy birthday. I sat down at the screen, hit the button, and he appeared. His Skype face was slightly distorted, his amiable features swollen. I suppose mine looked the same. I pushed my hair back from my face so he could see me.

'Hello, Juno! Happy birthday!'

I winced. He was altogether too loud for this hour of the morning but obviously felt he had to yell as South Korea is a long way off.

'Thanks, Brian.' I couldn't stop a cavernous yawn.

'Been out celebrating?' he asked.

'Hardly.'

'Good for you!' Brian is a diplomat but today he obviously had his listening skills switched off.

'How's things?' he demanded cheerily. 'How's it going in the shop?'

'OK, I suppose.'

'And all your dogs and grannies, you're still walking them?'

'Well, I don't walk the grannies, but yes, I still have all my clients.'

'I seem to remember your cousin Cordelia telling me once that your lot are supposed to be ambitious, you know, hard-headed business types—'

By *your lot* he meant people born under the sign of Capricorn. 'They are, yes.'

'—not that I believe any of that clap-trap, of course,' he added hastily. 'But what's gone wrong in your case?'

'I don't know,' I lied. I did know. Cordelia was an astrologer by profession, and she explained it all to me. My moon and Venus in Pisces, that's what had gone wrong, giving me too much empathy and unbalancing my supposed hard-head pragmatism altogether. Not that I believed it, either.

'Well, as long as you're happy. Listen, sweetie. I haven't sent you a present but I've transferred some money into your account.'

'Oh, Brian, you shouldn't! I owe you so much already.'

'You don't owe me anything,' he responded firmly. 'We've been through all this before. If your grandfather hadn't been such a stubborn old fool, he'd have left everything to you instead of tying it up and making it damn difficult for me to give you what's rightfully yours. But don't worry, I'll be over next year, and we'll get a few things sorted out.'

'It would be lovely to see you.' I was genuinely fond of Brian and I only saw him once every two years when he came back to England on leave. I thought I'd better enquire after his hag-wife. 'How's Marcia?'

'Oh, fairly perky, you know.'

The idea of a botox-stiffened mantis like Marcia being even slightly perky was impossible to imagine. 'Give her my love,' I said dutifully.

'You doing something nice on your birthday?' he asked.

I sighed. 'No, just working.'

'Sorry, what?'

'I'm spending the day with Ricky and Morris,' I explained.

'Oh, that pair! Well, don't let them lead you astray.'

'Too late.'

He laughed heartily. 'Well, you take care. And let me know if you need any more funds. Promise me, now.'

'I will,' I lied, crossed fingers hidden in my lap.

He promised to Skype again in a month or two and we said our goodbyes. I stared at a blank screen and experienced a rare moment of loneliness. My mother had died when I was too young to remember her, from a drugs overdose. My grandfather had disowned her, and me, and if it hadn't been for Brian I'd have been brought up in social care. He'd seen to my education and arranged for Cordelia to look after me in the holidays. But she had gone too, years ago. Talk of her always made me sad: Cordelia, my good witch mother. I felt suddenly bereft. Just birthday blues, I suppose. I reminded myself that self-pity is unbecoming, got up, put the kettle on and fetched my three cards from the mantelpiece.

The two cards in white envelopes were from college friends. I didn't recognise the postmark on the pink one.

The card had kittens on it and inside the message looked as if it had been scrawled by a spider with the shakes. It came from Maisie, still staying up north with her daughter. She wished me many happy returns and said she and Jacko were looking forward to coming home soon, from which I deduced that she was not enjoying her stay with Our Janet and her family up in Heck-as-Like, or whatever the northern town was called.

When I finally got ready to leave, I found offerings on the table on the landing: a bottle of white wine with a bow tied around its neck, a plastic box containing home-made chocolates and a card from Kate and Adam. I didn't knock on the door to thank them. In the winter they didn't open the cafe on Sundays and would be enjoying a good lie-in. I'd thank them later, when I got back home.

'So, Chloe's back on land, is she?' Ricky demanded as he let me in to the grand Georgian house that he and Morris shared together. 'How is the old sausage?'

I told him the latest. 'She thinks she's got ME.'

'ME my arse!' he scoffed. 'She wants to try doing a day's work.'

'Well, she does get very tired,' I pointed out, 'and she has a weak heart.'

I looked around the large, marble-tiled hall. I was expecting to see hampers full of costumes, but there didn't seem to be any.

'We've unpacked them already,' Morris explained, bustling up to greet me as he wiped his hands on a tea towel. 'We needed to get them out of the way. We've just piled them in the workroom . . .'

'. . . waiting for you to hang them up,' Ricky completed.

'Oh, right.' I shrugged off my jacket. Usually we had a cup of coffee before we started work but there was obviously none on offer this morning. 'Well, I'll get on then, shall I?'

'Yes, please, Juno,' Morris nodded. He was obviously deep in cooking mode, his bald head shining from the heat in the kitchen.

'Yeh, get a move on, there's a good girl,' Ricky said. 'We've got *Snow White* and *Cinderella* arriving back tomorrow.'

I carried on up the grand staircase. It seemed I would be working on my own. The costumes were in several piles on the workroom table. They'd clearly just been dumped and so far there had been no attempt at sorting them. I sighed. This was a bit like unpacking Chloe's suitcases all over again, except the contents of her suitcases were a lot more fragrant. There is a very particular smell to theatrical costumes, especially those that have just been worn. Performers sweat under the hot stage lights and costumes are often constructed from materials that cannot be washed. Few dry-cleaners will take responsibility for elaborate velvet robes, caged crinolines or animal costumes that cost hundreds of pounds to make. I opened the windows. Upholstery fabric spray is the only cure for the awful niffiness and I had no intention of breathing in a lot of nasty chemicals.

I dragged an empty clothes rail into the centre of the room and began sorting through the nearest pile, brushing the collar of each Chinese satin jacket from *Aladdin* to remove stage make-up, individually spraying and then pressing it. I could hardly lift Abanazar's trailing velvet robe, heavily encrusted with spangles. I pitied the poor actor who'd had to wear it.

I put it on a hanger and hung it from a window frame in the damp air where its crushed folds could be straightened out and its long sleeves allowed to trail on the floor. It would need steaming to get the creases out, but that was a job that could wait.

I began to work my way through a pile of crinolines. Each one had to be shaken out to ensure the hoops had not bent out of shape in transit. They took a long time and I began to get hot and bothered. I glanced at my watch. It was almost lunchtime and there had been no sign of the cavalry bearing refreshments.

Sudden strident chords sounded on the piano downstairs. '*Happy Birthday to you . . .*' began to drift up from the music room, Ricky and Morris in full voice, with some sort of backing group. I groaned inwardly and then ventured down, putting on a smile as I swung open the door.

'Didn't think we'd forgotten your birthday, did you, Princess?' Ricky demanded loudly.

I must be thick, I suppose. I did. Sophie, Elizabeth and Olly were standing by the piano, grinning at me.

Morris hurried up to give me a hug. 'Sorry about making you hang up all the costumes, Juno, but we had to keep you out of the way while we cooked lunch.'

'And sneak this lot in,' Ricky added, jerking a thumb towards the others.

'Come on.' Morris put an arm through mine and guided me towards the dining room. 'It's all ready.'

The table looked beautiful, spread with a white cloth laid with all the best silverware and decorated with a vase of tiny, early narcissi. There was also a very large parcel wrapped in paper and tied with a velvet bow.

I sat down at the head of the table and unwrapped it. From a cloud of tissue paper, I pulled a garment made of velvet, satin and silk, in shades of russet and peach. I wasn't sure if it was a blouse or a jacket. It had a stand-up collar, padded shoulders and long full sleeves.

'We designed it around that doublet you liked so much when we were unpacking *Twelfth Night* a while ago,' Ricky said as I held it up. 'Remember?'

'It's beautiful,' I breathed.

'Try it on!' Morris clapped his hands like an excited child.

I pulled off my jumper and slipped it on over my T-shirt. I was dragged to view my reflection in the mirror in the hall. It looked fabulous. I could wear it with jeans to a party or a long skirt to the opera, if I ever went. It fitted me exactly and the colours were perfect. It was unique and it was mine.

'Thank you so much!' I gave them big hugs and then packed it up carefully in its box before we all sat down to lunch. I got other presents: a huge bottle of my favourite hair conditioner from Sophie and a book on restoring antiques from Elizabeth and Olly. Pat couldn't come but sent me a fluffy brown scarf she'd knitted herself.

With a flourish Morris placed a napkin on my lap while Ricky popped the cork of a bottle of champagne.

'How old are you, anyway?' he asked as he filled all our glasses.

'You should never ask a lady her age,' Morris protested. He bustled out and in again, carrying a tureen of roasted vegetable soup and a plate of sweet-smelling home-baked rolls. 'Just ask him how old *he* is next birthday. I bet he won't tell you.'

Lunch took most of the afternoon – four courses, not counting the mint sorbet palate cleanser, and we were talking a lot. I gave them all an account of my time with Chloe and the appearance of the mystery couple who seemed to fill her with such dread. 'She said they were retired actors. You don't know who they are, I suppose? She thought his name might be Derek, and the woman was Amanda.'

Ricky asked me to describe them.

'He was greying and quite stocky, she was tall and slim with long, wavy, brown hair.'

'And her name was Amanda?' Ricky asked.

'That's what Chloe thought.'

He shot a look at Morris and grinned. 'You thinking what I'm thinking?'

Morris giggled. 'It sounds like them.'

'She said they were retired,' I said. 'She met them on a cruise.'

Ricky was nodding. 'I'd heard they ended up working the cruise ships as entertainers.' He laughed. 'Digby Jerkin and Amanda Waft.'

I wasn't sure I'd heard right.

'Husband and wife team,' he went on. 'We knew them way back when we were in variety. They performed duologues. This was back in the days when the variety bill would include scenes from plays, odd bits of Shakespeare and that sort of thing. They used to sing as well,' he added, sniffing. 'He had a good voice but hers wasn't up to much.'

'Digby Jerkin?' I repeated. 'That's not really his name? He sounds like a horse.'

Morris was nodding. 'And Amanda Waft.'

Olly giggled. 'She sounds like a fart.'

Ricky grinned. 'Wavy Mandy we used to call her.'

'They used to do a lot of Noël Coward,' Morris went on. 'They toured in *Private Lives*. Then, didn't they get some sort of television series together?' He peered at Ricky over his spectacles. 'A sitcom, wasn't it?'

'Why did they call her Wavy Mandy?' Olly asked.

Ricky frowned theatrically. 'You're too young to know.'

'She wavered in her affections,' Morris explained. 'And she had a funny walk . . .'

'She waved about,' Ricky added, 'pissed half the time.'

'It is her!' I remembered her odd walk. Her steps were exaggerated, one foot almost crossing over in front of the other at each step. I'd noticed it at the time, but I thought it was because she was having trouble balancing on her high heels. 'Now you mention it, she looked unnatural, as if she wasn't walking so much as . . . *performing* walking.'

Ricky slammed a hand down on the table and gave a crack of laughter. 'That's her!'

'And if these two are intending to settle in Ashburton . . . ?' Elizabeth asked.

He shrugged. 'They're harmless, nothing for Chloe to get her knickers in a twist about.'

Morris started to clear plates. He bustled off to the kitchen and came back staggering under the weight of a hefty cut-glass trifle dish. 'This is a rhubarb and elderflower trifle,' he explained, carefully setting it down in the middle of the table, 'but there's home-made lemon ice cream if you'd prefer.'

How we weren't all sick, I don't know, especially as dessert was followed, after a short interval to recover, by birthday cake.

During the slightly rueful silence that follows when everyone knows they have eaten too much, Ricky lit up one of his long, menthol cigarettes and I remembered the business card Pat had given me, dug it from my pocket and placed it on the table. 'Ken's nephew, Luke, is starting up a gardening business. He could clear all that jungle growing around your lake, if you felt like giving him a try: now is the time of year to get it done.'

'We will.' Morris picked up and read the card. 'Thank you, Juno.'

After the meal it took a lot of arguing to convince everyone that I was capable of driving home. I'd had too much to drink, they said. In truth, I hadn't had any more than they had – well, perhaps a bit – and it was only a short drive.

'You'd better let us drive you in the Rolls,' Ricky said.

Olly frowned. 'You haven't got a Rolls.'

'We have,' he insisted.

'I thought it was a Saab.'

'No. It's a Rolls Canardly.'

'What's that?'

'It rolls down the hills and can hardly get up 'em again.'

Everyone groaned. I promised to drive the narrow lane back into town very slowly and carefully, especially as it was still raining. Sophie decided to risk a lift with me rather than make Elizabeth drive around her way, so I couldn't have seemed too tiddly.

We almost made it home without accident. I nearly ran over Jessie Mole, but that had little to do with my reactions being slightly sluggish and more to do with her suddenly launching herself into the road and hobbling off as if all the devils in hell were after her.

'What's she doing up here?' I asked, after I'd screeched to a halt.

We were halfway down the hill from Druid Cross. The gateway from which she'd suddenly sprung belonged to a house that had been an empty derelict for years. We sat for a moment, peering down the muddy driveway through my swishing windscreen wipers. The old, wrought-iron gate hung open, the house hidden by a screen of overgrown bushes and tall weeds. There didn't seem to be anyone about. No one came chasing out after Jessie.

'She's always wandering around,' Sophie said. 'She must have been snooping about in there and got frightened by something.'

'We ought to offer her a lift.' I had no idea where she lived but it was raining and she was lame, after all. It would take her a long time to limp down into town. I drove on down the hill but we didn't catch her up. She'd disappeared. She must have got off the road somehow. Perhaps it was as well. She'd only have told the whole of Ashburton that I was driving under the influence.

CHAPTER EIGHT

I was unfortunate enough to encounter Jessie again next morning, and Mr Daniel Thorncroft. To be honest, I only saw him running in the distance as I was walking the Tribe down by the river. I recognised his long, lean figure on the skyline as he pounded along the ridge above us, little Lottie skipping daintily at his side. I thought he hadn't seen me in the dip below him, but he raised a hand in greeting as he passed, not stopping to speak or break his stride.

Jessie Mole spotted me as I was in town picking up prescriptions for Tom Carter, who I've recently taken on as a client. She grabbed my arm and clung like a leech, still pestering me with questions about the wretched effigy. I only got rid of her because I decided to turn the tables. 'What were you doing yesterday up at the old Owl House? I nearly ran you over. What were you doing there, Jessie?'

She scowled, the thick flesh of her forehead puckering as her brows drew together. 'What?' she muttered.

'The Owl House,' I repeated. 'I saw you come running out. Did something frighten you? Was someone there?'

She lowered her head, her eyes sliding furtively to one side. 'Wasn't me.'

'Yes, Jessie, I saw you.'

For a moment she looked uncertain what to do, the pink tip of her tongue peeping between her lips. Then she spotted another victim on the opposite pavement and hobbled off at high speed, almost getting mown down by a delivery van in her eagerness to cross the road.

'That's Juno Browne over there, with the red hair,' she announced loudly, pointing in my direction, 'her that keeps finding them dead bodies.' I beat a retreat around the corner.

There is a definite vibe between me and Tom Carter. There is too great a gulf of years between us for it to be any more than a vibe, but it's there, an unspoken subtext whenever we meet. If I had known him when he was younger, I'd have eaten him with a spoon.

He lives in Station Cottages, near the bottom of St Lawrence Lane, close to the old railway station, which still stands although the tracks are long gone. It isn't possible to drive all the way to his house. Station Cottages can only be reached by walking down a narrow alleyway, then the little terrace opens up to the left. A path separates the front doors from their allotment gardens, which rise up in a slope towards a screen of trees separating them from the A38 Expressway. It would be a peaceful spot if it weren't for the traffic whizzing by. I don't think it bothers Tom. He says he doesn't hear it any more.

As I passed his window I could see him working at a table, totally engrossed in what he was doing. I tapped the glass gently and he raised a hand in greeting without looking up. His front door was unlocked and I let myself in. Tom must have been vigorous in his youth, a farm worker, a member of Dartmoor Search and Rescue, a passionate fly-fisherman, chorister and a bell-ringer at St Andrew's Church. He was in his seventies now, grey, bearded, twinkly eyed, slightly bald on top, his powerful forearms fuzzed with white hair. He was crippled by arthritis, in constant pain and on a long list awaiting a hip replacement. It was his lack of mobility that had forced him to accept my help.

'Hello, my beauty,' he called as I came in. 'Have a seat.'

I slid into a chair at the side of him, careful not to obstruct his light, and watched him, fascinated. He was fly-tying. The trout fishing season would start in March and he always tied his own flies. On the table lay a selection of strange, tiny tools, with spools of thread and bunches of feathers, which together would produce imitations of bristly insects, which might be attractive to trout, but which I'd rather not have buzzing around my bedroom. There was an open leather case full of them, including one that looked like a particularly revolting caterpillar.

'What's that?' I asked, pointing.

He flicked a glance at it. 'Rhyacophila larva,' he told me, 'caddis fly.'

On the table in front of him was a vice holding the fly he was tying. I watched him carefully winding thread around a tiny filament of golden feather, viewing it through a lighted magnifier, his specs shoved halfway up his bald forehead. 'Pass me that whip finisher,' he said, pointing towards a wire instrument that looked like a badly bent crochet hook. Tom's interested in anything to do with rivers, so I started to tell him about the effigy I had found in the Ashburn, and the postcard attached to it. 'D'you know where the legend comes from?'

He snipped at the fly with a pair of tiny scissors. 'Old Cutty Dyer?' He gave a deep chuckle. 'He's been around a long time. My old auntie was frightened of him, would never cross a bridge at night for fear of him, and nor would any of her sisters.' He put down his scissors and sat back, readjusting his specs from his forehead. 'You know the story of St Christopher, don't you, maid?'

'Patron saint of travel,' I said.

'Of water crossings,' he corrected, holding up a finger. 'He carried the Christ child across the river on his shoulders.'

I nodded. 'He was a giant.'

'There was always a statue or shrine dedicated to him near any bridge or ford back in the old days,' Tom went on. 'Some folk think that Cuddyford Bridge on the way to Waterleat means the bridge of St

Christopher. There'd have been one here in Ashburton for sure, near King's Bridge. Course, all that lot got swept away during the Reformation. They didn't want people to worship the saints any more. Some folk think that Cutty is another name for Christopher, that the Protestant church turned him into an ogre to discourage people from having faith in him.'

He scratched behind his ear. 'Well, that's the story I've heard. Course, there may be others. Anyway, somebody's having a bit of a joke, by the sound of it.'

I chatted with him for half an hour and sorted out his shopping list. I offered to take his books back to the library but he shook his head. 'I'll stagger along with those. I've got to keep these bones moving and I can just about make it that far.'

'You'll be hopping about like a two-year-old when you've had this operation,' I promised him. He grunted. 'Still no date?' I asked sadly, and he shook his head.

After I'd dealt with Tom's shopping, I popped into Kate and Adam's cafe, *Sunflowers*, to blag a free coffee. My luck was in, and I got a free shortbread as well. Because of its quiet location, *Sunflowers* suffers long periods with no customers, a bit like *Old Nick's*, and for a while I thought I was the only person sitting at a table. This suited me. It meant I could enjoy a quiet perusal of a paper someone had left behind, even if it was a copy of the dratted *Dartmoor Gazette*.

On the front page was a photograph of a smiling couple: Digby Jerkin and Amanda Waft, with the headline *Famous Husband and Wife Acting Team Settle in Ashburton.* I couldn't help smiling. Chloe would be furious. And she wouldn't be the only one, I realised, as I read the accompanying article, in which Amanda stated that she and her husband hoped to introduce a little culture to the area. With this artlessly patronising remark she had without doubt alienated all the volunteers who ran Ashburton Arts Centre, the members of Dartmoor Operatic Society, Ashburton Players, the community choir, the Dartmoor Chamber Orchestra, all the local art and craft groups, the poetry society, archaeological society, International Cookery School and everyone else who had been enjoying a very fulfilling cultural existence without any help from her, thank you very much. Even Ricky and Morris would be miffed.

As I sat there, having a quiet chuckle, I became aware of a light pattering sound, a delicate clicking of nails on the stone-flagged floor. I looked up to find Lottie the whippet gazing at me soulfully, her head cocked enquiringly on one side, as if she was wondering if it was safe to approach.

I held out a hand to her. 'Hello, Lottie,' I said softly, and she came close, sitting by me and letting me stroke her smooth head gently. I heard another tapping noise then, and realised that around the corner, where I couldn't see him, Mr Daniel Thorncroft was making use of Adam and Kate's free Wi-Fi. Presumably, he couldn't see me either. Lottie and I stayed quiet, while she laid her slender muzzle on my knee and I continued to stroke her head. Sophie has a dark, soulful gaze that can melt your heart – she's been practising it for years – but she was barely a close runner up to Lottie. Her tragic stare was heartbreaking. She seemed such a sad little dog.

'Lottie?' Her master's voice. He had just noticed her absence. I heard his chair scrape back. There was a note of near panic in his voice. 'Lottie?' He appeared around the corner, his specs perched on his nose, and grinned with relief at the sight of her. 'There you are!' The tip of her tail wagged, but she stayed where she was, her head on my knee. He frowned. 'Are you seducing my dog, Miss Browne with an "e"?' he accused me.

'I am, Mr Thorncroft.'

'She seems to like you.' His voice indicated that he found this puzzling. All dogs like me, I could have told him, and cats. In fact, I've never met an animal yet that didn't take to me. I'd like to think I give off some spiritual vibe that attracts them, like St Francis of Assisi, but it's probably the way I smell.

'I thought you'd wandered off,' he told her, and Lottie, knowing where her duty lay, returned to his side. He crouched down and grabbed her narrow muzzle gently. 'Can't have that, can I, Lottie?' he asked, and then added to me, 'Lottie and I like to howl together.'

This was said with a grin, but for a moment I read in his eyes the desperation of a man drowning in a sea of sorrow and clinging to a life raft. What he was saying was not a joke. Up there, in that lonely farmhouse with only the cold stone walls to hear them, they howled their grief into the wind.

I felt an impulse to reach out to him, but before I could move the cafe door opened and a voice said, 'Oh, there you are, darling!' and in swanned Meredith, looking stunning in knee-high boots, jeans and a sweater, a red beret set on her dark, shiny hair, a cream pashmina thrown carelessly around her shoulders. As he stood up, she kissed him briefly on the lips. 'I've been looking for you in all the wrong cafes,' she confessed, smiling and taking his arm. She dropped her voice. 'I didn't know you meant *this* place.'

'It's quiet here,' he responded. 'Lottie gets nervous when there are too many people around.'

She glanced down at Lottie briefly. 'You and that dog!' Her tone was all warm indulgence, but her raised eyebrow suggested something cooler. They went back to the table around the corner where I could hear the rustling of papers, the snapping shut of a briefcase, the jingle of a laptop shutting down. Mr Thorncroft was gathering up his things. A moment later the two swept by me.

'Oh, hello, Juno!' Meredith pretended that she was noticing me for the first time but I knew damn well she'd clocked me as soon as she came in.

So much for the grieving widower, I thought, as I watched them go out, arm in arm, the sad little whippet trotting at their heels. And then I remembered the photograph I had seen propped on the mantelpiece in the kitchen of Moorview Farm, the face of the woman with straight dark hair, dark eyes and dazzling smile. Of course Daniel Thorncroft would be attracted to Meredith Swann: she and his dead wife looked so alike. The photograph had only shown me a face, but I was willing to bet that the deceased Mrs Thorncroft had the same strong, lithe physique. So, perhaps Mr Thorncroft was a grief-stricken man, after all, chasing the reflections of his dead wife in a mirror.

Thursday took me to Torquay. I drove Chloe to her appointment with her consultant at Mount Stuart, a private hospital. She was booked in for various tests, which gave me a couple of hours to myself before I picked her up again.

Torquay – jewel of the English Riviera, a gracious Victorian seaside spa set on a stretch of glorious Devon coastline, which a succession of short-sighted, blockheaded councils had done their best to destroy, allowing ugly sixties tower blocks to be built overlooking the harbour, ripping out the old shopping street, and replacing original shops with stores set in brutal blocks of concrete. Attempts to beautify by later, more enlightened councils have led to the mess which is the main shopping street today. I'm being harsh. It's nothing that a few tons of Semtex wouldn't fix in a jiffy. On the positive side, there is a pleasing selection of charity shops, and on any other day of the week I'd have happily truffled my way around these. But today was Thursday, which meant that the town hall would be hosting its weekly Grand

Flea Market. I hied me thither in my never-ending search for stock.

I did well. I picked up a very handsome carved Indian table with a brass top, a Carlton Ware buttercup design serving dish, some silver-plated button hooks, a pair of ivory glove stretchers and a fake crocodile handbag, circa 1960. I thought the bag was hideous, but the vintage clothes I sell on commission for Ricky and Morris in the shop mean that I often get customers looking for that kind of thing. I also found a small toque from about the same period, composed entirely of speckled green feathers. I dread to think whose feathers they had been originally and hoped it wasn't an endangered species. But it was too late to return them to their owner, so I bought the hat along with the bag.

As I was loading my swag into White Van, a gentle nudge from my mobile phone told me that Chloe had finished with her hospital appointments and wanted lunch. I picked her up and drove her down to the seafront and we ate tartes flambé in a smart bistro overlooking the sea. Under the January sky the water was flat calm, gunmetal grey, the tiny white triangles of sails in the distance. I'm not really a seaside person; I prefer my feet on dry land. But it was pleasant enough to gaze upon while Chloe told me all about the gallstones her scan had just revealed and begged me not to allow her to eat anything rich as she tucked into chocolate torte.

After lunch I persuaded her to walk the few hundred yards along the promenade to admire the expensive yachts and cruisers in the harbour, many of them gin palaces and floating tax dodges that never left their moorings, as ostentatious a display of wealth as you're likely to find anywhere in the world.

Around the harbour are some gift shops and galleries, as well as a smart independent department store where Chloe liked to shop. We emerged an hour later, Chloe exhausted and suffering from credit card fatigue, so I drove us to one of Torquay's prettier suburbs, the little village of Cockington, where thatched cottages, tea shops and craft workshops exist aplenty. We enjoyed the inevitable cream tea, and I spent half an hour resisting Chloe's attempts to buy me some handmade earrings in iridescent glass, which I had foolishly admired and which Chloe kept telling me would perfectly match the mint green pashmina she had bought me.

I returned to *Old Nick's* late in the afternoon, leaving Mrs Chloe Berkeley-Smythe resting on her sofa, moaning over a copy of the *Dartmoor Gazette*, a sherry at her elbow, proclaiming that now the famous thespians had arrived her life in Ashburton was ruined. I recommended a cruise.

'Luke's been taken on,' Pat told me happily as I struggled into the shop carrying the Indian table, the feathered hat sliding about on its brass surface, the handbag dangling from my arm. She held the door open for me. 'He's been up with Ricky and Morris the last two days, working in their garden, you know, round their lake.'

'Oh, that's brilliant! I'm glad they're giving him a try.'

'Thanks to you,' she said shyly.

'Well, they need a regular gardener so let's hope it works out. Any customers?' I added hopefully, as I set the table down.

'You sold a little jug.' She consulted the label. 'Torquay pottery.'

'How much?'

'Three pound fifty.'

'All my troubles are at an end.' I lugged the table down the corridor into my unit.

I told Pat to go home, removed my meagre profit from the cash tin and locked the shop.

The sky was fading to pink and I watched the rooks perform their evening swoop around the rooftops. They would fly around the town several times before they dropped down to roost for the night in the cedars and sequoias next to St Andrew's Church. I love to see them wheeling around the sky and walked out to the corner of West Street so that I could watch them. They landed, gathering on the top of the church tower, raucously chattering, a cawing, fluttering brotherhood. Then the church clock chimed the quarter-hour and they took off again, a fountain of dark shapes, away over the rooftops, and I turned my steps back to Shadow Lane, to where I'd parked the van.

As it happened, I came out again, when it was fully dark. I'd eaten my way through the last of the cafe leftovers the night before, forgotten there was nothing in the fridge except birthday cake and neglected to do any shopping. Despite lunch and cream tea, I was feeling peckish. I had to go out and get something for supper.

I strolled back down through the town. I had a choice of three small convenience stores that stayed open all evening, but I lamented the loss of Mr Singh's. The dear couple who had run it when Nick was alive had retired and gone to live with their daughter and her family in Plymouth. Their corner shop was now boarded up, a sign advertising it was to rent, so I trudged on down to the end of North Street.

The rooks were now a-bed and the town was quiet. I could contemplate its uniqueness. In the old streets of Ashburton, no two adjacent buildings are alike. Many have been turned into shops, but above street level lighted windows show as golden rectangles beneath the steep and crooked gables of buildings that have stood for hundreds of years, next door to grand imposing townhouses, Victorian or Edwardian, with wide bay windows looking down over the street. Meredith Swann's gallery was set on the ground floor of just such a townhouse, with an impressive stone frontage and three storeys above. I glanced up at its bay windows and wondered if she had the whole building to herself, lucky cow.

No sooner was the thought out of my head than I saw her strolling down the street towards me, a rolled-up yoga mat sticking out of the bag she carried on one shoulder. We stopped and chatted. She'd just come from a Pilates class, she told me. With that and running and swimming she kept herself pretty fit. In fact, she had won a medal for competing in a triathlon. Well, good for her. No wonder she possessed such a disgustingly healthy glow. We said our goodbyes and she let herself in through the front door next to her gallery. It must take her to the flat above. After a moment the large bay windows lit up. I muttered enviously and moved on.

By now, my guts were rumbling. It seemed a long time since my cream tea, so I decided to abandon the idea of shopping for groceries in favour of a nip to the Indian takeaway. I slipped down a side street to cut off a corner, down a lane where a terrace of cottages stood, their front doors edging the narrow pavement.

I glanced right. Jessie Mole was standing in my path. She didn't see me and I dodged back into a doorway where I could wait until she had gone. But she lingered. She must have been loitering in that lane a full two minutes, staring into the lighted window of one of the old cottages. Whether it was a living room or a kitchen I couldn't tell from where I stood, but the curtains must have been drawn back despite the winter darkness, allowing Jessie to gawp her fill at whatever was going on inside. She took a white envelope from her bag, glanced guiltily over her shoulder, first one way, then the other, stepped forward and slid it through the letter box. Then she hurried off, as fast as her strange, hobbling gait would let her, turned a corner and was lost to sight.

I'd love to have known what was in that envelope. Jessie's furtiveness suggested she was up to mischief and I was willing to bet she wasn't simply delivering a birthday card. As I passed by the cottage I couldn't help glancing in the window, but the curtains were now drawn tight. I could hear the faint sounds of a television from within. Had whoever lived there spotted Jessie peering in, or had they just felt that uncomfortable itch between the shoulder blades, a suspicion of being observed? Well, whatever Jessie was up to was none of my business, and I carried on towards my objective: a sag bhaji, a garlic naan and a prawn vindaloo.

CHAPTER NINE

Just so you don't think I'm disgustingly greedy, I saved half of my takeaway with the intention of having it for supper the following night. As it turned out, I'd rather gone off the whole concept of supper by that time, but it was no fault of the food.

Next morning, after dog walking, I went back up to Druid Lodge to help Ricky and Morris, as I had rashly promised while drunk on Sunday. I parked in their drive next to a small pickup truck, which I assumed belonged to Luke the gardener. I could smell woodsmoke and see a faint cloud, darker than the grey sky, arising from a bonfire at the end of the garden. The buzzing of a chainsaw was coming from amongst the trees by the lake and I walked down the sloping lawn for a closer look. A figure in an orange checked shirt was working, sawing up a chopped-off branch. He paused for a moment, put down the chainsaw and lifted his safety goggles up onto his forehead. 'You must be Luke,' I called out. 'Hello.'

He turned to look at me. He was younger than I expected, probably a few years younger than me, his light brown hair cropped very short. He had a thin face, pale and slightly sallow. His rolled-up shirtsleeves showed one arm inked in faded blue from wrist to elbow with a tattoo of thorns and roses, the flowers just outlines, as if he was saving up to get them coloured-in. I know ink is fashionable, but you either love it or loathe it and I'm not a fan of it myself. He nodded in greeting, flicking a glance at me from light blue eyes, but he didn't remove his leather work gloves so we could shake hands. 'You must be Juno.' His smile was a shy, fleeting thing. He looked awkward.

'You're making progress.' I could see where he had begun his attack, working to clear an area hidden by the green foliage of thuggish rhododendrons.

'It's a pity to chop these off,' he said, pointing to the fallen branches.

'The flowers are beautiful,' I agreed, 'but are very invasive.' The spread of rhododendrons was a real nuisance on parts of the moor.

'I'm going to clear all this lot here,' Luke described a wide arc with his arm, 'let the light in, give the native species a chance.' For a moment I studied the overgrown copse, the dark lake with the tangled mass of grasses and weeds obscuring the bank, the Gunnera plant with leaves as big as parasols, the willow that bent low to admire its own reflection in the mirrored surface. He certainly had his work cut out.

Luke pulled his goggles back in place. 'Well, I must get on.'

'Nice to meet you,' I said.

He nodded, started up the chainsaw and turned his back.

I could only spare Ricky and Morris the morning, so concentrated on unpacking the latest returning panto costumes with only the briefest of stops for coffee and a chat about the good progress Luke was making down by the lake. As I was coming out of the house a couple of hours later, he was loading the chainsaw in the back of his pickup.

'Finished for the day?' I asked, surprised.

'Ken's chainsaw's knackered,' he said with a fleeting grin. 'I'll have to take it into town and get it fixed.' He flicked me a shy glance. 'Fancy coming for a pint?'

I really didn't. I don't drink at lunchtime. But I didn't want to appear reluctant. I didn't want to hurt his feelings, or, more importantly, Pat's.

'Not if you don't want—' he began.

'Of course I do,' I said hastily, 'but it will have to be a quick one. I've got a client this afternoon. Look, I'll drive my van down and follow you. Where do you want to go?'

'Victoria?' he suggested. He grinned shyly. 'I could murder a pint of Jail Ale.'

I laughed and got in the van.

The Victoria Inn is an old pub at the far end of North Street, and used to be known as 'The First and Last' back in the nineteenth century, when there were more than thirty inns and taverns packed into the little streets of Ashburton, a fact that made John Wesley, travelling Methodist minister and all-time party-pooper, declare it the most sinful town in England. It's a place that often buzzes with live bands during the evenings, but would be quieter during the daytime. Perhaps that's why Luke had chosen it, because he preferred a quiet spot. How many people in Ashburton knew him, I wondered, knew his story? And if they did, did he care?

I followed his van down the hill and along North Street and swung around into Mill Meadow to park my van next to his. From here we were looking at the back of the pub across the stream of the Ashburn which slides around its walls on its way into town and separated it from its little beer garden. Our way to the back door of the pub lay across a narrow metal bridge. For a moment I stood on it, watching the water race along beneath me. As I glanced downstream I could see the end of a concrete access ramp that led from the bank down to the water a few yards away. Most of it was obscured by riverside greenery, but from where I stood I could make out a long trickle of red staining the sloping concrete, a hand lying palm upward and a tangle of dark wet hair.

'Look,' I breathed. 'There, on the ramp . . . there's someone . . . there . . . lying . . .'

Luke pushed me aside, and I hurried after him, back across the bridge. I was only a second behind him. When I reached him, he was standing at the top of the ramp, frozen, staring at the body lying there: her blue coat, her ankle socks, the bow in her tangled, wet hair. Jessie Mole was dead, a scarlet gash across her pale throat, a thin trail of her blood staining the concrete ramp. There was something pinned to her coat, a postcard inside a clear plastic envelope, a message scrawled on it in bold, red letters. I felt sick and gripped Luke's arm as he mouthed the words slowly: *Cutty Dyer Dun This*.

I wanted someone sane to talk to. When I got home, I phoned Elizabeth and she promised to be round within the hour. Meantime I ran myself a deep bath. I felt soiled by what I had seen, by the smell of death still lingering in my nostrils.

For what seemed like hours I had faced questions, first from a uniformed police officer, then from Detective Constable DeVille – beg pardon, Detective *Sergeant* DeVille – she has recently passed her exams, apparently. Whatever her rank, Cruella's icy violet stare and disapproving little mouth was not what I wanted to be faced with, but Inspector Ford was busy in the next room with Detective Constable Dean Collins, interviewing Luke.

They'd let him go by the time Cruella had finished with me. After all, he'd only seen what I'd seen – poor Jessie lying dead on the ramp by the water with her throat cut. Whereas, unfortunately for me, I had not only been one of the two people who found her body, I had also found the wretched dummy, which had suddenly assumed significance. Dean must have been getting brownie points for rescuing the thing from the river and for preserving it and, more importantly, for preserving the postcard. Forensic examination of both messages would be taking place, I'd been told rather primly by Cruella, to determine whether they'd been written by the same hand. Unfortunately, any useful DNA evidence was unlikely to be found on the dummy as it had been in the water too long.

I stayed in the bathwater too long and had only just hauled out and towelled myself off when I heard the doorbell announcing Elizabeth's arrival. I wrapped my dressing gown around me and trudged downstairs.

As I opened the door, she held up a carrier bag. 'I thought you could use a brandy, but I don't have any, so I come bearing gin.'

Excellent woman. We hugged.

'It must have been ghastly for you.' She sat on my sofa while I hunted for glasses.

We didn't bother with tonic, ice or lemon.

'It was,' I breathed, shuddering at the memory of the terrible scarlet split across Jessie's white throat. 'It seems I may be the last person to have seen her alive.' I told Elizabeth how I'd seen her loitering in the lane the night before, peeping in the window of the cottage before posting something through the letter box.

'Do you know who lives there?' she asked.

'I haven't a clue. But the police are going to interview the owner, to talk to everyone who lives on the lane in case anyone else spotted her.' I stared down at the clear glass of gin I was cradling and sighed. 'Do you know what really bothers me? I wonder if I hadn't reported finding that damned dummy, if that story had never appeared in the paper, perhaps Jessie wouldn't have been murdered.'

'Of course she would,' Elizabeth cut in firmly. 'It may amuse the twisted imagination of the person who killed her to make a reference to Cutty Dyer, perhaps prompted by the story in the paper, but no one is going to cut a woman's throat for a joke.'

'I'm not so sure. You hear about psychopaths all the time. And Ashburton's not immune from loonies.'

'If there's a psychopathic killer abroad in Ashburton,' she responded calmly, 'then he would have killed anyway. He either had a motive for picking her as his victim, or poor Jessie was in the wrong place at the wrong time. Either way, the story in the newspaper is irrelevant. And presumably I don't need to point out that if the latter is true, the victim might just as easily been you.'

I considered this and puffed out my cheeks in a sigh. 'I was home again in half an hour. We don't know what time Jessie was killed. For all we know, she was roaming about all night. She was always wandering around the town, snooping.'

'And we don't know how long she'd been lying on that ramp?' Elizabeth asked.

'No. It was just chance that Luke and I were the first people to go to the back door of the pub this morning and go out onto the bridge. Anyone parking in Mill Meadow might have seen her on that ramp. It must have been a quiet morning.'

My phone suddenly began ringing. 'Oh God,' I muttered. 'News is getting around.'

Elizabeth told me to ignore it, but I shook my head. Before I could answer it, she reached out and picked up the receiver. 'Hello? Yes, this is her number,' she answered in a quietly authoritative voice. 'Who's speaking?' She listened a moment then covered the mouthpiece with her hand. 'It's Luke,' she said softly. 'He wants to see you.'

'Tell him to come over.'

Elizabeth raised her brows. 'You're sure?'

'Yes. It's OK.'

When she put the phone down she gave me one of her quizzical looks. 'Do you want me to stay?'

'No, thanks. It's all right. He had just as big a shock as I did. I'm sure he wants to talk things over.'

She waited until Luke rang the doorbell while I dressed hastily.

'Thanks for coming,' I said.

'My pleasure. Call me again if you need me.' She indicated the bottle on the coffee table with a nod of her head. 'I'll leave you the gin.'

I heard her exchange a word with Luke when she opened the front door and tell him to come up. He arrived a few moments later. I thought he had looked pale when I had first met him that morning. Now he looked ill. 'Vulnerable' was the word that came into my mind. I felt like giving him a hug but feared I might embarrass him.

'We never did get as far as that drink,' he said, after an awkward moment looking round him.

'Gin?' I offered.

He shook his head. 'I'd settle for a cup of tea.'

He followed me into the kitchen and I put the kettle on. 'I wanted to thank you, for putting in a word for me, for getting me the job.'

'It was nothing.'

'No, I'm grateful.' He smiled. 'Looks like it might keep me busy for a week or two.'

'Several weeks, I should think.'

Mugs in hand we returned to the living room. 'That's why I wanted to buy you a drink this morning,' he went on, 'to say thank you, only . . . well, the other thing got in the way.'

'It did rather,' I agreed weakly. We were silent, remembering the moment when we found Jessie's body.

'Did you know her?' he asked eventually.

'Not really. I mean, everyone in town knew Jessie. She made a nuisance of herself.'

His hands cupped around his mug as if he was drawing warmth from it, one knee jigging up and down restlessly. 'I know Pat told you about me, being in prison . . .' He stole a glance at me. 'It was just one punch. This bloke was being an arsehole, mouthing off in the pub and I took a swing at him. But he hit his head on the corner of a table on the way down and . . .' He shrugged.

'And the court didn't accept that it was an accident?'

'I pleaded guilty. I didn't mean to kill him, but I couldn't say I didn't mean to hit him. The judge said I had to learn that actions have consequences. He gave me three years. I only served eighteen months. I'm still on licence for good behaviour.'

'Well, thanks for telling me, Luke, but you really didn't need to.'

'I like to be straight with people. I told Ricky and Morris before I started. They were fine about it.' He flashed a nervous smile, then began looking around him, as if now he'd said what he came to say, he was searching for a way to escape. Just at that moment Bill leapt on the arm of the sofa and chirruped a greeting. Luke began stroking his head and he responded with a deep, rumbling purr. 'What happened to him?' he asked. 'He's only got one eye.'

'Fight with a chicken,' I told him. I watched his face as he stroked the cat. Despite the brutal haircut his features were gentle, almost aesthetic; his pale skin, high cheekbones and delicate brows would have suited a young monk, or a medieval saint in a stained-glass window. Bill slid neatly onto his lap with every intention of settling down. That cat is a complete tart.

Conscious of my scrutiny, Luke looked up. 'Did the police ask you a lot of questions?'

I told him about my interview and the fact I'd seen Jessie hanging about in the lane the night before. 'The police didn't give you a hard time, did they?'

'What, cos of me being in prison?' He shook his head.

'No. They were all right.' He put down his mug. 'I'd better be off. I've got to get up early. I want to get a good day's work in and I still haven't got that chainsaw seen to.'

We said our goodbyes. Luke submitted, diffidently, to a brief hug.

As soon as he left, the phone started ringing. I picked up.

'Sandy Thomas here,' a Welsh voice breathed excitedly, '*Dartmoor Gazette.*'

'Eff off!' I advised her and slammed down the receiver.

CHAPTER TEN

Detective Constable Dean Collins sounded unconvinced on the phone. I was still feeling the after effects of consuming half a bottle of gin the night before, a mug of tea clutched in one hand, the phone in the other as I tried to prevent Bill, who was sitting on the kitchen table, from licking the butter from my breakfast toast.

'You're certain, are you, Juno, about the number of the cottage?'

'I don't know the number of the cottage,' I admitted grumpily, 'but it was the second one from the end. It's got a green front door and reddish curtains.' I remembered the pink glow the light had cast as I had walked past the window, a few moments after Jessie Mole had skulked off around the corner. 'Why do you ask?'

'Because we sent some uniforms down to interview the owners . . .' He paused briefly, I could imagine him consulting his notes '. . . a Mr and Mrs Williams live there with two teenage children . . . and they say nothing came through the letter box during the evening. I wondered if perhaps you'd got the wrong house.'

I knew I had the right cottage, just as I remembered very clearly the white envelope in Jessie's hand as she posted it through the letter box. 'They're lying,' I told him, 'about nothing coming through the letter box.'

'Why would they?' he asked.

'It could be a motive for murder, couldn't it, whatever was in that envelope?'

He laughed. 'You think Mr and Mrs Williams killed Jessie? You think one of them is Cutty Dyer?'

'Well, anything's possible.' I put my tea down, successfully elbowed Bill off the table and rescued my toast. 'You should get a search warrant.'

Dean laughed. 'Don't get carried away! You thinking you saw Jessie put a note through their door isn't sufficient cause—'

'I don't *think* I saw anything,' I responded indignantly. 'Anyway,' I added after a moment's thoughtful chewing, 'they've probably destroyed that note by now, if it's incriminating.'

I heard Dean give the sort of weary sigh that I usually associate with Inspector Ford.

'What about the postcard on Jessie's coat?' I went on. 'Was it written by the same person who put one on the dummy?'

'I can't tell you that!' He sounded shocked. 'You want to know that sort of thing you'd better join the force.'

'No, thanks,' I responded, a little tartly. Saving his life only a short while ago had obviously not entitled me to any favours in the information department.

'Anyway, forensics is still working on it,' he admitted.

'Is anyone going up to Owl House?' I asked.

'We'll take a look around, see if we can find out what she was doing up there. I don't suppose we're likely to find anything . . . I will tell you one thing, though, if you can stop crunching down the phone for a minute.'

I swallowed. 'What?'

'You'll have to keep this to yourself, mind.'

'What?' I whispered, all attention.

'This Cutty Dyer thing, it doesn't . . . Oh sorry, Sarge!' The voice I could hear slicing through the air in the background could only have belonged to Cruella, who was now, it had to be remembered, Dean's superior officer. 'I'll come right away!' And he put the phone down on me.

'Bugger!' I muttered.

Despite my conviction, Dean had sown a seed of uncertainty in my brain and on my way to the shop I detoured down the lane to check that the cottage I had told the police about was the right one.

It was. I knew it was. So, what if the envelope had been missed? If it had been shoved under the door then it might have slipped under the doormat, but it was difficult to see how that could have happened when it was dropped through the letter box. But if the message it contained had been innocent, why wouldn't the Williamses admit to receiving it?

But maybe, of the four people living in that house, three of them genuinely knew nothing about it. I imagined the family gathered in their living room, curtains drawn, watching television, one of them getting up to make a cup of tea or use the bathroom, and spotting the envelope on the mat, picking it up and hiding it in a pocket, tearing it open and reading it later, alone, reading in appalled silence something so sordid and incriminating that they couldn't tell anyone about it. In which case, Jessie could be involved in blackmail and I wondered which one of the four of them the note had been addressed to.

It was bedlam in the shop all day. In the few minutes of quiet I got, first thing after I'd opened up and put the lights on, I managed to polish the filthy glass on the Millais print and hang it on the wall. It looked so much better cleaned, the details of the flowers floating on the water glowing like little jewels. Then Pat came in to see that I was all right after discovering Jessie's body, followed by Sophie, to see that I was all right, followed by Ricky and Morris, who came in with more vintage clothes and to see that I was all right, and finally Elizabeth, who knew I was all right but decided to come in anyway.

The story of poor Jessie's murder was all over town by now, the ramp by the river where we had found her hidden by a little tent, the whole area taped off, police everywhere, making house-to-house enquiries, trying to track her movements on the night she was killed. Ashburton was in shock, horrified by the callous brutality of her murder, but also agog for gruesome details. We had a string of so-called 'customers', most of whom claimed to be 'just browsing' but I'm sure had come in to gawp at me. Ricky suggested standing me in the window. The talk was all of Jessie, and of Cutty Dyer and whether Ashburton now had a lunatic on the loose, some crazed killer who'd assumed Cutty's identity, and whether he would be cutting the throat of some other poor unfortunate soon. Women in Ashburton were no longer safe and should not be venturing out alone after dark, it was decided. When a young man sidled up to me and said casually, 'So, Juno, you found another body?' we threw him out. He might as well have had *Dartmoor Gazette* stamped on his forehead.

Ricky and Morris hung around quite a while, refreshing their stock and re-dressing Mavis the mannequin, whose 1960s hippy outfit had begun to look a little tired. They replaced it with a full-skirted dress, circa 1950, in green taffeta, changing her long black wig for a short blonde one. So they were there when two completely unexpected visitors wandered in. At least, Morris was upstairs in the kitchen making everyone a cup of tea and cutting up the cake he'd made while Ricky was sorting through things on the clothes rail. At the sight of the couple who appeared in the back room, he concealed himself behind the dressing screen.

'Oh! Vintage clothes! How lovely!' Amanda Waft pronounced as she meandered across the floor to the clothes rail, each foot placed down very precisely, like a lioness stalking its prey. At close quarters she was older than I had thought. I could see that she had once been beautiful, a finely boned thoroughbred. But she was too thin, all knees, wrists and elbows, and had no boobs at all. I wondered if she was ill, but Ricky informed me later that she had always been as flat as Norfolk. With one long arm she pulled out a feather boa and wound it around her tanned but wrinkled neck. She turned to the man who had followed her into the room. 'What do you think, Digby?'

Digby was a short and burly figure with slightly protruding eyes, his black crinkly hair silver at the temples. He looked like a frog in a wig. 'Oh, very chic, darling! Digby Jerkin, hello!' he introduced himself suddenly, thrusting out a hand for me to shake.

'Juno,' I responded. 'You're new to Ashburton, aren't you? Are you settling in?'

'Oh, we're just looking around you know,' he assured me heartily, 'for our dream home. We've found a very pretty house to rent in town while we look about.'

Amanda, meanwhile, had discovered the Millais print. 'Oh, poor Ophelia!' She heaved a deep sigh and began to intone: '*There is a willow grows aslant a brook, that shows his hoar leaves in the glassy stream; there with fantastic garlands did she come . . .*'

I have to admit her rendition of the Shakespeare was a lot better than mine. For one thing, she knew it all, and despite her obvious theatricality, her voice was deep and mellifluous, like flowing caramel, and she was able to inject it with genuine sadness.

'*Of crowflowers, nettles, daisies and long purples . . .*'

I wondered if she was going to do the whole thing. She was. Silence fell over the shop. As she continued the speech, Sophie, Pat and Elizabeth gathered in the doorway of the back room to listen. I glanced at Digby. His face was absolutely rapt and I realised that here was her most adoring fan.

'*. . . from her melodious lay to muddy death*,' she finished. There was a moment's pause and she looked around, smiling expectantly, her eyebrows raised in enquiry.

Digby began to applaud. 'Bravo!' he cried. Feeling that something was required of us, we began to clap too, while Amanda executed a gracious little curtsey. Digby grabbed her hand and kissed it. 'It gladdens my heart to hear you give that speech again.'

'Oh, darling,' she murmured.

'Oh for Gawd's sake, Mandy,' Ricky told her, stepping from behind the screen, 'do stop showing off!'

'Rickeee!' Her voice soared from contralto to soprano in one long glissando as she flung her arms around his neck. 'Oh, Ricky, what absolute bliss! What on earth are you doing here?'

There followed a conversation filled with *darlings* and *old chaps* as the three luvvies – four once Morris returned with the tea – caught up on the intervening years. The thespians were offered tea and cake, and while Digby looked as if he might have enjoyed a slice, Amanda declared that she never ate cake with much the same shudder that she might have sworn she never chewed worms.

'I did notice a rather attractive wine bar in the main street,' Digby said, and to my huge relief, the four of them swept off to continue their reminiscences there, Amanda still sporting the feather boa, Ricky favouring me with a frankly lewd wink as they left. I was so relieved they'd gone. After ten minutes in their company I felt exhausted. I could just imagine the effect they'd have on Chloe Berkeley-Smythe.

'What the hell was all that about?' Pat demanded, venturing back into the room. I explained about Ashburton's famous new residents.

'Thank God they've gone!' Sophie crept in from the front of the shop.

'Yes,' I surveyed the loaded tray that Morris had brought down with him, 'there's all the more cake for us. Tuck in!' I looked about me. 'Where's Elizabeth?'

'Serving a customer,' Pat told me.

'Well, I'm glad someone is.'

As a matter of fact, we had a steady stream of customers during the afternoon. Notoriety obviously pays off. Even Meredith Swann came in, on the arm of Mr Daniel Thorncroft, to take a look around. She bought one of Sophie's paintings, a tangle of purple foxgloves in a summer hedgerow. 'It'll look beautiful above my bed, don't you think, Dan?' she asked.

He'd obviously been in her bedroom because Dan agreed. He must be her sex slave. Today there was something different about him. It took me a minute to work out that he'd simply had a decent haircut. Ms Swann was exerting an influence. I wondered if she'd wielded the shears herself.

I was pleased for Sophie making a big sale, even though it was an obvious part of Meredith's campaign to seduce her, to poach her work for her own gallery. After she and her acolyte had departed, I put it to Soph that I really didn't mind if she wanted to display some of her paintings there, as long as she didn't abandon *Old Nick's* altogether. But she was adamant. 'No, thanks! She'd rob me blind. She'd want exclusive rights, and she'd put a massive commission on top of my price. I've met her sort before. Remember your friend, Verbena Clarke?'

Like Meredith, Verbena had offered to sell paintings for Sophie and had taken it for granted that as the middleman, or -woman, in those transactions, she should take the lion's share of the profit. Sophie had other ideas.

Elizabeth left early to pick Olly up from Honeysuckle Farm where he was helping Ken for the day, but we continued to be busy with people wandering around till closing time. Sophie and Pat left together, after counting out their profits, leaving me to lock the shop. Before I left,

I popped into the back room to make sure everything was tidy on my unit. As I cast a last glance around the walls, I noticed that the picture of Ophelia had undergone a subtle alteration. I frowned, drawing close, touching the glass that I had cleaned only that morning. There was a mark on it now: blood-red, drawn with something like a marker pen, scribbled back and forth across Ophelia's pale neck. Someone had cut her throat.

CHAPTER ELEVEN

'Someone is playing games, Juno,' Detective Inspector Ford told me as he studied the Millais picture with a heavy frown. 'And you're sure you saw no one touch it?'

'The shop's been really busy all day today,' I told him. 'As far as I know, the only person who showed any interest in it was Amanda Waft, and she didn't go near it. She just stood in the middle of the room and quoted Shakespeare at it . . . The painting illustrates a scene from *Hamlet*,' I added as he gave me a puzzled glance.

'Yes, I'm aware of that,' he responded. 'I just wondered who Amanda Waft might be.'

I explained, as the inspector seated himself carefully on the edge of a small table, his arms folded, and listened patiently. There was a weariness about him these days, as if responsibility weighed heavily on his broad shoulders. I wondered why he'd come himself when I'd phoned to report the incident, not just sent Dean Collins or Cruella to talk to me. 'You say you have no idea where this painting came from?'

'No,' I answered with a shrug. 'It was delivered by someone about a week ago. Pat was the only one here at the time. The parcel had my name written on it, but that was all. There was no note. I've no idea who sent it.'

'And this was *after* your discovery of the effigy in the water was reported in the *Gazette*?'

'Yes, it was.'

The inspector stood up and returned to the painting, his lower lip sucked in thoughtfully.

'This red mark on the glass, it's not paint. It must have been made by some kind of marker. Do you have anything in the shop that could make a mark on glass?'

'We've got some markers we use for pricing in a pot on the counter. There's a big red one.' I stood up. 'I'll fetch it.'

'No,' he said quickly. 'I don't want you to touch it, just show me where it is.'

I took him through to the counter, but while the pen pot was in its usual place, there was no sign of the red marker. I hunted underneath around in case it had been dropped and rolled underneath the counter, but I couldn't see it. 'One of the girls might have used it and put it down somewhere else,' I said.

'Or, someone, anyone, could have picked it up and used it to make the mark on the painting, on impulse,' he suggested. 'You say the painting came wrapped up. You didn't, by any chance, keep that wrapping paper?'

I shook my head. 'Sorry. It only had my name written on it, in black ink.'

The inspector grimaced. 'It might have been useful to compare the handwriting.'

'. . . with the note on the effigy?'

He nodded slowly.

'And the note on Jessie's body?'

'As I say,' he answered evasively, 'it might have been useful. But I don't think we should leap to conclusions here. I think someone is playing games, someone who's read about you in the paper, came in here, saw that picture and thought it was a good joke to scribble on it. There are some very sick people about.'

'One of them being Jessie's killer,' I retorted with some heat. 'And perhaps the same person who wrote the postcard attached to her body and who happens to carry a red marker in his pocket has been here today, in my shop.'

The inspector said nothing, just favoured me with his stare. 'I am not dismissing this as a trivial incident,' he told me with a note of reproach. 'I will send someone from forensics to dust this picture for fingerprints . . .'

Now I felt embarrassed by my outburst. 'Um . . . I'm afraid I gave it a jolly good clean before I hung it on the wall,' I confessed awkwardly.

He gave a wry smile. He got up to leave and I walked with him to the shop door. 'One more thing, Juno,' he added, fixing me with his steady gaze, 'no sleuthing.'

'What do you mean?' I asked innocently.

'You know what I mean. I don't want you going around Ashburton asking questions, trying to find out who killed Jessie.'

'Well, as if I would!' I protested.

'I mean it. You listen to me now,' he insisted, pointing a stern finger in front of my face. 'Whoever killed Jessie is a dangerous customer. You leave finding him to us.'

Now I knew why he'd come himself: to warn me to behave. 'I will . . . I promise,' I added as he continued to give me the hard stare.

'You've been lucky in the past, Juno, but luck can run out.' The bell on the shop door jangled as he opened it. 'I don't want to have to fish your body out of the river.'

My promise to the inspector ruined my plan, which had been to go to the Williamses' house and ask them openly about the note Jessie pushed through their letter box. Now I'd have to be more subtle about it – subtle, and ever-so-slightly unethical.

I rolled up unannounced at Olly and Elizabeth's house just as they were putting supper on the table. They immediately offered to lay another place and the slight guilt I felt was put to flight when I considered that all I had to eat at home was the congealed remains of a prawn vindaloo. Whereas, the home-made lasagne Olly had just brought out of the oven looked and smelt delicious. He had cooked it, Elizabeth assured me, all she'd done was prepare the salad and warm the garlic bread. I'd only meant to pop in, I told them, and apologised for not bringing dessert.

'Of course, what this really begs for is a glass of red wine,' Elizabeth sighed, 'but I'm afraid we're out.'

'Nothing wrong with water,' Olly told us, a little primly. He'd been brought up by his great-grandmother and disapproved of alcohol.

Elizabeth hid a smile. 'Now, to what do we owe the honour?'

While we ate, I told them what had happened to the picture of Ophelia, and how Inspector Ford had warned me against sleuthing.

'He's giving you excellent advice,' Elizabeth said drily, 'I suggest you take it.'

Olly's eyes had grown round with wonder. 'Do you think Cutty Dyer's been in your shop today?' he breathed. 'Just think, you might've served him, sold him something!'

It wasn't a comfortable thought. 'Do you know any kids at your school called Williams?' I asked. 'There would be two of them.'

He rubbed his freckled nose thoughtfully. 'There's a Williams in my year. His name's really Philip but everyone just calls him Will. He's got a sister in the sixth form. I can't think of any others.'

'Do you know where they live?' I told him where I had seen Jessie posting her envelope through the letter box.

He was nodding. 'Yeh, that's them.'

Elizabeth shot me an enquiring glance. 'Why are you asking Olly?'

'Because they deny receiving the envelope,' I answered. 'I just wondered if Olly knew anything about the family, that's all.'

'Juno, you are not to drag Olly into this,' she warned me firmly.

'Blackmail!' He announced dramatically, rising to his feet, his little pixie face alight with excitement. He held up a thin forefinger. 'That's what this is! Blackmail! That Jessie Mole was blackmailing Will!'

'Why would she have been blackmailing Will?' I asked.

'Because of his maths homework,' he breathed in a whisper.

Elizabeth and I exchanged glances.

'Calm down, Olly,' she told him. 'Sit down and tell us what you mean.'

'Will is best friends with Pierce,' he began, 'he lives three doors down. They walk home together, and cos Will's mum doesn't get home from work till later, Will has always gone and done his homework in Pierce's house until his mum gets back. But Pierce's mum, she works at home, got her own office like, up in the attic and she never comes down till it's time to make the supper. But as soon as he gets in, she makes him do his piano practice . . .'

'This is Pierce?'

'Yeh,' he nodded. 'She's making Pierce learn the piano. She leaves her door open upstairs so she can hear him practising his scales . . .'

'While Will sits there doing his homework?'

'That's it. Only Pierce don't want to learn the piano, he *hates* learning the piano and he hates practising scales. Anyway, one day,' he went on, glancing at each of us to make sure he still had our attention, 'Will – who's been listening to these scales for years – says to him, "I reckon I can play them scales just as well as you." So, they have a bet on. Will bets Pierce that he can play the scales and that his mum won't even notice the difference. So he did, and she didn't.'

'She didn't realise it wasn't Pierce playing?'

'No. So ever since, every day, when they come home, Will practises the scales instead of Pierce.'

'And what does Will get out of this arrangement?' Elizabeth asked.

'Pierce does his maths homework.'

'How long has this been going on?' I asked.

He rubbed his nose thoughtfully. 'Oh, a couple of years.'

I laughed. 'And nobody knows?'

'Well, everybody at school knows except for the maths teacher and the music teacher, and Pierce's mother.'

'But what happens when Pierce has to take a piano exam?'

'Ah, well, that's easy, isn't it?' Olly grinned. 'Examination nerves! Poor Pierce, he gets 'em terrible!' His face grew serious again. 'But if this Jessie Mole found out . . . and was blackmailing Will . . .'

'I doubt if someone else doing your homework—' I began.

'They could of done it together . . .' His blue eyes grew wide.

'Could *have*,' Elizabeth corrected.

'They could *have*, him and Pierce, cut her throat,' he carried on dramatically, 'all that blood . . . there would have been gallons of it . . .'

'That will do, Olly!' Elizabeth said firmly. 'This isn't a fantasy. A real person has been murdered.'

'Sorry,' he murmured awkwardly.

'It's my fault.' I smiled apologetically at Elizabeth. 'I shouldn't have brought the subject up. That lasagne was excellent,' I added to Olly, and said no more about the Williamses or Jessie Mole.

CHAPTER TWELVE

Detective Constable Dean Collins was not pleased to receive my phone call. It was nine-thirty on a Saturday evening, he'd not long come off duty and he and Gemma had only just got baby Alice off to sleep. Well, he shouldn't have given me his private number, should he? And after he'd warned me off, I could hardly ring Inspector Ford. But I apologised for the intrusion and told him about what happened at the shop.

'When we were talking on the phone this morning,' I said, realising this now felt like a century ago, 'you were about to tell me something about Jessie's murder before Cruella cut you off.'

There was a suspicious silence at the end of the line. 'Was I?'

'So, was the postcard found on Jessie's body written by the same person who wrote the one attached to the dummy?'

'We're not sure,' he admitted after a pause. 'It could

be that the murderer had read about the dummy in the *Gazette* and thought it was a good joke, the sick bastard.'

'Just like the person who put that mark on my painting today. Perhaps he just enjoys the idea of getting the town stirred up, getting everyone talking about Cutty Dyer.'

Dean hesitated. 'Look, Juno, you've got to keep all this to yourself, right?'

I dutifully gave my word.

'The boss would have my hide if he knew I'd been talking to you. There's something else about that postcard. After we found her body yesterday morning, we searched Jessie's cottage. In her kitchen we found a drawer stuffed with those *From Devon With Love* postcards, with her handwriting on . . .'

'*Cutty Dyer Dun This*?' I asked.

'In her handwriting,' he confirmed, 'almost as if she'd been practising.'

It was my turn to be silent, to try to understand the significance of this. I remembered Jessie hobbling along on the pavement beside me, pressing me with questions about that dummy. Suddenly, it made sense: her eagerness for details, the almost triumphant leer on her face. She already knew what that dummy looked like. She wanted to hear the details from me so she could feed off my feelings of horror, my sense of revulsion. But could she have made the thing herself? It would have been simple enough for her to stuff a pair of overalls with packaging, but somehow, I couldn't imagine her fashioning that mask. It seemed too sophisticated.

'We've been trying to find out if masks like that are

sold anywhere,' Dean went on, 'but it looks as if this was a home-made job, a one-off.'

'Perhaps Jessie's murderer made the mask.'

'We don't know that. At the moment, the only connection between the dummy and the murder is the postcard about Cutty Dyer.'

'But why would Jessie write more of those? Was she planning another dummy?'

Dean grunted. 'I would say she just enjoyed making mischief, judging by some of the stuff we found in that cottage of hers.'

That much was true. Stealing Chloe's messages to the milkman had been a simple way of making mischief, posting poisonous notes through people's letter boxes was another.

'She was definitely a weird one,' Dean went on. 'She had owl ornaments everywhere in that cottage, hundreds of 'em.' I could hear him shudder at the end of the line. 'Gives me the creeps, all those eyes staring at you.'

'Perhaps she and the murderer made that dummy together,' I went on, trying to figure things out. 'Jessie wasn't very bright. Perhaps, for her, it was just a joke or the murderer convinced her that it was.'

'What? And then the two of them fell out and he killed her?'

'Unless she was his intended victim all along,' I suggested.

'He got Jessie to collude in her own murder?'

'Unknowingly,' I said. 'That would have been a real joke, wouldn't it?'

* * *

Next day was Sunday, which meant there was no Tribe to walk and no shop, so naturally what I wanted to do was to go up to the abandoned Owl House, have a poke around and see if I could discover what Jessie had been doing there. But as I drove up to the front gate in White Van there was already a police car parked in the drive. I thought perhaps my presence might not be welcome, so I tootled on past, nonchalantly.

I decided to activate plan B. I'd seen a clearance sale advertised in a house near Dartington, so I drove there to see if I could pick up any stock for the shop. I'd made up my mind I would spend half of Brian's birthday money on paying the shop's bills and half on increasing my rather sparse hoard of stock.

The sale was in a Victorian house recently inherited by a young couple and full of furniture and family belongings they didn't want. They were planning to rip out all of the panelling, they told me proudly, the original fireplaces, oak staircase and the kitchen range, replace the mullioned windows with bi-folds and commit other acts of vandalism too barbarous to mention in their quest for the fashionable, bare, minimalist look. Apart from lamenting the fact that the house wasn't listed, I wondered how it is that people like them get to inherit such places. It just isn't fair.

On the positive side, they had no idea what anything was worth. This didn't stop them trying to be greedy, though. Their advertisement had attracted dealers from all around, several of my fellow traders from Ashburton, and I could soon see there was no point in my competing for any of the furniture or larger items when I lost a bidding war for a pretty davenport. So I concentrated on smaller things, things the owners couldn't believe anyone would want: odd brass weights for kitchen scales, a chipped enamel coffee pot, stone ginger beer bottles, tiny medicine bottles in blue ridged glass, walking sticks, a biscuit barrel, glass stoppers minus their decanters, a tin full of spoons – silver jam spoons unnoticed – and a Victorian brass beehive-shaped pot for containing balls of string, with a hole in the top for the string to come out and – best of all – still with original scissors still attached.

I came away, well pleased with my swag, especially as I'd also managed to negotiate a good price for a broken nursery chair. Children's chairs are always popular. I'd have to pay for the cane seating to be repaired, but there would still be a profit in it. The van bumped along the drive, and before I turned out of the gate, I noticed a scattering of snowdrops across the lawn, mingled with pale mauve crocuses. Spring was happening in this garden, at least this year. Next year, if things went according to plan, it would be lost under decking.

On the way back home, I stopped at Staverton where the medieval bridge spans the water in four solid but graceful stone arches. Next to the bridge is a tiny station for the steam train that in the summer, laden with visitors, chugs the line between Totnes and Buckfastleigh. The station was deserted now, the little engine parked for the winter behind the gates of the level crossing.

Built as a crossing place for wagons, the bridge is barely wide enough to take a car. But I parked up so that I could walk across. I paused in one of the tiny jutting refuges along its length, spaces just big enough for a person to stand in and not be mown down by a horse and cart as it crossed the bridge. I sat my bum down on the stone parapet and gazed down at the water.

This was not the little River Ashburn which flowed through Ashburton but an arm of the mighty Dart, a very different kettle of river indeed. There's a legend that every year the Dart claims a heart. But it was peaceful now, the water almost still beneath the winter sky, bare trees mirrored in its surface. In summer, when they were in full leaf, the lights on the water would have been dappled in green and gold. Now in winter they were platinum and silver. There was good swimming here, a long stretch of water deep even in summer because of the weir further down. A dark head, sleek as a seal, suddenly broke the glassy surface, shattering its ripples into fragments. I watched in surprise the fluid, sinuous turns of the body, the long graceful strokes of the arms. It was rare to see a swimmer here in January. A few moments later an arm came up out of the water and waved at me.

'Juno!' a voice called. It was Meredith Swann. 'Come on in!' She laughed. 'The water's lovely!'

No, thanks. For a start, she was wearing a wetsuit. 'I'll meet you on the bank,' I called back.

There was no way to reach the river from the bridge.

I'd have to walk along the footpath to get to the water's edge. Meredith signalled me with a thumbs up and turned to swim in that direction.

The water was clear, right down to the bottom, every pebble on its stony bed sharply visible, but it was brown as ale, nourished by the peat bogs that it had passed through on its journey from the moor. I reached the place on the bank where it was easy for a swimmer to haul out and found Meredith waiting for me, sitting on a rock, one leg swinging in the foamy water that rippled round it. Her wet hair was drawn back into a knot and her face glowed from the exercise of swimming. She looked energetic and healthy, only very slightly breathless.

'Juno!' she greeted me with a smile. 'I knew it could only be you, with all that glorious hair!'

I ignored the compliment. 'You swim a lot?' I asked, taking a seat on the bank.

She nodded, laughing. 'Every day, if I can.'

'You must be careful. The Dart can be treacherous. The currents are stronger than people realise. Swimming alone—'

'I'm a very strong swimmer,' she interrupted, a touch sharply, 'and I'm not alone.' As if on cue a long arm broke the surface as someone made lazy backstrokes upstream. Of course I didn't need to guess who it was. I suppose he had swum down as far as the weir and was now making his way back. He must have spied me on the bank because he suddenly called out, 'Miss Browne! With an "e"!' and began to swim towards us. Why did the very sight of the man annoy me so much? Why couldn't he call me Juno like everyone else? I would cheerfully have left then, but felt obliged to sit and make conversation.

'Are you going to join us?' he asked, when he reached the rock where Meredith sat like a Lorelei, and hauled himself out.

I gestured at his wetsuit. 'Not equipped, I'm afraid. To be honest, I'm not that fond of swimming.' As I've said before, I like my feet on dry land. 'I might take a dip in Ashburton lido occasionally.'

'That's a shame,' Meredith sighed, 'when there are so many wonderful places around here for wild swimming.' She looked across at her adoring swain perched on the rock beneath her.

'My favourite spot is near Pennsland.' She described it to me. I knew the place well, had often walked there, although I'd never swum in the river there myself. 'It's a pity we didn't have time to get there today,' she told me. 'We're meeting friends for dinner.'

'Where's Lottie?' I asked.

She shrugged. 'Snoring in her armchair, I imagine.'

'She'd have wanted to come in the water with us,' Mr Thorncroft added, 'and it's a bit cold for her today.'

'Well.' I stood up, ready to make my escape. 'I have things to do. You'll have to excuse me.' I nodded at the water. 'Have fun.'

As I turned away I heard the gentle splash as they slid back into the water and Meredith's low, sexy laugh. I didn't need to turn around to know that wetsuits were entwining. As I walked back across the bridge to the van

I couldn't help wondering where they were going for dinner. The Sea Trout Inn, perhaps. That was nearby.

I didn't think about them for long. I had stock to rub my hands over when I got home, to sit like Fagin and contemplate small profits, and I still had half a birthday cake in the fridge.

The police car had gone I saw as I pulled up outside of Owl House. There was no police tape sealing off the drive. Obviously it was not considered part of any crime scene so there was no reason why I shouldn't take a snoop around. Now was as good a time as any. I couldn't see the house from the gate. It was hidden by a bend in the driveway and the overgrown tangle of its garden.

It wouldn't be dark for a while, but the late afternoon light was failing. I fished my torch from the glove compartment, locked the van and walked up the path, watched by the stone owls that glared from either gatepost. It was very quiet. A magpie chattered an alarm as I crunched up a driveway where a tangle of weedy grasses grew tall, save where they'd been flattened in two straight lines by the wheels of the police car.

As the house came into view, I felt a surge of disappointment. The name 'Owl House' had conjured up the romantic vision of an old building: gothic, creepy, mysterious – possibly haunted, a pale face glimpsed through the shattered pane of an upstairs window, unexplained footsteps on the stairs, a banging shutter, a creaking weathervane – not a hideous between-the-wars bungalow with a big sign on the door declaring it was condemned because of concrete cancer. I realised as I trudged my way around the building that I would not be going inside. All the windows and doors had been boarded up, and judging by their weathered appearance and the ivy encroaching over their surfaces, they had not been disturbed for years, certainly not recently, by Jessie or the police.

I puffed out my cheeks in a sigh and turned to look around the garden. Bindweed, brambles and ivy had strangled whatever had once grown in the flower beds, and apart from a monstrous pampas grass squatting in the middle of an overgrown lawn looking as if it was waiting to mug someone, there was nothing to see except for a few brave little crocuses, and owls – statues in stone and plaster dotted the low walls and the rockery everywhere I looked. An owl fetishist had lived here, obviously.

I realised then what Jessie might have been doing in the garden. Dean had mentioned her house was full of owl ornaments. Perhaps she'd been owl-rustling.

So what had sent her running off like that? Something must have scared her – a stray dog, a tramp, teenagers doing drugs? I don't suppose I'd ever know now.

I put myself and the torch back in the van and headed back down into town, where the remainder of my birthday cake was still waiting.

CHAPTER THIRTEEN

I had a very indignant phone call from Chloe Berkeley-Smythe when I got home.

She wasn't indignant with me but with Digby Jerkin and Amanda Waft. 'They were in church!' She couldn't have sounded more scandalised if they had been a pair of practising Satanists. 'I spotted them a few pews in front of me. They didn't see me, and I sneaked out at the end of the service. I thought I'd got away with it, but just as I was about to get into my taxi I heard them call my name. Well, I couldn't be rude! Now, I've had to invite them around for a cup of tea. It really is too exhausting,' she sighed. 'I don't suppose you could be an angel in the morning and pop along to the deli or that lovely artisan baker in West Street and buy me some goodies? I'm bound to offer them something.'

'I don't think you need to worry about Amanda,' I told her frankly. 'I don't think she eats.'

'Hmm, maybe not,' Chloe responded, unconvinced, 'but that Digby's jerkin looks pretty well stuffed, so I'd better provide some eats. You don't want to join us, I suppose?' she added hopefully.

'Sorry,' I lied without looking in my diary, 'I'm definitely working tomorrow afternoon. But I should be able to get your things in the morning,' I went on as she gave a martyred sigh, 'and pop them round to you before lunchtime.' We then had a discussion about exactly what she wanted me to buy and how much I should spend, and decided to leave all the choices to me. She'd pay me when she saw me. She signed off with an air of deep long-suffering.

Next morning, I was in town, actually carrying the aforementioned bag of goodies from the bakery, when who should I bump into but Digby Jerkin himself, and not just Digby, but Morris. Amanda, it transpired, was in the hairdresser's. Ricky was home in bed.

'You know how every little cough and cold goes down on his chest,' Morris tutted. He was carrying a loaded bag from the chemist.

Digby shook his head sadly. 'He wants to give up the old coffin nails.'

'I've spent a lifetime trying to get him to do that,' Morris told him primly. 'Last year we tried the nicotine patches.' He shuddered. 'Talk about a bear with a sore head!'

'How's the house-hunting going?' I asked Digby before Morris could get too emotional.

'Slowly,' he admitted.

'Was it really because of Mrs Berkeley-Smythe that you decided to come to Ashburton?'

'Well, we've always loved Devon, and she showed us such wonderful photographs. Of course, I'm not sure precisely where we'll end up,' he confessed. 'Morris and I are going for a coffee, fancy joining us?'

Why is it that people think I have nothing to do all day except sit about drinking tea and coffee? I explained I was busy, and after hugging Morris and promising to visit the invalid sometime in the week, I took my leave.

I popped into *Old Nick's*, said hello to Sophie, laid Chloe's goodies carefully on a shelf in the fridge upstairs for safekeeping, and dashed out to spend two hours cleaning at the Brownlows'. Then I was off to see Tom Carter. He was still sitting at his table, tying flies, as if he hadn't moved since the last time I'd visited him. I put the kettle on. 'Do you ever swim in the River Dart, Tom?' I asked.

'Sometimes accidentally,' he admitted, 'if I've been struggling to land a big fish.'

I told him about seeing Meredith swimming at Staverton and he shook his head. 'It's foolishness at this time of year,' he said gravely. 'I've seen what the river can do, seen what it can bring down off the moor after heavy rain. I wouldn't do it.'

Neither would I, I agreed silently.

I went back into town for his shopping, which I delivered before driving up to Simon the accountant's house, where I let myself in and spent an hour climbing the north face of the pile of ironing he'd left me. I wrote him a brief note, informing him that I didn't consider underpants or tea towels worth ironing, before I rescued Chloe's goodies from Nick's fridge and delivered them to her just as she was beginning to panic.

'Are you sure you won't stay?' she asked, gazing at me wretchedly.

'Chloe, they are only coming to tea! They probably won't stay an hour . . .'

'An hour!' she groaned faintly. 'I must lie down.'

'That's right,' I recommended cheerfully. 'Get your strength up!'

I almost wished I could have stayed for tea. I'd love to have been a fly on the wall.

I grabbed a sandwich from the deli by way of lunch. As I was heading back to *Old Nick's* to devour it, I passed No. 14, a rather lovely wine bar in North Street. Seated at a table in the window, deep in conversation, were Meredith Swann and Verbena Clarke. Their heads were almost touching, one sleek, shiny and dark, the other a cloud of angelic fair curls. *Now, there's a match made in heaven*, I thought. Verbena, my erstwhile employer, was a designer by profession, and the fashionably expensive artefacts in Meredith's gallery were right up her street. They ought to be in business together. They'd be tearing one another's eyes out within the month.

After my hastily crammed sandwich I went to the post office to pay some bills, stopping to gaze in the window of *Keepsakes*. It is the kind of antique shop I would like

Old Nick's to be: absolutely crammed with interesting things. There is not a table that is not loaded with piles of plates, saucers and odd bits of dinner service; not a shelf, crammed with glasses, vases and figurines, from which rows of jugs and teacups do not hang on hooks. Dolls and old teddy bears take up every seat and a dangerous assortment of glass fishing floats, model boats, old diving helmets, coal scuttles and chamber pots hang from the ceiling, which, as it's low and dips perilously in the middle, means I have to watch my head. The glass counter, lined with dusty velvet, is a treasure chest glittering with jewellery, medals and small pieces of silver, and a trip up the winding stairs, walls lined with paintings, leads to two more rooms just as crammed as the one downstairs, although here the emphasis is more on the dusty and long-forgotten. A stuffed grizzly bear, moth-eaten and sad, has taken up permanent residence and helpfully holds a mirror, which allows customers to try on top hats and pith helmets and gives Ron and Sheila, the owners, a sneaky peek at who's gone upstairs.

As I stood there, staring in the window, it began to rain again, large sploshes darkening the pavement and falling on my head. It rapidly turned into a downpour. I took refuge inside, grabbing an armful of paintings that had been left on display outside, propped against the wall, on my way in.

'Thank you, Juno!' Ron called, dodging past me onto the pavement to rescue a box of bric-a-brac and an old rug from getting wet.

I sheltered in the shop while the violent little shower blew over and just missed banging my head on some wooden item hanging from the ceiling. It turned out to be a sledge, probably Edwardian. I avoided injury but managed to set the thing rocking and reached up to bring it to a stop before it could damage anything else. I remarked on how nice it was, slender and highly polished, with graceful, curved lines, the kind of sledge you see racing through the snow on old-fashioned Christmas cards.

'We did have two,' Ron told me, 'but we sold one just before Christmas. I said to the man who bought it, if he was hoping for snow, I think he was going to be out of luck.'

'You don't think we'll get any this year?'

He pulled a face. 'I was talking with old Ted Barton who farms up around Widecombe t'other day, and he doesn't think we'll get any. Bleedin' rain's bad enough,' he added gloomily.

'Perhaps your customer should have bought a boat,' I suggested.

He chuckled. 'You might be right.'

The storm passed, as brief as it had been heavy, and I proceeded on my way, leaving Ron and Sheila wondering whether or not to put their stock back out.

I might not be able to rival *Keepsakes* but at least I had some new items to display, and I spent part of the afternoon happily sorting, polishing and pricing, an activity that always satisfies some strange little corner of my soul.

Elizabeth had come in to mind the shop, allowing Sophie and Pat to get off for the afternoon. 'I'm taking Olly to a concert at the arts centre this evening,' she told me, 'some sort of jazz collective. One of the teachers involved in the youth band is performing and Olly is very keen to go. I don't suppose you'd like to join us?'

'Why not?' I have very wide musical tastes and I wasn't averse to a spot of jazz. I glanced at my watch. I'd shortly have to dash off to see my last client of the day, a recent addition: Mrs York, an elderly lady who lived in a bungalow on the way to Woodland. 'Probably best if I meet you there. If I get there before you, I'll bag some comfy seats.'

I was driving into town on my way back from Mrs York, having washed her floors, cleaned her bathroom, helped her with turning her mattress and a few other things she found awkward, when I spotted Luke standing outside the Silent Whistle, talking to a man I didn't recognise. I would have minded my own business and driven past but something about the two of them made me slow down and glance in my nearside mirror. Luke's rigid stillness told me he didn't like what the other man was saying. I didn't know him. He was big, flabby and pale as if he was making poor lifestyle choices. I saw Luke push him away as if he wanted to end the conversation. The other man, smiling, laid a hand on his shoulder. Suddenly Luke lashed out. I braked hard. He was still on licence. He couldn't afford to get into an argument, couldn't afford to swing another punch. I threw the van into reverse and backed down St Lawrence Lane. His flabby friend had dodged out of reach, laughing. I flung open the passenger door. 'Want a lift?' I called out.

Luke turned to stare at me, his fists clenched, his whole body tense and wired for a fight. He blinked, as if he was waking from a dream and I saw his shoulders relax. 'Yeah,' he said in a low voice. 'Thanks.'

Flabby fella's plump lips were twisted in a smile. 'Bastard!' Luke snarled at him before he ducked into the seat beside me and slammed the van door.

His face was grim, eyes bright with anger, his jaw clenched so tight I feared for his teeth. A glance in the rear-view mirror as I drove off showed the other man still standing outside the pub, arms folded, smirking.

'Who was that?' I ventured after a steady silence, during which time I'd turned into East Street and then around the corner into Kingsbridge Lane.

'Just some wanker I used to know.'

I waited for him to elaborate but it seemed that was all the information I was going to get.

'You don't want to tell me who he is?' I asked. 'He doesn't live round here, does he?'

'Forget him!' Luke's face was twisted with distaste. 'You can let me out here,' he instructed as I turned by the town hall. 'My truck's parked just here.'

'Luke, if you're in any trouble—' I began.

He cut me off. 'No, I'm not.' He took a moment to get control of himself and when he spoke again his tone was softer. 'I'm trying to stay out of it.'

'Anything I can do?'

He flicked me a shy glance and smiled. 'You've done it already. Thanks.'

'Fancy a pint?' I asked.

He hesitated, but only a moment.

I parked and we slipped down the ginnel that took us onto West Street and walked up the hill to the old Exeter Inn. I got the Jail Ale in and we sat down at a table.

'I've never been in here before.' Luke looked around at the yellowed walls and the low beams overhead. 'It's a really old pub, isn't it?'

'It was this pub Sir Walter Raleigh walked out of and got arrested and taken to the Tower of London,' I told him, 'and it was an old pub then. I think it's at least eight hundred years old.'

Luke nodded and sipped his pint.

I shut up and sipped mine. My enthusiasm for all things Ashburton led me to sound like a guidebook if I wasn't careful. For a minute we sat in silence.

'How'd it go today at Ricky and Morris's place?' I ventured.

He nodded again. 'Good.'

Silence again. The words 'blood' and 'stone' came to mind, but it was Luke who spoke next.

'Pat says you go up on the moor a lot.'

'Well, I used to,' I said sadly. 'I like to tramp about. But this last year I've hardly been up there. I don't get much time these days, with the shop . . .'

'I'd like to live up there,' Luke said, 'roam about like a Gypsy.'

'Like Micky.'

'That old tramp with the big dog?' he asked. 'I've seen them up there.' He shook his head in wonder. 'Biggest dog I've ever seen!'

'Duke? I think his ancestors can trace a direct line back to the Hound of Hell.' I smiled. Duke and I had history; we were old mates.

Luke laughed and for a moment his eyes were far away, as if he was gazing at wide-open spaces, not sitting in the pub with me. 'I like all the old industrial stuff,' he said, returning his gaze to me, 'stuff leftover from the mines and quarrying, like up at Haytor Quarry. I've been up there sometimes, by myself, just sketching.'

'I didn't know you could draw.'

He shook his head. 'I'm not very good.'

'I bet you are,' I said. 'Got a sketchbook on you?'

He frowned, his light eyes narrowing. 'How do you know that?'

'Just guessing. Sophie never goes anywhere without one, a tiny little one, just fits in her pocket. She's likely to whip it out anywhere and start drawing.'

He grinned and pulled a black notebook from his inside jacket pocket. It was quite a large pad and he had a job to wriggle it out.

In shades of grey the moor opened out on his pages. He worked in pencil, sketching familiar landmarks like Haytor, bluff and rounded like a clenched fist dominating the landscape, and Great Mis Tor with its stacks of deeply fissured rock. I recognised the jutting overhang of Crow Tor and Brentor with its church. But he'd drawn many tors I couldn't name: some solid blocks of granite like castle keeps, brutalist sculptures carved by the wind, others with rocks round as pillows. His sketches of the landscape were stark, bold, and impressive. But it was where he had come in close to his subject that his work was really good. Almost microscopically he had rendered the weathered surfaces of the rock – ice-cracked, wind-scoured, blotched with lichen or glittering with quartz and mica. My favourite was a simple sketch of a drystone wall. It occurred to me I ought to introduce him to Sophie.

'These are stunning,' I told him truthfully. 'Do you sell any?'

'No.' He smiled, amused by the idea.

'Well, I'd be very happy to put some in the shop, if you wanted me to,' I told him, although, to be honest, a more fitting place would be Meredith Swann's gallery.

He shrugged. 'Maybe, one day.'

I glanced at my watch and realised that if I wanted a seat at the jazz concert, I'd better get going and we said our goodbyes.

Fortunately, Elizabeth and Olly had got to the arts centre before me and had already grabbed three of the comfortable chairs. There were a dozen or so of them, grouped around small tables. But it was first come, first served; the only other seats were the old chapel pews, which despite the donation of dozens of home-made cushions are very hard on the buttocks after a short period of time. The Methodists obviously believed a numb bum was good for the soul.

The place filled up around us. I hunkered down, trying to sit as low as I could. Someone tall like me, with a mass of curling hair, is the very last person that anyone wants sitting in front of them in a concert. I have often felt the burning of hostile stares from shorter people sitting behind me in theatres, and if I'm booking seats, usually choose the back row. But in this case, I was down the front and feeling rebellious. Even tall people have rights, so sod it.

The music was excellent, although a little busy for my taste. I prefer jazz that's melancholy and soulful rather than hectic and frenetic. When the band took a break, Elizabeth got up to refresh our glasses at the bar. Olly grabbed my arm before I could follow her and beckoned me close to him.

'It was Hannah got that envelope,' he whispered fiercely.

I didn't know anyone called Hannah and didn't catch on for a moment.

'Hannah Williams,' he said, seeing my blank look. 'Will's sister. She got the envelope through the letter box.'

'From Jessie Mole?'

He nodded excitedly. 'Will caught her burning the postcard in the sink when their mum and dad were out.'

I cursed softly. That postcard was evidence.

'She made him swear never to tell a living soul,' he added dramatically.

'So he told you?'

'Well, I asked him.'

'Do we know what was written on it?'

Olly cast another look over his shoulder, in case Elizabeth was returning. We both knew she wouldn't approve if she found he'd been poking around in things which shouldn't concern him. 'Hannah wouldn't say. But Will says she's got a boyfriend at school, and on their way home they take a walk through the woods so that they can . . .' he blushed slightly, 'you know!'

I had a fair idea. 'And Jessie had seen them?'

'Hannah said she thought someone was watching them once from behind the trees, spying on them, someone who ran off.'

'Do we know if Jessie threatened to tell her parents about her boyfriend?'

'Don't know. But she told Will she was glad Jessie was dead.'

I frowned. Somehow I couldn't see a teenage girl as Jessie's killer.

'Anyhow,' Olly went on, 'she's paying Will half her Saturday job money not to tell their mum and dad.'

'He's quite the entrepreneur, your friend Will, isn't he?'

'He's what?'

'Never mind.'

'The message was written on one of those corny postcards with a Dartmoor pony on the front,' he went on, 'and *From Devon With Love* printed on it.'

'Irony, I suppose.'

Olly frowned. 'What?'

I spotted Elizabeth returning from the bar. 'We'll talk about it later.'

Olly went to talk to his music teacher, and I watched Elizabeth taking a rather circuitous route back to our table. She'd stopped to talk to someone sitting over the other side of the chapel, someone I hadn't noticed come in, Daniel Thorncroft. I looked around for Meredith but there was no sign of her. Somehow I couldn't imagine her in this setting, couldn't see her roughing it on one of those hard pews, even to listen to good music.

As Elizabeth came back to our table and set the glasses down, she said, 'You've met Daniel Thorncroft, haven't you?'

'He's a bit of an oddball if you ask me,' I grunted. 'How do you know him?'

'He's come in the surgery a couple of times. We got chatting once when the waiting room was empty.' She sat down and gave me a rather challenging look. 'I like him. He lost his wife just over a year ago. He's been through a rough time.'

'How did she die?' I was curious despite myself.

'Cancer,' she told me. 'It was all very sudden, from the time of diagnosis only a few weeks.'

I cast a glance in Mr Thorncroft's direction to find he was watching us. He raised his glass in silent greeting. I gave a nod in return. I wondered if he knew we were talking about him.

'He's been struggling with loss, feelings of guilt

and anger – all quite usual. Anti-depressants didn't help in his case, made it all worse.' She smiled sadly. 'Grief can make people behave very strangely, you know. Perhaps you should remember that,' she added, patting my arm affectionately. In her voice there was the merest hint of reproach.

Olly reappeared at that moment, the band was returning to the stage, and I didn't get the opportunity to reply. Later, I glanced across at Daniel Thorncroft sitting on his pew, his long legs out in front of him, rapt in the music. I wondered what he had said about me to Elizabeth that should have made her speak the way she did. I was comforted to think, by the end of the evening, how much his backside would be hurting.

CHAPTER FOURTEEN

'So Jessie Mole's got herself murdered,' Maisie said with a sniff. 'Well, it was only a matter of time.' These were almost her first words as she entered her cottage on her return. I wondered how she knew.

'Nelly phoned me,' she explained.

Nelly was one of Maisie's regular churchgoing friends. 'Nelly Mole?' Mole is a common name in Devon and I hadn't made the connection. 'Are she and Jessie related?'

'Distant branch of the family,' she said, 'from up Okehampton way.' She dismissed the lot of them with a wave of her hand. 'Well, I ain't surprised she got murdered, that Jessie was always a nasty piece of work.'

'That's not a very kind thing to say, Mum.' Our Janet hovered behind her, still carrying the cases from the car. She'd lived so many years up country that her voice had taken on a northern quality, a slight flattening of the vowels. Jacko, Maisie's bristly, self-important little terrier, had already gone on ahead, leaping onto the sofa and up to his favourite seat on the window sill, settling down and shoving his evil little snout through the lace curtains as if to announce to the occupants of Brook Lane that he was back.

The day before, after a warning call from Our Janet, I'd opened up and aired the cottage, switched on the fridge and the heating, made up Maisie's bed and one in the spare room for Janet, who wouldn't begin her long journey back to Heck-as-Like until next morning, and fetched some essential shopping. Now I helped her with the cases and together we got Maisie settled in her chair and sorted more shopping, which Janet had brought with her.

'How's it been?' I muttered as we stood together in the kitchen, unpacking the shopping and putting it away. Her response was to roll her eyes heavenward and shake her head. Our Janet is a kind woman, with a husband, large family and a job. She is full of concern for her ninety-four-year-old mother who lives far away and stubbornly refuses to leave Ashburton to be near her. 'I'll be glad to see the back of that bloody dog,' was all she said.

'What's that?' Maisie demanded from her armchair.

'Are you better now?' I asked, ignoring her question. 'Fancy a cup of tea?'

She tutted. 'I thought you'd never ask.'

A few minutes later, when we were all suitably equipped with refreshment, I brought the subject back to

Jessie. 'What did you mean about her being a nasty piece of work?' I asked. 'Surely Jessie was just a bit simple.'

Maisie grunted in disgust. 'I don't know about simple! Police took her in for questioning more than once, warned her off. She had to leave Okehampton in the end.'

'What had she been doing?'

Maisie sniffed. 'Writing letters.'

Our Janet and I exchanged glances. 'How do you mean, Mum?' she asked. 'Blackmail?'

'Now, I don't know about blackmail,' Maisie admitted. 'I don't know she tried to get money. Poison-pen letters is what I mean, just saying nasty things about people, upsetting 'em. Everyone knew it was her doing it. Police knew too but they couldn't prove it was her, not for definite – crafty baggage, she was – but there was trouble and they warned her off.'

'What sort of trouble?'

'Well, that I can't say,' she responded with a shake of her head. 'Nelly don't like to talk about it. All I know is she disappeared upcountry for years before she turned up here like a bad penny.'

Now it seemed she'd started letter writing again, at least, I'd seen her posting that envelope through the Williamses' letter box. But why risk posting it herself? I wondered. Why not send it through the mail, or the Internet? On reflection, I doubted if Jessie had ever been near a computer; she would almost certainly have become a troll if she had. Perhaps she derived evil satisfaction from getting as physically close to her victims as she could. Perhaps the danger of getting caught was part of the thrill. I thought about all this as I drifted off to sleep, as January became February and the rain began to fall.

Next morning, we waved goodbye to Our Janet, after a slightly strained farewell, and she set off back to Heck-as-Like.

'Didn't you enjoy yourself up there over Christmas, Maisie?' I made us a cup of tea. I could tell she was gagging to talk. 'Apart from getting the chest infection, I mean.'

'No, I did not!' she declared roundly, sitting herself down in her chair. 'All those bleedin' kids!'

'Those are your great-grandchildren,' I pointed out.

'Well, there's too many of 'em!' She held up her hands in horror. 'The noise, come Christmas Day, with all that lot running around screaming!'

I laughed. 'You're just not used to them.'

This wasn't really what had upset her. Our Janet, she told me with disgust, had made the mistake of taking her to visit what sounded like a beautifully appointed residential home nearby, on the pretext of visiting one of Janet's old friends.

'"Isn't it lovely here, Mum?"' Maisie sneered in an imitation of her daughter's voice. 'I knew what she was up to. She must think I was born yesterday.'

'She worries about you,' I said in her defence.

'Putting me in with a load of old biddies!' Her apricot curls shook in outrage. 'Loony, half of 'em are!'

'She wants you close by, where she can come and visit you.'

'Don't you start!' She eyed me wrathfully. 'I told her, I was born in Ashburton, and I'm being buried here.' She held up a crooked finger. 'The only way I'm leaving this cottage is in my box. Mind you,' she went on sorrowfully, 'Ashburton's not what it was. They ripped the heart out of the old town when they stopped the cattle markets . . .'

'Well, foot and mouth—' I began.

'It did for the old farming families around here.'

'There's still lot of farming—'

'They used to hold cattle fairs right out in the street,' she carried on, 'where North Street joins East and West Street. The Bull Ring, they used to call it . . .'

'They still do,' I told her, although you have to look hard to find the sign.

'They used to drive the cows and sheep straight down to the railway station, right onto the train.' She grunted. 'Now we don't even have a railway station any more . . .'

'No,' I sighed.

'And they tore down the pannier market.'

That was before Maisie was born. She was getting muddled. 'All those pubs we used to have when my dad was a nipper . . . now we just got antique shops.'

'Mm.'

'Who buys all these antiques? That's what I want to know.'

So do I.

'Antique shops, wine bars,' she sniffed indignantly. 'What's the old town coming to?' She rapped her knotty knuckles on the surface of her little table in protest. 'The banks have gone . . . and now they're trying to close down our fire station . . . It'll be the hospital next, you'll see.'

I listened to another ten minutes of this before I escaped to take Jacko out for his constitutional and to fill up the gaps in Maisie's food supplies.

Jacko felt it was his duty to remind everyone who was boss after his long absence and snapped and snarled at every dog we met, as well as giving it large to anything on the pavement that had wheels, like pushchairs and mobility scooters. He visibly swelled in importance during these encounters, bristling. He looked like a pot-scourer with teeth. I understood Our Janet's happiness at parting from him, but wondered if it wasn't only the dog she was glad to see the back of.

I was kept awake all night. Rain came down hard, tap-dancing on the roof of the conservatory beneath my bedroom window. It gurgled down drainpipes, filled the weed-choked gutter and overflowed in a drizzling cascade onto the concrete path below where it tap-danced some more. My landlords, whose bedroom is on the other side of the house, were undisturbed by all this, and slept on.

It was still pouring, though not as hard, as I took the dogs for their walk in the woods next morning. They didn't mind muddy paths and dripping trees. They loved the swollen streams and wet undergrowth, the smell of damp earth. But I arrived in *Sunflowers*, after I'd delivered them home, looking and feeling a touch bedraggled. Adam, who I'd come to have a word with, was not best pleased to see me, my shiny yellow mac dripping onto the nice clean floor of his cafe and my wellies leaving muddy boot-prints.

'You just come off a fishing boat?' he joked, surveying me from behind the counter. There was a slightly apprehensive look in his eye. There usually is whenever I turn up in *Sunflowers* because my presence often means I shall demand something that involves him in DIY.

'Well, I feel as if I've been at sea all night.' I tore the sou'wester off my hair and deliberately shook out my curls, spraying the place with drips. I didn't care. There didn't seem to be any customers about. 'When are you going to get that damned gutter cleared?'

'It's the magpies,' he complained, wisely deciding he'd better make me a coffee. 'They pinch the moss off the roof and drop it in the gutters.'

'Well, I don't know if magpies are responsible for the buddleia that's taken root halfway along, but it all needs clearing out.'

'I'll get round to it,' he promised.

'Before it rains again?'

He sighed. 'As soon as I've got time.'

'That's what you said the last time.'

To be fair, Adam got up early and worked long hours in the cafe. He didn't get much free time. He always looked tired. Also, he really didn't like going up ladders. I decided not to nag him any further and accepted the large cappuccino as recompense for my nocturnal suffering.

It was only as I turned, cup in hand, that I realised that this exchange had been observed from the corner of the cafe by Lottie, who was standing with her head on one side, the tip of her tail wagging, and Daniel Thorncroft, who seemed mightily amused as he surveyed me over the top of his specs.

'Miss Browne with an "e",' he said, grinning, 'come and sit with Lottie and me.'

I couldn't very well refuse, and he moved his laptop so I could put my coffee down. Lottie was pleased to see me, and we greeted each other enthusiastically before we settled down.

'Did you enjoy the jazz, Miss B?' Mr Thorncroft asked. I noticed he was no longer wearing the scary specs with the heavy frames, but had swopped them for smaller, wire-framed ones that suited him a lot better. Ms Swann's influence, no doubt, I thought cynically. She'd be dressing him soon. Actually, that was a nice shirt he was wearing.

'I thought it was a little frantic in places, but yes, on the whole.'

'You know, I wonder about you, Miss B.'

'Oh?' I did my best not to sound interested, wondering if it was his constant tone of amused mockery that I found so infuriating.

'I wonder what you're doing here in Ashburton, that's all. You don't sound Devon born and bred.'

'No, I was born in London,' I admitted. 'I'm what people around here call a blow-in.' He was obviously waiting for further information, so I went on. 'When I was growing up I used to spend my summer holidays with a cousin in Totnes . . .'

He frowned. 'Why? I mean . . . sorry to interrupt . . . but why with a cousin?'

'I'm an orphan.' As soon as I'd spoken, I wished I'd chosen my words differently. I'd sounded as if I still thought of myself as a lonely child.

'Do you think an orphan always feels apart?' he asked suddenly. 'From other people, I mean?'

I was taken aback by this sudden switch to what seemed like a serious question. There was no hint of mockery in his voice now, no twinkle of amusement in his storm-grey eyes. This was personal. I wondered if he was an orphan too.

'Yes,' I answered, telling the truth despite myself.

'Sorry,' he said with a sudden grin, 'that was probably a very strange question. It's just something Meredith and I were discussing the other night.'

'Oh?'

'She lost her mother when she was quite young,' he explained. 'But I interrupted you. Please, carry on.'

I wasn't really sure if I wanted to. 'Anyway,' I continued after a moment, 'we'd spent a lot of our time exploring the moor. I decided then I never wanted to live anywhere else.'

'But not in Totnes?'

Totnes was too sad for me since Cordelia died but I wasn't going to tell him that. 'Totnes has become very . . .' I struggled to find the words for it, 'conscious of itself . . . Ashburton seems more real, somehow.'

He nodded as if he understood. 'It certainly has its charms.' I assumed by that he meant Meredith. 'But this murder is a terrible thing,' he went on. 'I think I met her once, the victim.'

'Jessie?'

He nodded. 'I'm sure she was the woman my aunt used to employ as a cleaner until a few years ago.'

'You don't know why she stopped employing her?'

He shrugged. 'Something to do with her move to Torquay, I expect.'

'Probably.' I pointed to his laptop 'What about you? What do you do?'

'I'm an environmental analyst.'

I paused in lifting my cappuccino to my lips. 'I don't think I'm any the wiser.'

'I crunch numbers, do costings, carry out feasibility studies, that sort of thing.'

'Feasibility studies into what?'

'Various environmental projects.' He was being evasive, definitely cagey. 'I've been working up in Scotland the last few months, took a couple of months off to try and sort out the mess my aunt left me with. My employers are very understanding, but I'll have to go back there soon.'

'And are you getting anywhere?' I asked. 'With Auntie's mess?'

He gave a grunt of laughter. 'Not really.' He was staring at me, smiling. I seemed to be amusing him again for some reason. 'You've got foam on your top lip.'

I groaned inwardly and wiped it away.

'Well, it's been lovely talking to you, Miss Browne with an "e",' he announced, suddenly standing up, 'but Lottie and I have things to do.' With that, he pocketed his specs, shrugged on his coat, packed his laptop under one arm and strode out.

'Don't let me keep you,' I muttered to myself. Lottie, who'd been resting her head on my boot, rose and trotted off after him, turning in the doorway to look at me with an expression of sad enquiry before she left.

CHAPTER FIFTEEN

The only good thing you can say about February is that it's short. Next to January, it's probably the worst month to get born in, especially for people like poor old Morris who arrived on the 29th and only gets a real birthday once every four years. The upside of this is that technically he's only eighteen and a half. But I'm getting ahead of myself. For a short month, it certainly packed a lot into itself, especially rain. It came down heavily almost every day, the deluge pouring off waterlogged fields, sending a slick wet glaze down the tarmac roads and churning the dry lanes to mud. It turned lambing into a miserable business and prevented me from doing many of my usual winter gardening jobs, tidying up herbaceous flower beds and pruning. Even the Tribe began to get unenthusiastic about going out in it. Schnitzel the sausage dog's mum even bought him a raincoat. The clear, shallow stream that was once the River Ashburn, so quiet and well-behaved, turned into a deep, brown, boisterous torrent that frolicked noisily through the town, burbling as it went, sweeping along rafts of sticks to get stuck under bridges.

After two weeks of my moaning about the downpour, my landlord finally climbed nervously up a ladder and dredged the muck from the gutter beneath my bedroom window, allowing me to sleep undisturbed.

I settled back into my routine with Maisie while Chloe Berkeley-Smythe, utterly exhausted by the wet weather, began packing for her next cruise. Speculation about poor Jessie Mole's murder continued, but more sporadically, the sense of shock fading as tales of sheep-rustling and theft of farm machinery superseded the identity of Cutty Dyer as the main topic of conversation.

'No, madam, I'm very sorry,' I could hear Morris on the telephone as I let myself into Druid Lodge. 'I am afraid we never hire out costumes for parties . . . Well, because they come back damaged . . .' He turned to give me a little wave as he listened to the strident female voice on the other end of the line. 'I am sure you would be very careful with it,' he went on, sounding genuinely apologetic, 'but it's other people, you see. It's *their* glasses of red wine we have to worry about. It's not as if you can stuff beaded chiffon in the washing machine . . . Well, you could try that fancy-dress shop in Exeter . . .' He dropped the receiver as if it had burnt his fingers. 'Rude cow!' he muttered, shaking his head as he replaced it properly on its cradle. 'That was for the Spring Ball up at Moorland Manor,' he told me. 'We've had a whole rash of these calls over the last couple of weeks.'

The Spring Ball at the Moorland Manor hotel was a very swanky and expensive occasion held every year at the beginning of March. Tickets cost a fortune. 'Sophie's entered a competition in the *Dartmoor Gazette* to win tickets,' I told him.

'This year they've decided to make it fancy dress,' Morris sighed, 'the roaring twenties!'

'Do you really not loan out for parties?' I asked. 'I didn't realise.'

He shook his head. 'No, no! People don't take care of them. We've had stuff come back covered in wine, vomit . . . and worse.'

'But you loaned clothes to me and Sophie when we went to that party at Moorworthy House,' I reminded him.

'Well, you're different,' he said, giving me a hug.

'Where's the invalid?'

'He's in the breakfast room.' As we headed across the hall I became aware of a sweet, sickly smell and a convoluted ribbon of white smoke rippled through the doorway.

'Don't worry, we're not on fire,' Morris sighed, propelling me forward, 'it's only Puff the Magic Dragon.'

Ricky was lounging at the breakfast table, resplendent in a silk Chinese dressing gown, and holding a metal implement in his hand that I did not immediately recognise. Then he raised it to his lips and was almost lost to view in a miasma of scented smoke.

'You're vaping!' I cried in horror.

'Oh, don't you bleedin' start!' he gasped irritably, flapping the smoke away with one hand. 'Everyone complains cos I smoke, now I'm trying to give up the fags everyone moans just as much!' He subsided into a rasping cough. He looked awful, his skin pale and dry as old parchment, his eyes red-rimmed and bloodshot.

'By *everyone* he means me,' Morris explained quietly.

'And her!' Ricky pointed an accusing finger at me.

'Sit down, Juno, love.' Morris seemed unimpressed by all the retching and coughing. 'I'll make some tea.'

'No, it's good that you're trying to give up,' I told Ricky, trying to sound conciliatory. 'I'm impressed.'

He growled. 'Don't patronise me.'

'She's come to see how you are, you miserable old bastard,' Morris reproved him, smacking him across the back of the head in a rare moment of temper. 'Try and be nice.'

I tried to mollify him. 'I've brought you some grapes.'

Ricky's eyes narrowed. 'Green or red?'

I pushed the bag across the table to him. 'Black.'

'Ooh, sexy!' He opened the bag with his fingers and peered inside as if he suspected a rat was going to leap out and bite him. After a moment he reached inside, drew out a solitary grape and popped it in his mouth. 'One of my five a day,' he mumbled.

Morris made a harrumphing noise, pouring tea.

'But you are feeling better than you were?' His chest infection had been so bad he hadn't been up to seeing visitors.

'I had to call an ambulance one night.' Morris sighed, placing a plate of biscuits on the table. 'They wanted to take him to hospital.'

'I didn't know this.' I was horrified, felt neglectful.

'He refused to go.'

Ricky shuddered. 'They're not getting me in one of those places. I'm allergic!'

'But he is better?' I asked Morris, talking over the invalid's head.

'Now that he's getting visitors, yes. Mandy came to see you yesterday, didn't she?' Morris added slyly.

'She came to do her ministering angel act,' Ricky said ungraciously. 'Daft cow!'

'Digby seems very sweet,' I commented. 'Have they found anywhere to live yet?'

'Don't think so. Yes, Digby's a gent.' He turned to Morris. 'We met him when we were doing *Wind in the Willows* that Christmas, remember?'

Morris nodded. 'Must be forty years ago.'

'Was he Toad?' I asked. He'd be perfect with his portly stature and bulging eyes. He only needed painting green.

'He was.' Ricky grinned. 'I was Ratty and *Maurice* here played Mole.'

Morris performed a little bow and made it somehow mole-like.

'Oh, do it again!' I urged them. '*Wind in the Willows*

would be wonderful! Put it on next Christmas!'

Before anyone could reply the phone rang again. 'That'll be someone else after costumes for this ball,' Morris sighed, getting up to answer it.

'Well, they're not having 'em!' Ricky rasped, trying not to cough. 'Remember what happened to all those claw-hammer suits we loaned out for that Tory Party bash? If all they can teach them at public school is how to start food fights . . .' He lapsed into another fit of coughing, shaking his head to refuse a glass of water when I suggested it. He'd settled down by the time Morris returned from his phone call and turned his attention back to me. 'So, Juno, tell us what's happening in the world of murder and mayhem.'

Another thing about February is that it contains Valentine's Day. In recent years this has meant absolutely nothing where I am concerned, and I had begun to view the appearance in the shops of cards with hearts on and bouquets of red roses with growing cynicism, because I wasn't getting any. But this year, I got invited to dinner.

The invitation came from Luke. My heart sank, to be honest. Although I think he's a nice lad, and very talented, I didn't nurture any romantic feelings for him, and I found the thought he might be harbouring them towards me a bit worrying.

Actually, his invitation couldn't have been less romantic. I was alone at the time, in the shop. It was towards the end of the day and I was thinking about cashing up. With the coming of twilight, the rain, which had fallen for most of the day, had dwindled to a fine drizzle, forming a nebulous mist that hung in Shadow Lane, turning the single street light into a pale blur.

I wasn't expecting any more customers and was surprised by the jingling of the bell. Luke sidled into the shop, nodded as I said hello, and then hovered, hands in his pockets, one foot tapping nervously. He looked as if he wanted the ground to swallow him up. There was obviously something on his mind.

'Can I help you?' I asked, hoping he might want to buy something.

He cleared his throat. 'I was wondering,' he began, flicking me a nervous glance from beneath lowered lids, 'if you were doing anything on Saturday night?'

I knew I wasn't. I also knew what date Saturday was. 'Well . . .' I began.

'Only I wondered if you fancied coming out . . . if you haven't got anyone else . . . I mean . . . any*thing* else to do. Just friendly, like,' he added hastily, seeing my hesitation. 'I just thought if you didn't already have a date . . . and you're not going anywhere, and I'm not . . .'

'We might as well go out together,' I completed, putting an end to his misery. I felt sorry for him. He probably hadn't asked a woman out since he'd come out of prison. His chat-up line could certainly do with some improvement.

'I thought we could go to that place near the arts centre.'

'Coljan?' I named the nearest restaurant.

'Yeh, that's the one. Pat says it's good in there. I haven't been out anywhere like that since I've come out of jail and I just thought . . .'

'You need to get back in practice.'

He nodded. 'Something like that.'

'You sure you don't mind being seen out with an older woman?'

He hunched a shoulder, grinning. 'I don't mind . . . you're not that much older than me, anyway,' he added hastily.

'In that case, I'd be delighted,' I responded graciously, 'providing we split the bill.'

'Oh, yes, if you like.'

He was supposed to argue about that a bit more, but I let him get away with it. I certainly had no intention of letting him pay for me. We fixed a time to meet, exchanged contact details and he went away happy. I heard him whistling as he wandered off down the street.

I sat where I was for a few moments, deep in thought, not sure I had done the right thing.

As I stared into the misty gloom of Shadow Lane a solitary figure seemed to melt out of the mist, crossed in front of the shop window, visible for just a few moments before it was swallowed by the gloom again. It was almost like seeing a ghost. For a moment I wasn't sure I'd seen anyone. And yet I had recognised him: heavily built, flabby-looking, wearing the same jacket as when I had first seen him arguing with Luke outside the Silent Whistle.

I ran to the door and looked out, but already he was lost to the fog. I hurried to the end of the lane, looking up and down the road, but I couldn't see anyone on the narrow pavement, nothing but the glistening paving and the fog hanging in the air. A little country bus trundled down the street towards me, but the sweep of its headlights as it turned the corner towards the centre of town showed me nothing more. There was any number of ginnels and passages the man might have turned down. But was he following Luke?

I ran back to the shop, locked the door behind me and phoned his mobile number on the shop phone. The call went straight to voicemail. With any luck, Luke was safely in his pickup and driving back to Honeysuckle Farm by now. I left a message asking him to call me.

How likely was it, I asked myself as I put down the receiver, that this man just happened to be walking down Shadow Lane a bare few moments after Luke had left the shop?

The phone rang a few moments later. Luke had been driving and had pulled over to see who'd called.

'What's up?' he asked.

I told him who I'd just seen and where. He grunted. 'He's still hanging about, is he?'

'I was worried he was following you, that he meant you some harm.'

'Well, if he was, he didn't catch me, but thanks for the heads-up.' He paused. 'Was that what you phoned about?'

I told him it was.

'Oh, that's all right, then.' His voice warmed suddenly. 'When I saw your number come up I thought you might have had second thoughts about our date on Saturday.'

'No, of course not,' I assured him, with a lot more certainty than I felt.

We ended our call and I got my things together to go home. As I stood outside the shop, locking the door, I had a sudden idea where the man I had seen might have gone to. I debated for a few seconds, and then, instead of heading off to the place where I had parked White Van, I turned out of Shadow Lane and made my way through the misty streets towards the Silent Whistle.

He was sitting in the bar, alone, at a table. There could be no mistaking that this was the same man I had seen with Luke. In the well-lit pub I recognised his flabby features straight away, even though I was peering at him through the window as I stood on the pavement outside. He seemed to be waiting for someone, one foot tapping restlessly. He kept checking his watch. I ducked back out of the way as he turned his gaze towards the window. I didn't know how clear a view he'd got of me when I was sitting in my van, but I didn't want him to spot me staring at him. He wasn't anywhere near Luke at this moment and that was all I'd wanted to know. I turned to go home, almost bumping into two men who must have seen me staring in through the pub window. They stepped back, one preparing to open the door for me. In the light coming through the pub door I could see he was darkly handsome. He might have been Italian or Greek. 'Are you going in?' he asked. However exotic his origins, his accent was pure Essex.

'No, thank you.' I smiled politely and turned away.

As I passed the windows I cast a last glance inside at the man waiting at the table. It struck me that he didn't simply look as if he was waiting for someone, he looked afraid.

CHAPTER SIXTEEN

My dinner with Luke on Saturday gave me an opportunity to wear my latest acquisition, the doublet that Ricky and Morris had made for me. I decided to wear it open like a jacket, its elaborate fastenings left undone, with a chocolate brown T-shirt underneath. I teamed it with brown jeans and boots. I wanted to look as if I'd made an effort, but not too much. I didn't want to give Luke the wrong impression. I didn't want him getting a crush on me.

Coljan was a small restaurant on West Street, set in part of an old building that had once been a brewery and The London Inn. Its old stables had been converted into flats and the restaurant was housed in what had once been the inn kitchen, its low ceiling and open fireplace retaining the homely feel. It was a relaxed, informal place, with pine tables and unpretentious decor, but the menu was based on locally sourced foods and standard of fare was excellent. It also boasted a comprehensive gin menu, which I blurrily remembered sampling with Elizabeth at New Year.

It had dressed itself up for Valentine's Day with red and pink flowers and a scattering of paper hearts on the tables. The menu offered heart-shaped panna cotta with strawberry coulis or ruby chocolate and passionfruit parfait. I always look at the desserts first. But before then Luke and I had choices to make. I started with sweet potato and pear soup and he went for pan-fried scallops. He was wearing a leather jacket and cream shirt with jeans and trainers. He looked nice, but perhaps, like me, he was anxious not to look as if he was trying too hard.

I hadn't told anyone I was having dinner with him and I was rather hoping we wouldn't run into anyone I knew. He'd obviously told Pat, though; she'd mentioned it in the shop with a nudge and knowing grin that made me want to sink through the floor. I was ashamed to have such feelings. It wasn't because Luke had been in prison that I didn't want to be seen out with him. I couldn't care less who knew about that. I didn't mind anyone knowing we were friends. I just didn't want anyone to think we were more than that. Perhaps I shouldn't have agreed to dinner and should have suggested going to a pub.

He was obviously feeling a bit shy. Conversation stalled while we waited for our starters to arrive. 'Are you enjoying living at the farm?' I asked, feeling it was up to me to make the effort if this wasn't to be a very quiet evening.

'It's OK. It's good of them to take me in.' He hesitated then leant forward slightly, lowering his voice. 'I was lucky I had somewhere to go. A lot of blokes who come out of prison don't have anywhere, a lot of them will be back sleeping in police cells in a few days, just to get under a roof.' Then he smiled. 'I was lucky.'

'Yes, you were.'

Suddenly, as if he felt the need to change the subject, Luke pulled his sketchbook from the inside pocket of his jacket and showed me his latest picture.

'My God!' I breathed as I took it from him. 'It's me!' I was staring at a head and shoulders portrait of myself, drawn in pencil. I had to admit it looked uncommonly like the woman I see in the mirror, face framed by a riot of curls. 'When did you do this?'

'The other night, after we'd come out of that old pub up the road.'

'You did it afterwards?' I stared at the accurate detail of the drawing, the wide shape of my mouth, the freckles across my nose. 'Do you have a photographic memory?'

He shrugged. 'Pretty much.'

'You're like one of those courtroom artists,' I told him. 'You know those pastel sketches you see on the television news of defendants in trials? I thought they were done in court, but I read somewhere that the artists aren't allowed to sketch while the trial's in progress. They have to come out and do them afterwards. You could be one of those.'

'I don't think I want to spend any more time in a courtroom, thanks.'

I felt like a twerp. 'I'm sorry, I didn't think.'

He grinned, slipping the sketchbook back into his pocket. 'It's all right.'

Fortunately, the starters arrived so I could occupy my mouth for a while without putting my foot in it.

The restaurant began to fill up around us, but it wasn't until we had already embarked on our main course – roasted crispy duck for Luke, salmon florentina for me – that a couple entered the restaurant who knew me. Meredith Swann drifted in wearing a dress in midnight blue, her hair in an elegant twist at the nape of her lovely neck, her silver swan necklace her sole item of jewellery. She was followed in by Daniel Thorncroft, who'd scrubbed up very nicely in a charcoal-grey suit. Meredith nodded a greeting as she passed our table, her eyebrows slightly raised.

'Miss B.' Mr Thorncroft acknowledged me as he guided Meredith towards their corner table and smiled briefly at Luke. From the corner of my eye I could see Meredith as she settled in her seat, conscious that her gaze was still upon us.

I couldn't help wishing that Luke had kept his jacket on, not rolled up his shirtsleeves to show that tattoo. His tongue loosened by alcohol, he chatted through the rest of the meal, talking about the work he was doing at the lake and how it was turning into a much bigger project than he'd thought, but I was acutely conscious of the couple in the corner. I found myself straining my ears to catch snippets of their conversation in case they were talking about us. I knew what cocktails they ordered, which dishes, which bottle of champagne. I was being paranoid, projecting my own prejudices onto them and assuming that they would think things that may not have entered their heads.

Later, when I went to powder my nose, I found Meredith waiting for me to come out of the ladies. She smiled as she plucked at the sleeve of my jacket. 'Where on earth did you buy this gorgeous thing?'

'Oh, I had it made for me,' I answered sunnily, and moved away before she could ask me any more questions.

I hoped I hadn't spoilt the evening for Luke. I reviewed it as I lay alone in bed. I think he could tell that during the latter part of our meal my attention hadn't been focussed totally on him. Although why I should give a toss about what Meredith Swann and her acolyte might think was still a mystery to me. I reproved myself for childish feelings, probably rooted in jealousy. She was richer and more attractive than me and her business was considerably more successful than mine. OK, she'd tried to poach Sophie, but business is business, and apart from a slightly supercilious manner, she behaved towards me with unfailing politeness and I really had no reason to dislike her.

Luke was more of a problem. I liked him a lot. We shared a passion for the moor and agreed to go walking up there together once the weather improved. But the warmth of his smile and the increasingly adoring look in his eyes made me want to shrink back, to hold my hands up defensively. I wasn't sure what to feel about the picture of me he had drawn. Did he draw pictures of everyone he met, or was this a sign of infatuation? I hoped he wasn't developing an attachment to me. I wasn't sure I could put him off without hurting his feelings, without crushing his self-esteem. And he didn't need that.

He insisted on walking me home and I couldn't argue: Jessie's murderer was still at large, although her murder was something we had pointedly avoided talking about all evening. He was clearly disappointed that I didn't invite him in when we arrived at my door, but he didn't try to press the point, and said goodnight after a chaste kiss on the cheek.

I watched him wander away, a lost and lonely soul. I felt sorry for him but perhaps I was to blame. Perhaps it was wrong of me to have gone out with him in the first place.

CHAPTER SEVENTEEN

I'm glad to say I did not discover the next dead body, nor was I acquainted with the victim, which made a pleasant change. I didn't find out there had been a murder until I popped into the shop late in the afternoon, by which time it was already common knowledge around the town. Sophie and Pat were full of it. Apparently, the victim had been found by a farm worker near Barnsey Bridge that morning, his body dumped at the mouth of an outlet pipe, part of the town's flood defences. 'They say he'd had his throat cut,' Pat told me, voice hushed with horror, 'just like Jessie Mole.'

'And there was a postcard attached to his jacket,' Sophie added, 'like the one you found on Jessie.'

'He'd had his throat cut?' I repeated. 'You're sure?'

Pat nodded. 'That's what they're saying. Blood everywhere! And they say his hands were tied. There's a lunatic on the loose,' she went on. 'At least, that's what the television people said. Serial killer, that's what they're calling him.' She'd gone up to Barnsey Bridge as soon as rumours of the murder began to trickle down the street and hung about with a knot of curious onlookers, their view of the crime scene blocked by a solid police presence. It was while she was there that a television news crew had arrived from Plymouth. But it seemed there was little in the way of factual information and all the news people had done was fuel speculation. No one knew who the victim was.

'Who's going to be next?' Pat asked and assured an already nervous Sophie that she would drive her home. 'It's not safe out on the streets.'

After I'd locked the shop, I phoned Dean Collins.

'You know I can't talk about it,' he said.

I ignored that. 'Seeing that Jessie's dead, I'm guessing that the note on the victim isn't in her handwriting?'

'Well, no it's not,' he admitted.

'So, who was he, the victim?'

'I can't tell you that, either.' He hesitated a moment. 'You can read all about it in the *Gazette* tomorrow,' he went on, 'but you didn't hear it from me.'

'And did he have his throat cut?' I asked.

'He certainly did. It was a very nasty killing.'

'Aren't all killings nasty?'

'This was brutal. They practically took his head off. The poor chap who discovered him is in shock.'

'Rumour is, that the victim had his hands tied.'

'I'm not commenting on rumours,' he responded pompously.

'You're no fun any more.'

'Have a good evening, Juno,' Dean said, and put down the phone.

There's nothing like the recent activities of a serial killer to make a girl go wandering about the streets of Ashburton in the dark on her own. I had to, in order to get home. Pat had not offered me a lift. She assumed I'd driven to the shop in the van and parked around the corner, which is what I usually do, and I hadn't enlightened her. After my morning's activities I'd left White Van at home. But I didn't feel in the mood for a car ride packed with fear-fuelled gossip, so I said nothing. Something was niggling at me and I didn't know what it was.

I wandered up towards Barnsey Bridge, but long before I got there I could see the bright lights set up by the police so that they could work at the crime scene through the night. I knew I wouldn't be allowed to hang around there – a pity, as I wouldn't have minded a look at where the victim had been found.

Years ago, the Ashburn regularly flooded after heavy rain. I'd seen black and white photos in the museum of times when the river had burst its banks and roared through the town, pouring out of shops and gushing from the doorway of the town hall. Back in the seventies, a flood alleviation scheme had been installed. It had tamed the Ashburn, turned it into little more than a stream, although from time to time its swollen waters still found ways to escape: Love Lane became a bubbling torrent just a few years ago. But the flood defences blocked the way from Barnsey Bridge onward, forcing anyone who wanted to take a riverside walk to backtrack, cross the road, and pick up the path on the opposite bank. And it was here, in a dry culvert, that Cutty Dyer's second victim had been found, just a few hundred yards from where Luke and I had found Jessie.

It was a thought to make me shiver. I turned back into town, along Cleder Place, where the river ran unhindered past the little green, down North Street and turned by the town hall to stand on King's Bridge – Cutty's bridge – and peer over the low stone wall.

I could barely see the water in the dark, just the barest glimmer as it slid behind the houses on Kingsbridge Lane. But I could hear it, the water babbling softly to itself as it swept over its stony bed. Then there was a gulping noise. I don't know what it was, nothing probably, a hiccup in a drain, but it sounded too much like Cutty Dyer licking his lips for me to linger. I felt the hair prickle on the back of my neck, a cold thrill of fear shuddered through me and I hurried away, turned my steps towards the safety of home, not another soul abroad in the dark, empty streets.

I suppose I only have myself to blame that I had nightmares that night. I dreamt I was standing by the river, in town. But as in all dreams, it wasn't quite the town, and it wasn't quite the river. Cutty's huge eyes were shining out from the darkness under a bridge. The effigy floated by, except it wasn't an effigy, it was Jessie Mole: Jessie, floating on her back with a purple gash in her throat, but talking, talking all the while as she floated slowly along, trying to tell me something that I couldn't hear. And as she floated on out of sight I turned to see Cutty's giant hand come up from the darkness under the bridge, his fingers splayed against the stonework, the webbing between them green like frog skin and I woke up in a sweat.

I grabbed a copy of the *Dartmoor Gazette* early next morning and the murder of Cutty Dyer's latest victim occupied the entire front page. '*Serial Killer in Ashburton?*' the headline screamed. '*Second Victim Found. Murderer Adopts Identity of Mythical Fiend.*' Sandy Thomas must be wetting herself. The victim's name, it turned out, was Dave Bryant. He was a resident of Princetown where he served as an officer at Dartmoor prison. There was a photograph of him in uniform. A cold, sinking feeling settled in my guts. I did know the victim, after all. I'd seen him crossing in front of my shop window in the fog, seen him sitting at a bar table waiting for someone, seen him arguing with Luke outside the Silent Whistle.

I must find him. I drove up to Druid Lodge but his pickup truck was not parked in the drive. I ran down to the water's edge to check if he was there. He wasn't by the lake. I stared at the rain pitting the surface of the dark water, and then looked around the path. I shouted his name but there was no answer, so I called in at the house. Ricky and Morris hadn't seen him either, although he was supposed to be working that morning.

At the shop, there was no sign of Pat.

'Isn't she supposed to be coming in?'

Sophie looked up from her copy of the *Dartmoor Gazette*, pale and serious, dark shadows under her eyes as if she hadn't slept. 'Yes. She's late.' I hadn't got beyond the front page myself, but leaning over her shoulder I could see that the first two pages of the paper were devoted to the legend of Cutty Dyer: *Ashburton's Own Jack the Ripper!* It seemed the editors of the *Gazette* had dredged up every version of the myth they could find and come up with some highly imaginative artwork. They had talked to various experts on Dartmoor folklore, but opinions differed on exactly what form Cutty took. In some accounts he was described as a nimble water sprite, in others a huge ogre. They all agreed that he had eyes as big as saucers, and these were well represented by the *Gazette*'s artist who made him look like a goblin on speed. There was also general agreement about his nasty habits: lurking under bridges and drinking the blood of those unfortunate enough to stray within his grasp.

'Were you told about Cutty Dyer when you were a kid?' I asked Sophie.

She shook her head. 'No, but Mum was. My gran used to warn her to stay away from the bridges or Cutty would get her.'

The only 'eyewitnesses' who claimed to have encountered Cutty and lived to tell the tale were two drunks wandering home one night in the nineteenth century, who claimed to have seen the horrible vision rising from the river, and their account can hardly be considered to be reliable. As far as I could tell, there was no account of a real person ever being found dead in the river with their throat cut – until now.

'It's horrible, isn't it?' Sophie shuddered. 'Someone who lives around here, someone we might know, has murdered two people, cut their throats. I hardly slept last night. Every little noise scared me. I kept thinking someone was trying to break in.'

'Well, we don't really know the facts,' I pointed out, trying to calm her down. 'It may be that Jessie and this man Bryant were connected in some way, that the killer had a motive for murdering them both. It doesn't mean he's going to kill again. It doesn't mean there's a serial killer on the loose, whatever the papers and the television say.'

She sighed. 'No, I suppose not.' She didn't sound convinced, and the truth was, I wasn't that convinced either. I left her and ran up the stairs to phone Honeysuckle Farm, hoping I could speak to Luke.

But it was Pat who answered and she sounded tearful.

'I'm sorry I've not come in, but we're all in a state here. Luke's been taken to the police station.'

'He's been arrested?' I asked, shocked.

'Well, no, the police said he'd just be helping them with their enquiries.'

'When was this?'

'Early this morning, before breakfast. He knew this bloke, you see, the man who got murdered.'

'In the paper it said he was a prison officer.'

'Well, there's a bit more to it than that,' Pat admitted. 'Luke put in a complaint against him, when he was inside.'

'Against Dave Bryant?'

'That's right. I don't know what it was all about. But Luke got beaten up because of it. He ended up in hospital. He was naive, I suppose . . .' She hesitated. 'What if the police think he held a grudge, that he killed Bryant?' Her voice broke in a sob. 'Well, they must think that, mustn't they, otherwise why have they taken him in?'

'Even if they do, they have to have evidence,' I said. 'And there won't be any, will there?'

'Well, no . . .' Pat admitted.

'We know Luke's not a killer. He couldn't cut anyone's throat. I'm sure he'll be home soon. Ring me later, will you? Let me know he's back. And try not to worry.'

When I got downstairs, Sophie was still poring over the paper, turning its pages.

'You're not still reading about that murder?' I was ready to snatch the wretched thing away from her.

'No,' she said, without looking up. 'I'm trying to find the results of the competition I entered to win those tickets for the Spring Ball.' She turned over another page.

'What did you have to do for it?' I asked.

'Oh, just answer this really simple question.' She looked up. '*Where in Ashburton would you find a site for sore eyes?*' She tutted. 'Well, everyone knows that!'

I nodded. 'Saint Gudula's Well.' Saint Gudula was a patron saint of the blind and there is a tiny spring, which is supposed to have healing properties, marked by a stone cross at the western end of town.

'The well is a *site*,' Sophie explained, just in case I was too thick to get the pun.

I made a face. 'I wouldn't fancy bathing my eyes in that water.'

Suddenly she shrieked. 'I've won!'

I bent to look over her shoulder. 'You're kidding!'

'No, look!' She pointed. 'My name's printed here. It says winners will receive their tickets by post.' She turned to gaze up at me, her big dark eyes suddenly serious. 'You will come with me, won't you? The prize is a pair of tickets, you see.'

I should have been delighted at her offer, but my mind was still fixed on Luke. 'Isn't there a man you want to take?'

'No one!' she sighed tragically. 'I might meet someone there, though.' She prodded my arm. 'We both might.'

'Don't you want to take your mum?'

'God, no! She'd hate it, anyway. Oh, come on, Juno!' she urged as I hesitated. She adopted her pleading orphaned puppy look. 'It'll be fun!'

I laughed. 'Of course I'll come.'

'D'you think Ricky and Morris would loan us costumes?' she asked, gazing at me innocently. Suddenly her reason for asking me rather than any of her other friends became a little clearer. She knows I have influence. 'They loaned us costumes when we went to Moorworthy House.'

'Well, Morris informs me that they don't usually loan out for parties,' I told her loftily, 'but I think our chances are good. Leave it with me.'

Before I left the shop, I tried to ring the police station, but I couldn't speak to anyone involved in the investigation. The officer on the phone promised someone would return my call but couldn't say when.

The rest of the day was taken up with clients. I didn't mention Bryant's murder to Maisie or to Chloe Berkeley-Smythe. There was no point in alarming them with tales of Ashburton's serial killer. They'd find out soon enough when their copies of the *Gazette* dropped through their letter boxes.

I popped into the shop before closing. Elizabeth had taken over from Sophie but there had been no word from Pat. I phoned her when I got home. She was even more upset. Luke had still not returned from the police station. I phoned the station again, got the same response. Someone would return my call.

I was still waiting when my doorbell rang early in the evening. I hoped it might be Luke, or Dean Collins, but instead, Detective Sergeant Cruella DeVille was standing on my doorstep. She said she wanted a word and reluctantly I showed her upstairs.

'Have you released Luke Rowlands yet?' I asked, before she had a chance to sit down.

'Mr Rowlands is only helping us with our enquiries,' she responded primly. 'He is free to go at any time.'

'So, he's not a suspect?'

She paused, giving me her iced-violet stare. She had no intention of answering my question. 'How well do you know Mr Rowlands?'

'Well enough to think he's not a killer.'

There was a tiny tug at the corner of her mouth, almost a smile. 'He's killed before.'

'Is that why he's helping you with your enquiries?' I asked. 'Because he was convicted of manslaughter?'

'Rowlands knew Bryant from when he was in prison,' she responded. 'They were recently seen arguing outside the Silent Whistle . . .' She paused. I said nothing. 'We received an anonymous tip-off,' she added, 'from someone who saw Rowlands get into a white van driven by a woman with long red hair. That wouldn't be you, would it?'

I wasn't going to lie. 'We went for a drink.'

'Where?'

'The Exeter Inn.'

She wrote that down. 'I see. And did you talk about the incident?'

I shrugged. 'Luke didn't want to talk about it.'

'Did he identify Bryant?'

'No, he just said that he was someone he'd known before, someone he wanted nothing to do with.'

'He didn't show any further hostility towards him?'

'Not at all.'

'He didn't threaten him, swear to get even with him?'

'No,' I said emphatically. 'He didn't.'

'You didn't go inside the Silent Whistle yourself?'

'I didn't get out of the van.'

'Were you aware of any other witnesses to the incident?'

'No,' I responded, giving it a moment's thought. 'There was no one else on the pavement, not outside the pub. I couldn't swear there was no one further up St Lawrence Lane who might have seen what was happening. But, you know, it was hardly an incident, Luke just gave the man a shove, that's all. It wasn't a kerbside brawl.'

She gave me the Medusa stare again. She clearly didn't believe what I was saying.

'So what did you talk about,' she asked at last, 'in the Exeter Inn?'

'Archaeology on Dartmoor,' I told her, thinking back. 'We weren't there long. I was off to a concert at the arts centre.'

'You didn't know Rowlands well, yet you offered him a lift in your van?'

'Look, he's the nephew of a friend. I knew he'd been in prison. I could see he might be about to get into a fight, and I wanted to stop him getting into trouble.'

'Very noble of you,' she said and put away her pen and notebook. 'I don't think I need to trouble you any longer.'

Thank God for that, I thought. I wondered afterwards if I'd have been more helpful if it had been Dean Collins asking the questions, or Inspector Ford. Probably not, on balance. I hadn't withheld anything and I'd told the truth. I hadn't mentioned I'd gone out for a meal with

Luke on Saturday evening, but I'd have told her if she'd asked me. Why was it, then, that Cruella left me with the feeling that I had either said something I shouldn't or not said something that I should?

When the doorbell rang again it was close to midnight. I was already in bed and went downstairs tying my dressing gown around me. It was too late for visitors and I opened the door a little cautiously. Luke was on the doorstep in the rain, his hair flattened, the shoulders of his jacket sodden. As I dragged him inside, I could feel him shivering but I guessed he wasn't trembling from the cold. Upstairs I helped him out of his wet coat and offered him the last of Elizabeth's gin. This time he didn't refuse. He sat on the sofa, glass in hand, peering into it for several seconds before he knocked it back. He almost choked, but nodded his head for another when I held out the bottle.

'When did they let you go?' I asked.

'Couple of hours ago,' he answered. 'I've been home, seen Ken and the girls. They didn't want me to come out again, but I needed to talk to you.' He smiled nervously. 'I'm sorry it's late.'

'It doesn't matter.' I sat next to him. 'The police were questioning you all that time?'

He gave the ghost of a laugh. 'Well, they left me on my own, kicking my heels in an interview room for a few hours, but that's the kind of thing they do. They kept asking me what Bryant was doing in Ashburton, if he had come here to meet me. Well, I don't know, do I?' He took another drink, his hand still trembling. 'Wasn't it too much of a coincidence, they kept asking, Bryant being found dead in Ashburton not long after I'd come out of prison and come to live here . . . ? And wasn't it another coincidence that he'd had his throat cut when it was me found Jessie Mole like that? Is that what gave me the idea, they wanted to know.' He shook his head. 'I thought they were going to accuse me of killing her too.'

I didn't know what to say. For me, the police had always been the good guys; for Luke, it seemed they had become the enemy. He had lapsed into silence, gazing into some different, darker place.

'Pat said you'd made a complaint against Bryant when you were in prison,' I ventured at last.

He nodded, rolling the empty gin glass between the palms of his hands. 'He was a bully, used to beat people up – or stand by with his back turned while other cons beat them. He was into all sorts – smuggling in drugs and phones – these things can't happen in a prison without a bent screw somewhere. And I talked about him to another prisoner.' He shook his head at his own folly. 'God, I must have been stupid.'

'What happened?'

'I had a nasty accident in the showers, didn't I? I'd have been dead if the right person hadn't come along.'

'And do the police know what kind of man Bryant was?'

His mouth twisted. 'If they do, they're not telling me.' He put the glass down.

The gin bottle was empty. I offered him coffee, but he shook his head.

'So, how come the two of you were quarrelling outside the pub?' I asked.

He held up his palms in a gesture of defence. 'I didn't want any quarrel. I walked into the pub thinking I'd watch a bit of the football match – you know they have those big screens in there? I thought I'd get in early, before the place filled up. Anyway, I hadn't got as far as the bar when I saw Bryant there talking with these two blokes. As soon as I saw him, I wanted to get out of there. But he'd already spotted me and he followed me out.'

'What did he want?'

'Just to wind me up, that's the kind of bastard he was. He said he was looking forward to seeing me back inside, that sort of thing.' He smiled grimly. 'Then you came along . . . and what I wanted to ask you was,' he said, turning to look at me directly, 'did you see either of these other men, the ones Bryant was talking to?'

'No,' I said, shaking my head. 'I didn't notice anyone outside the pub except for you and Bryant.'

'I'm sure they were standing by the windows looking out, watching what was going on. And I keep thinking, it must have been one of them that tipped the police off about the argument.'

'I suppose anyone who was in the pub might have

known that there was an argument going on outside. And once his picture appeared in the paper . . .'

'But that's just it,' Luke objected, 'there wasn't anyone else. It was early, the place was deserted, only Bryant and these two blokes. And not many people in Ashburton know me, to put the finger on me . . .'

'So, it must have been one of them. Did you mention them to the police?'

Luke nodded. 'They asked me to describe them. I told them I could do better than that. I drew them a picture.' He smiled. 'They seemed to get a bit excited then.'

'Have you still got the picture you drew?' I asked.

Luke shook his head. 'They took it away. They kept asking me if I was sure these were the men I'd seen, that I wasn't just making them up.' He turned to face me. 'And I thought if you'd seen them through the windows, maybe the police would believe that they really existed.'

'Could you draw them again?' I asked.

'Sure,' he said. 'Got any paper?'

I handed him a pad and a pen, watching as he began to draw. As a face began to take shape on the paper, I knew I had seen it before, in the light cast through a pub doorway. Dark and handsome, he'd stepped back to hold open the door, to ask if I wanted to go inside.

During the night I realised what had been bothering me so much. It was blood. Olly had mentioned it first, said that when Jessie had been killed there must have been a lot of blood: except there wasn't, just a thin trickle staining the ramp. If Jessie's throat had been cut while her heart was still pumping there would have been a lot more blood. Even if she had been killed elsewhere, her clothes would have been drenched in it. It had flowed copiously from Dave Bryant's body. So maybe that's not how Jessie died. Maybe whoever killed her just wanted it to look that way.

CHAPTER EIGHTEEN

'Juno, just bloody calm down!' Dean Collins yelled at me. 'We're only doing our jobs!'

'Fourteen hours you held that boy yesterday,' I flung at him.

'He was free to leave—'

'Oh, come on!' I yelled. 'He was shattered.' I took a deep breath. I hated this, feeling antagonistic towards Dean, towards the police. I felt unbalanced, as if a solid plank I had always relied on had suddenly become a seesaw. Dean was right, I needed to calm down. *Old Nick's* was no place to be having a blazing row. It was likely to alarm the customers. Fortunately, at that moment, there weren't any. 'You could have let him go. You held him in the hope that you could break him—'

His voice dropped to a fierce whisper. 'Look, the lad's killed once – maybe accidentally,' he admitted holding up a hand to fend off my protest. 'He knew Bryant. He'd been on the end of some rough treatment from him. He was seen quarrelling with him – you were a witness to that yourself, you've admitted it. Now, Bryant's found dead in the town where Luke Rowlands has recently come to live . . .'

I tried to interrupt.

'With the same message attached to his body,' he carried on, 'that was found on the body of Jessie Mole, a body you and Rowlands discovered. Adding all that up, Juno, do you think we were wrong to bring him in for questioning?'

Put like that, no, I didn't, but I wasn't going to bloody admit it. 'Different killer,' I said.

Dean frowned. 'What?'

'Jessie Mole and Dave Bryant were not killed by the same person.'

'Who told you that?' He was visibly shocked.

'No one told me. I worked it out. There was hardly any blood where Jessie died, despite the gash in her throat. Because when her throat was cut, she was already dead.'

'Listen, Juno,' he lowered his voice. Although the shop was empty, he glanced over his shoulder as if to assure himself no one was listening. 'This is very important. You haven't told anyone this, have you?'

'Of course not.'

'Good. The only people who know this are the police, and it may help us catch the bastard who killed her.'

'The men who killed Dave Bryant didn't know it, did they?' I retorted. 'They only knew what they'd read in the paper, and that's why they cut his throat, to make it look like a copycat killing.'

Dean nodded. He didn't look comfortable with the conversation.

'So, how did Jessie die?'

He hesitated, wrestling with his better judgement. 'She drowned. Someone held her head under the water.'

'There, on the ramp?' It was horrifying to think she might have been murdered so close to the pub, struggling with her killer while people just a few feet away were drinking and enjoying themselves.

'We don't know.'

'And he cut her throat, why? As a theatrical gesture?'

He nodded reluctantly. 'We think this is a narcissist at work. Displaying her body like that, with the postcard attached.'

'Well, that wasn't Luke.'

'And how do you know that?' Dean asked gently. 'Because he's a friend and you like him?'

'Yes.'

'And haven't you liked killers before?'

I crumpled, felt as if he'd punched me. 'That,' I told him steadily, when I had recovered breath to speak, 'was below the belt.'

He nodded sadly. 'It was and I apologise. But you get my point?'

I didn't answer. 'Those two men Luke drew for you,' I went on, 'I saw them, going into the Silent Whistle, when Bryant was inside.'

'Seriously? In that case I want you to come to the station,' Dean said, 'see if you can pick them out from some photographs.'

'And if I do, does that mean Luke's off the hook?'

He rubbed the back of his neck thoughtfully. 'Look, Juno, we know Bryant was a bad apple . . . there's likely more than one person had a motive for killing him. It'll be helpful if you can confirm the sighting of these two men, but it doesn't mean Rowlands may not have been involved.'

I gave a frustrated sigh.

'I'm sorry, Juno,' he said simply.

'Was there something you came in for?' I asked. I'd flown at him the moment he'd come in the shop door. I still didn't know what he'd wanted.

'Well . . . yes.' He became awkward suddenly, his gaze fixed on his shuffling feet. 'I came in to ask you . . . Gemma wanted me to ask . . . well, me as well . . .' he cleared his throat, 'if, well, after what you did for us at Moorworthy House we didn't want anyone else . . . if you'd consider—' He held up a finger. 'Now, you may want to think about this—'

'For God's sake, Dean!' I cried, unable to stand it any longer. 'What?'

He drew a deep breath. 'Would you be godmother to little Alice?' he asked in a rush. 'We're having her christened in April.'

I laughed, my anger melting away. 'I'd be honoured,' I told him.

His broad features creased into a smile. 'Oh, that's great!' He eyed me a little uncertainly. 'Are we friends again, then?'

'Of course we are.' I wasn't sure if a hug was appropriate at this point, and clearly, neither was he. We sort of shuffled.

'Well, that's all I came in for,' Dean said, as if he'd suddenly been relieved of a great burden. 'I'd better go . . . Listen,' he touched my elbow lightly. 'As soon as I can tell you anything I will, I promise.'

I smiled. It was the best I could hope for.

So, I'm going to be a godmother, I thought, trying to turn my mind to a more cheerful subject. I haven't got the remotest idea what a godmother does. I think it's something to do with pumpkins and coaches, but whatever it is, I'm up for it.

Later I went to the police station. I sat down in a room with Dean and was given about two dozen photographs to look at. I picked out Handsome straight away, the dark-haired man who had held open the door for me. He didn't look so handsome in the photograph. His expression was more murderous than polite. His companion, who'd been hanging back behind him, was more difficult to identify. I'd only got a partial view of him in the light through the pub door and his face had been enclosed in a hoodie, but there was something about the staring eyes of a thin-faced individual in one photo that made me point a finger and say, yes, I was pretty certain that was him.

'And you're a hundred per cent sure about this man?' Dean asked, pointing at Handsome.

'Yes,' I said.

'Excellent!' He thumped the table with his fist in glee. 'You've identified the same photographs as one of the bar staff.' His face fell. 'I haven't just told you that, by the way,' he added guiltily. He stood up. 'Hold on there a minute, Juno.'

He left the room and returned a few minutes later, accompanied by Detective Inspector Ford.

He asked me to identify the photographs again. When I did, he actually smiled.

'Who are these men?' I asked.

'Members of a criminal gang,' he informed me. 'Our colleagues in the Met are searching for them now.'

'And they killed Dave Bryant?'

'They were certainly involved with him in some way. The girl in the pub says she'd seen them with him there before. But as yet, we can't place them in Ashburton on the night of the killing. We're relying on forensics to come up with something there.' He fixed me with his stare. 'Listen, Juno, even if we find these two charmers are responsible for Bryant's murder, that doesn't mean that Rowlands wasn't involved.' He held up a hand as I opened my mouth to object. 'He knew him from the prison, knew the stuff that Bryant was involved in—'

'Yes, and he got beaten up when he talked about it!' I protested.

'That doesn't make him innocent.' He gave me a moment to digest this. 'So, what I'm saying is, you keep quiet about all this. Don't go talking to anyone, and above all, don't talk to Rowlands about it. I don't want any arrest or future prosecution blown away because someone fed a suspect with information.' He gave me a broad smile. 'You've been very helpful to us in the past, Juno. I wouldn't want to have to arrest you for perverting the course of justice,' he went on as I gaped at him, 'now would I?'

The discovery of Cutty Dyer's second victim had a far greater effect on the town of Ashburton than the discovery of the first. People had reacted to Jessie's death with a sense of shock, but a general acceptance that her killer was someone who knew her, someone with a motive, who was unlikely to kill again. But with this second killing, it seemed there was a maniac on the loose. It wasn't just Sophie and Pat who were frightened. Kids were ordered to go straight home after school, to be in safely before dark, and above all, to stay away from the river. Shops started to close a little earlier to let staff get home. People were wary of being out alone after dark and the streets, never exactly throbbing during dark February evenings, became deserted. It was as if snow had fallen, sealing everyone inside the safety of their warm living rooms. Snow had fallen and muffled every footfall.

I hated it, hated the fear-spread rumour, because apart from the police and the killer, only I knew that Jessie had not been killed by the same person who had killed Bryant and that Cutty Dyer was unlikely to kill again. Or so I thought.

If the spectre of Cutty Dyer wasn't off-putting enough, there was another good reason for staying away from the water's edge: the worsening weather. The level of the Ashburn had risen alarmingly with all the rain and gushed between its banks gurgling and swirling in a muddy brown torrent, certainly capable of sweeping away any small child who fell into it.

One person who refused to venture out was Chloe Berkeley-Smythe, but as she rarely left her cottage anyway, this made little difference to her lifestyle. She was happy to send me out – in daylight only – to do her food shopping. Despite her assertion that she had more than enough clothes for her next cruise and never needed to buy another thing, she was rarely off the shopping channel and parcels and packages arrived for her nearly every day. But when I next came to her cottage, she was far more interested in showing me the photos stored on her tablet than packing for her next voyage.

'All this talk about Cutty Dyer made me think,' she told me, after insisting that I poured us both a sherry, 'of the river festival they held here – oh, several years ago now. Do you remember it, Juno, dear? There was a procession through the town with all the children and they'd made these lovely figures.' I watched her manicured fingernail skimming through one photo after another in a dizzyingly blurred line until it stopped at the one she wanted. 'There! I think they spent weeks making them. Aren't they lovely?'

I found myself staring at a picture of a procession on East Street headed by two larger-than-life figures: one dressed in shades of blue and green, with a narrow silver face, pointed ears and an elongated nose: a water sprite. The other figure was huge, with eyes the size of dinner plates, long fangs and strange, webbed hands and feet: Cutty Dyer. The procession was watched by cheering crowds, all back on the pavement, except for one figure standing out in the road, in everyone's way, in her blue coat and ankle socks, waving at the procession.

I pointed her out to Chloe. 'Look, there's Jessie Mole.'

'So there is!' She took the tablet from me for a closer look.

'Quite ironic really,' I said, 'in view of how she died.'

Chloe gave a shudder. 'You know, I shall be glad to get away from Ashburton for a while, safe on the high seas, away from all this horror.' She frowned at me. 'Are you sure you don't want to come?'

'Quite sure, thank you.'

'There's more to life than Ashburton, you know,' she reproached me gently.

'I know, but just at the moment, it's got more than enough to keep me interested, thanks.'

'Well, if you're sure . . .' Her glossy fingernail was busy again, skimming through photos. I decided it was time I got on with her packing, but she stopped me.

'Look! Look!' she cried in disgust. 'It's them!'

I found myself staring at a photo of Digby Jerkin and Amanda Waft. They were dressed for dinner on the cruise boat, Digby in a dinner jacket and Amanda in a long blue gown, champagne flutes in hand, standing next to Chloe, looking plump and sparkly in purple.

She sucked in her breath, her eyelids fluttering. 'Just too exhausting, the pair of them! I wish I'd never shown them my photos now.'

'They may not settle in Ashburton,' I told her, 'they're looking all around the area.'

'Let's hope they find somewhere far away,' she muttered.

'Well, you're going to be far away soon,' I said, getting up, 'and you won't be ready in time if I don't get on with your packing. In the meantime,' I nodded in the direction of the tablet, 'do you want me to put that thing on charge?'

'Oh, yes, please, Juno, dear,' she said, thrusting it to me as if it had suddenly become a hand grenade. 'You know I'm not good at these things.'

I went to Druid Lodge next day in the hope that Luke would be working by the lake. The rain had stopped for once, although heavy drops pitted the smooth mirror of the water whenever the wind stirred dripping branches overhead. The path around the lake was clear to walk. Trees had been crown-lifted, weeds ripped out and thick shrubbery pruned back. Hellebores, long hidden, nodded their drooping flowers in clumps of speckled white and purple. Crocuses and daffodils planted years ago, and for so long kept secret in the undergrowth, sparkled along the edges of the path.

'This looks lovely,' I told Luke when I eventually found him, sawing his way through the pale branches of a fallen silver birch. He had let light into the little woodland glade. He stopped work to listen to me. I know the inspector had warned me not to speak but I could at least tell him that the police were following other leads.

But he shook his head, still certain that they were trying to set him up.

'I keep thinking about what we were talking about the other day,' he said, 'about getting out of here, going on the moor, living up there by myself.'

'If you disappear, Luke, that will only make the police think you have got something to hide.'

'Doesn't matter.' He resumed his sawing, his face set in stony lines. 'They'll never find me.'

When I left Luke, I called up at the house to see how Ricky was. I'd promised to give Morris some help with costumes, anyway. Their refusal to loan out clothes for the Spring Ball had a knock-on effect at *Old Nick's*. We were selling vintage dresses like they were going out of fashion – if you'll excuse the pun – even though most of them weren't right for the roaring twenties at all.

'Silly bitches!' Ricky groaned when I told him about our customers. He was looking a lot better and sounding far more his usual vitriolic self.

'There's nothing easier than making a flapper dress,'

Morris said. 'You just buy a slip and attach fringe or scarves to the hem. That's it. It couldn't be simpler. All you need then is a ribbon and a feather for your headdress.'

'Well, that may be what Sophie and I have to do. She's won tickets and asked me to go with her and I was wondering if . . .'

'You're not going in any bleedin' slip!' Ricky rasped at me, falling into a fit of coughing and sucking on his vaping machine.

'No, no, no!' Morris cried, patting my hand. 'We've got lovely, lovely things you and Sophie can wear!'

'I was hoping you'd say that.' I gave him a little hug as we were both enveloped in a cloud of sickly smelling smoke. 'Thank you!'

'You'll look dazzling!' he promised. 'Just leave it to us!'

This crucial point having been established, we left Ricky resting in an armchair and worked on packing up costumes for *School for Scandal*, which, I am glad to say, did not involve sending off any flapper dresses, but a lot of very large petticoats and powdered wigs. We worked all day and I told Morris about Luke, that I was worried that he might do something stupid.

'Well, he's not very communicative even on a good day,' Morris sighed. 'But as long as he's working here, we'll try to keep an eye on him.'

At the end of the day I said goodbye to Ricky and checked, once more, that Sophie and I would be able to borrow costumes. 'Yes, we said so!' Ricky groaned at me. 'How many more times?'

I ignored the groaning. 'It's just a pity we haven't got two gorgeous men to go with.'

Ricky gave a sly grin. 'I wouldn't be so sure about that.'

I frowned. 'What do you mean?'

'He means,' Morris said coyly, giving my arm a little pat, 'that we've got tickets too.'

Another person refusing to leave her house was Maisie, but her refusal had more to do with the rain than Cutty Dyer. She'd recovered from one chest infection and didn't want to risk going out in the damp. The water in the tiny stream, which separated her garden gate from the road, and gave Brook Lane its name, had risen so much that it lapped the granite stepping stone, which gave access to her property. Jacko tried snarling and snapping at it when I took him for his walk, but it refused to subside.

'I remember them floods before the war,' Maisie told me, shaking her curls at the memory. 'I was only a nipper at the time. Six feet deep the water was in North Street,' she went on, pursing her lips, 'it carried down these rocks from the moor, tore up all the roads. I remember Hamlyns the butchers . . . o'course, it's not there any more . . .'

'How is Nelly Mole?' I asked, before we got lost in too much reminiscence. 'Have you seen her since you've been home? She must be very upset by what happened to Jessie.'

Maisie had little sympathy for Jessie and dismissed

her with a wave of her gnarled little hand. 'Bad lot, that's what Jessie was! Nelly would tell you just the same if you asked her.'

'The police still have no idea who killed her.'

Maisie gave a snort of disgust. 'I reckon she must have started on her old nonsense again.'

'Poison-pen letters?'

She nodded. 'Anyone's likely to murder her if they got one of them.'

'But they'd have to know it was from Jessie,' I pointed out.

'Ah, well,' Maisie sniffed. 'Mud sticks.'

'You think someone in Ashburton knew that Jessie had been in trouble before?'

'Well, I don't know about that,' Maisie admitted. 'But when she had to leave Okehampton, no one knows where she went then or what she got up to . . . least, no one in her family.'

'And Nelly won't talk about why she had to leave?' I asked.

Maisie glanced around the room and dropped her voice to a whisper as if she suspected the ornaments might be eavesdropping. 'I think a death was involved . . . y'know,' she mouthed the word, 'suicide.'

'Because of one of Jessie's letters?'

'Well, they couldn't absolutely prove it was her who wrote it, but that's when Jessie had to leave town.'

'And how long ago was this?'

Maisie held up her hands helplessly. 'I don't know.

I just know it was a long time ago. And wherever she went, who's to say she didn't carry on with her mischief?'

Later that night I spent some time on the Internet, trawling through *Dartmoor Gazette*'s online archive. Unfortunately, I didn't have much to go on. Apart from the recent ones, I could find no references to Jessie Mole and no references to poison-pen letters or suicides in Okehampton. Not knowing what year I wanted didn't help. It was possible the online archive just didn't go back far enough. And what Maisie had said was true: Jessie might have carried on with her mischief somewhere else for years – which meant there could be an awful lot of people out there with a motive to kill her.

CHAPTER NINETEEN

We got a round of applause as we entered the ballroom, but then, our costumes were superior to everyone else's.

'Are they originals?' Sophie had squeaked in delight when we had first tried them on.

'They're better than originals,' Ricky had told her. 'These were made for *Thoroughly Modern Millie*. They're much more glam.'

We couldn't just walk in discreetly, of course. Ricky and Morris made sure we were noticed. They refused to shed their silk top hats, capes and silver-topped canes until we reached our table, where they helped us out of velvet wraps with wide shawl collars, to reveal the divine dresses beneath. It was like putting on a show, but with Ricky and Morris everything is. From their immaculate white ties and waistcoats to their gleaming patent shoes, they were every inch the gentlemen. Morris had abandoned his little spectacles in favour of a monocle, and Ricky had oiled his hair and given it a central parting, which did give him a slight look of Count Dracula, but as they both in perfectly synchronised motion flipped up their tails, sat down and crossed one leg over the other, I had to admit they had style.

Sophie wore a classic flapper dress in purple, strings of beads in gold, purple and black hanging from the hem; a purple ribbon circled her dark cap of hair, with feathers in black and gold standing up from her head. 'Very Sally Bowles,' Ricky had commented.

My dress was a deep, dark forest green and fringed, from the shoulder to the hem, in strings of shimmering bugle beads in emerald, green and turquoise. It sparkled and glistened with every move I made. How anyone ever danced in it I don't know, because it weighed a ton. Ricky had tormented my hair back into coils at the back of my head, except for one looping spit-curl in the middle of my forehead, which was held firmly in place by a green velvet ribbon, with a cluster of feathered and beaded flowers hanging down over one ear. I'd have felt ridiculous if I hadn't looked so fab.

Secretly, Sophie and I were more than a little dismayed to see an orchestra playing twenties-style music in the corner of the ballroom. We'd been hoping for a disco. The presence of a live band meant that they were almost certain to be playing a Charleston at some point, and we would have to dance it. Ricky and Morris had spent all afternoon trying to teach us the steps, and there was no way they were going to let us get away with not trying them out. We'd managed the basic forward and back reasonably well, although I was deplorably short on swivel, but when it came to all that knee-weaving I really wasn't very good. I like to think of my own dancing style as less structured, more primeval.

But before the dancing we had drinks and dinner to get through and this gave us a chance to get a good look at everyone else. Many of the ladies had obviously made their own costumes or had them made, their efforts rated with varying degrees of scathing rudeness from the corner of Ricky's mouth.

There were one or two ladies whose costumes were outstandingly good. Meredith Swann looked stunning in a heavily beaded evening gown in shades of red. It looked like a modern creation, but suited the period well. Her dark hair was looped back into a simple chignon. Above all, she wore her usual effortless elegance in a manner that made those of us in fancy dress feel silly. Sitting with her was Verbena Clarke. I suspect she'd probably designed her dress herself, a gauzy, floaty number in a colour that wasn't quite white, wasn't quite silver and wasn't quite blue – something to do with the way it was layered, probably. She looked ravishing, although a spiteful observer – Ricky, for example – might have commented that it was really a dress for a slightly younger woman. Sharing their table was Mr Daniel Thorncroft, one of the few gentlemen to have come properly attired in white tie and tails. There didn't seem to be a fourth member of their party and I could only assume he was acting as squire to them both.

'Blimey!' Ricky murmured to me. 'He's got his hands full!'

'Did we tell you,' Morris asked, tapping me on the arm, 'they turned up at the house the other day?'

'Who did?'

'Verbena and her new friend, Meredith,' Ricky said slyly.

'Were they after costumes?'

'No. They're putting on an exhibition, the two of them, at Meredith's gallery – some swanky artist friend of Verbena's,' Morris explained. 'They brought us an invitation to the opening.'

I made a face. 'They haven't brought me one.'

'They're after our money.' Ricky grinned.

'They know you haven't got any,' Morris added.

They were right.

I spotted one person amongst the crowd who I wasn't expecting to see: Detective Sergeant Cruella DeVille. I don't know where she had got her dress from but she had chosen the perfect colour, an icy violet that matched her astonishing eyes. She wore a matching hairband around her black, bobbed hair and looked the perfect flapper. She was sitting at a table amongst a large group. I'd have loved to have known which man she was with but couldn't work it out. I pointed her out to Ricky. 'She looks lovely,' I said.

He pulled a face. 'Pity she always looks as if she's sucking a lemon.'

Sophie choked on her champagne, nearly spraying it over the tablecloth. 'She can't help her mouth!' she protested.

'She could smile occasionally, that might help.' His eyes widened at the sight of someone entering the ballroom. 'Oh my God!' he murmured. 'I think it's Miss Havisham!' Morris and Sophie dissolved into fits of giggles and I turned to see who he meant.

Amanda Waft, trailing yards of cream chiffon, did give the impression that she might be wearing a wedding dress, an original probably, with a wide lace headdress worn very low over her brow, which added to the suspicion that she might be slightly drunk. She was valiantly supported by Digby as she minced across the ballroom. There was a smattering of applause, from people who presumably recognised them from their old television series, which led Amanda to stop and give a wobbly curtsey before she continued on her way across the ballroom, turning from side to side and waving a gloved hand like visiting royalty. With some determined steering from Digby she eventually alighted like a giant cream butterfly at the table next to ours. Digby sat next to her and I saw him puff out his cheeks in a sigh, like a man who'd just safely landed a dodgy aircraft.

'How lovely everyone looks!' Amanda cooed graciously, gazing rather unsteadily around the room. 'Is there champagne?'

A waiter with a tray was soon at her elbow, furnishing her with a glass. 'You'd better get a bottle, Digby, darling,' she told him and Digby darling hurried off to the bar to do her bidding. After reminding Amanda who Sophie and I were – she had a vague recollection of having met us before somewhere – we chatted about how their house-hunting was going. She couldn't remember much about that either, so the conversation flagged a bit until Digby returned, then came dinner, which filled a couple of hours nicely. But as soon as the last of the coffee and mints had been cleared away, the band struck up a Charleston.

Everyone stayed resolutely in their seats. Sophie and I would have liked to do the same, but Ricky and Morris had other ideas and we were dragged, resisting, into the middle of the dance floor. The initial forward and back steps, performed in hold, Sophie with Morris, Ricky with me, weren't too bad, but it was the side-by-sides I was dreading. All too soon we opened out. 'Scarecrow!' Ricky yelled at me. 'Elbows out, knees together, elbows out, knees together,' he shouted above the music as I flailed at his side. Whichever direction I moved in, the weighty strings of beads seemed to swing in the opposite one. Sophie was doing much better than I was: small and compact she had better balance, and she was dancing with Morris who, like a lot of fat men, was light on his feet.

Some of those seated watching us soon caught on to the fact that Ricky and Morris knew what they were doing, and lined up behind us, attempting to mimic our steps. 'Bees knees!' Ricky yelled and we all tried knee-weaving. Gradually, the dance floor filled and became one giant dance class with Ricky at the helm. Fortunately, Amanda was either too drunk or not drunk enough to attempt to dance – that or Digby had nailed her to her chair.

'Scarecrow!' Ricky yelled again. 'Goony birds!' and the whole crowd turned sideways and waved its arms up and down like crazy. I turned the wrong way and found myself chest-to-chest with a wildly flapping Daniel Thorncroft and turned away again. The rhythms got faster and the room grew hotter than the tropics. I swear the blasted band played the tune through twice. Eventually, the music stopped, and the whole crowd erupted in applause and breathless laughter. Most people decided to take a break and staggered back to their seats. Ricky, who was looking grey after all his exertions, went outside for a vape, and I headed off towards the ladies' loo.

On my way back I passed Cruella's table. I was still curious to see who she was with. She was chatting with a fair-haired young man whose slightly beefy good looks could have fitted a young farmer or a fellow policeman. My speculating meant I wasn't looking where I was going and suddenly found myself accosted by Mr Daniel Thorncroft.

'You really do look quite lovely Miss Browne with an "e",' he told me. He was smiling but for once there was no hint of mockery in his voice. 'Would you care to dance?'

By now the band was playing something slow and intimate. I hesitated.

'I should warn you,' he went on, seeing my hesitation, 'that I can't dance, really, only shuffle.'

I was about to refuse and then saw Meredith and Verbena watching us from their table.

'Me too,' I admitted and let him lead me onto the dance floor. We assumed the same hold as those dancers around us, my hand on his shoulder, his arm around my back, my other hand resting lightly in his. It was too close for casual acquaintance. I could feel his warmth, smell the tang of his aftershave. I felt awkward and didn't know what to say so I lowered my gaze.

'My bow tie really is quite fascinating, isn't it?' he remarked pleasantly after he'd endured a minute of my mulish silence. 'I expect you're wondering how I managed to tie it. It took a bit of doing, I can tell you.'

I couldn't help laughing and looked up at him.

'That's better.' He smiled. 'Tell me, who are those gentlemen who are with you? They're brilliant dancers.'

How do you explain Ricky and Morris? But I was grateful to clutch at any straw of conversation if it would distract attention away from myself, from our awkward proximity, and explained about their theatre hire company, and how they entertained as Sauce and Slander, until we were interrupted by a nudge from a slightly drunken man dancing beside us.

'You're a bit greedy, aren't you?' he accused my partner. 'Not content with that beautiful blonde and gorgeous brunette, you've grabbed this ravishing redhead as well.'

'So much beauty in the room,' Mr Thorncroft responded blandly, 'so little time!' and spun me away with a whispered 'idiot' in my ear. 'And the lady in the cream?' he asked. But by this time the music was coming to an end, and I begged to be released, conscious of the pairs of eyes that were watching us. It was a wonder I didn't have scorch marks on my spine. 'You mustn't abandon your harem.'

He crooked a dark eyebrow. 'Verbena's partner let her down at the last minute,' he explained.

'Awkward,' I acknowledged, 'trying to keep two ladies happy.'

'Trouble is, Miss B,' he said, leaning towards me confidentially, 'Lottie doesn't like either of 'em.'

I sighed sadly. 'A dog is such a very good judge of character!'

'We're in agreement, Miss Browne,' he said, relinquishing my hand and letting me drift back to my seat.

Morris and Ricky's faces were already alight with mischief when I sat down at the table, but I knew in advance that they would be annoying. 'And just who was that you were dancing with?' Ricky demanded.

'That's Daniel Thorncroft,' I responded irritably.

Sophie gave me a puzzled frown. 'I thought you didn't like him.'

'I don't much.'

She insisted on turning round to stare at him. 'I think he's rather gorgeous. You looked great dancing together.'

I could have slapped her. 'We were hardly dancing.'

'Well, whatever you were doing,' Ricky grinned, 'that pair in the corner,' he nodded in the direction of Meredith and Verbena, 'weren't happy about it.'

Morris gave his coy little smile. 'You should have seen their faces.'

I did.

Ricky gave a low chuckle. 'They looked like slapped arses.'

Sophie's voice dropped to a whisper. 'D'you think they're fighting over him?'

'I don't think there's anything much to fight over,' I responded. 'In any case, it makes no difference to me.'

This wasn't quite true. I was rather pleased at the idea I'd annoyed them, that I might actually have made them jealous.

The dancing didn't break up until the early hours, the band stopping at midnight to be replaced by a disco. This meant that far more people got up to dance, at least to jig around in the loose fashion that Sophie and I found more comfortable. It also allowed Daniel Thorncroft to dance with both Meredith and Verbena at once. We kept going until the effort made Sophie a bit wheezy and she confessed that she'd forgotten to bring her inhaler and had left it back at Druid Lodge.

'Time to sit down and take it easy for a bit,' I told her as we returned to our table. 'In fact,' I added to Ricky and Morris, 'perhaps we should be thinking of going.'

'I think it's time I took Amanda home,' Digby added.

I hadn't noticed what a state she was in. I don't know how much champagne she'd got down her, but she appeared to be asleep, her head down on the table. She resisted all attempts to rouse her with gentle shaking, and beyond a few mutterings, refused being returned to consciousness. I felt sorry for Digby; he must have felt embarrassed but he refused to show it.

'Shall we ask a waiter to make her some coffee?' Sophie suggested, but Digby shook his head.

'Probably best just to get her home,' he said, catching her arm and trying to drag her to her feet. 'Come along, darling.'

It was clear the poor man was going to need help. Together, we managed to get her more or less upright and between the two of us, Digby and I walked her out of the ballroom, weaving between dancers as the coloured disco lights swept over us and the music blared. Ricky, Morris and Sophie had gathered up all the hats and capes and were coming on behind. Digby kept explaining to anyone who expressed concern that his wife wasn't ill, just very tired, which made her drunken state all the more obvious.

'Did you come by taxi?' I asked.

'No, I brought the car,' he said and went off to fetch it, leaving Sophie and me on a low wall either side of Amanda, holding tightly to stop her falling off it backwards.

'I'm going to have to go back with Digby,' I told Ricky. 'I can't just abandon the poor man, he'll never manage her by himself.'

'Oh, we'll all come!' he yawned. 'The night is yet young, we might as well have a laugh.'

'Young?' Sophie repeated. 'It must be two in the morning.'

Digby arrived back with his car. It took considerable effort to wedge Amanda, moaning softly, into the back seat. I crawled in next to her and Sophie climbed into the front seat next to Digby. Ricky and Morris were to follow in their Saab. Before we drove off, Ricky rapped on the passenger window. 'Don't let her vomit on your dress,' he warned me.

'Now, there's a cheery thought,' I muttered.

We made it back to Digby's rented cottage without any colourful upsurgings, but getting Amanda out of the back seat was more difficult than getting her in and took a long time, even with Ricky hauling her by the arms and me pushing her from behind. After what seemed an age, she popped out like a cork and for a moment seemed to recover consciousness, tottering about like a newborn giraffe on the pavement before collapsing again into Digby's sturdy arms.

Sophie took his keys and opened the door while the rest of us carried Amanda in and up the stairs. We managed to get her onto the bed, took off her shoes and the trailing scarf that was threatening to strangle her and left her to Digby's tender and well-practised mercies.

Morris drove us back to Druid Lodge, which was where Sophie and I had left our clothes.

'Nearly time for breakfast,' Ricky announced along the way.

We both groaned. 'I think I'll sleep all day,' Sophie yawned. I was just grateful that it was Sunday and I wouldn't have to get up to walk the dogs.

'Nah, a couple of hours' nap and you girls will be fine,' Ricky insisted, 'ready for a nice fry-up.'

When we staggered from the car it was close on five. It wasn't yet dawn, a bleary-eyed moon was still visible, and the remnants of the night were grey. We tottered indoors where Sophie and I retired to the spare room, took off our finery and collapsed onto the spare bed.

I don't know how long I slept. When I awoke, my sandpaper tongue cleaving to the roof of my mouth, Sophie was still sleeping, snuffling gently into her pillow and I decided not to disturb her. I pulled on my sweater and jeans and let myself quietly out of the bedroom, in search of a drink of water.

Ricky and Morris were already up, in their dressing gowns, sitting at the breakfast table with the Sunday papers and a large pot of coffee. 'Haven't you two been to bed at all?' I asked.

'We just had a nap for an hour,' Ricky answered, yawning and stretching his long arms.

'The best thing, when you've been up all night, is to stay awake till bedtime, if you can. It's like coping with jet lag.' Morris lifted the pot and pointed, but I shook my head and reached for a glass before pouring myself water from the cold tap and taking a long glug. I sat down at the table with a sigh.

'Sophie still asleep?' Morris whispered and I nodded. 'Tea?' he asked and I gave him a grateful thumbs up.

'Aspirin?' Ricky enquired softly, raising his brows.

'I'm OK.' I hoped I looked better than he did. His pallor had not improved overnight. Perhaps it was just the morning light, but he was still recovering from his chest infection and he'd certainly overdone it last night with all that wild dancing.

'I think what I could really do with is some air,' I

told him. 'I might take a walk down to the lake.'

'Good idea,' Morris nodded. 'I'll put the kettle on.' He poked Ricky on the arm. 'You too, go on! Go with Juno! A few lungsful of air wouldn't do you any harm!'

'I'm in my slippers!' he protested.

Morris pointed at his boots, placed by the garden door. Ricky rolled his eyes and muttered, but didn't argue, pulling the boots on over the legs of his pyjamas and shrugging his overcoat on top of his dressing gown, and winding his blue scarf several times around his neck. I opened the garden door and we trudged down the sloping lawn together. The sky was overcast, grey, threatening more rain and the grass was wet.

'You can actually see the lake from here now,' I said, as Ricky vaped, sending a ribbon of white smoke rippling along behind him like a scarf.

He stopped suddenly, pointing at the water. 'Hello? Is that a swan?'

I stared for a moment. There was something white floating on the surface. 'No,' I breathed, my heart starting to pound. 'No, it's not.' And I began to run.

Ricky came stumbling after me, coughing. 'Wait, Juno!' I heard him call out, but I couldn't stop. I kept running, my trainers slipping and sliding on the wet grass. I crashed down onto the path, and began stumbling along the water's edge, picking my way along the lake's edge until I reached the spot that brought me closest to the pale form floating on the dark surface, all the time praying that it wasn't real, that what I was looking at was just another effigy. I stopped, my heart throbbing in my chest. I didn't have the breath to cry out, to give voice to the moan I felt welling up deep inside me. There was no point in wading into the water, in trying to save her. It was too late. I sank to my knees on the muddy path.

Her body had come to rest at the water's edge. She floated on her back, her fair curls slicked back by the water, her pale dress shimmering just beneath its surface. Her dead blue eyes were wide, gazing sightless at the willow branches above her. Around her slender neck was tied a scarlet ribbon.

Ricky caught up with me at last. 'Oh God!' he cried, gulping in breath as he doubled over, his hands on his knees. 'It's Verbena Clarke.'

'She's dead,' I said needlessly. Ricky sank down next to me, folding an arm around my shoulders.

'The ribbon,' he breathed, his voice still coming in gasps. 'She wasn't wearing it before . . .'

'It's a message,' I told him numbly.

'Message?'

'Don't you see who she's meant to be?' I gazed at her face, her lips parted, eyes staring upward, the weight of her silvery dress gradually dragging her down in the water. 'She's meant to be Ophelia.'

CHAPTER TWENTY

'I might be wrong,' Dean Collins said uncertainly, glancing from me to Inspector Ford, 'but Ophelia didn't get her throat cut in *Hamlet*, did she? She drowned.'

The inspector nodded. 'The scarlet ribbon is significant in that it's an apparent reference to the mark made on the picture in Miss Browne's shop.'

The three of us were sitting at the table in the breakfast room. In another part of the house Ricky was being interviewed by Det. Sergeant DeVille and in the living room Morris was comforting a distraught Sophie.

We had all been interviewed already about the ball and our last sightings of Verbena. We could remember her on the dance floor with Daniel Thorncroft and Meredith during the disco, but none of us were sure if they were still dancing when we left. We'd had our hands full with Amanda. Through the garden door I could see a police car parked at the bottom of the lawn, near the lake, the comings and goings of police in uniform, men in white suits under a grey sky. It all seemed unreal.

'But why the ribbon?' Dean persisted. 'Why not cut her throat?'

The inspector rubbed his brow and sighed. 'Why indeed?' he asked softly.

'And why no postcard?' he asked. 'There's no mention of Cutty Dyer this time.'

'Because the ribbon is the message,' I said. 'It's telling us that Verbena was killed by the person who made that mark on the picture, someone who must have been in my shop.'

Dean frowned. 'It still doesn't make sense to me. Is the killer taunting us?'

The inspector leant forward, his elbows resting on the table. 'Juno, this is very important,' he said slowly, 'I want you to think back to the day you discovered Jessie's body . . . I know we've been through it all before but bear with me . . . You met Luke Rowlands for the first time that morning, here by this lake. Who suggested you go for a drink?'

'He did.'

'And who decided on the Victoria pub?'

'Luke.'

'And when you got into the pub,' he went on, with deliberate slowness, 'why didn't you use the front door? Why did you decide to use the back entrance, by the river?'

'Um, because we'd parked in Mill Meadow.'

'There was nowhere to park on North Street?'

'I don't really remember. I was following Luke's pickup in my van.' I frowned. I wasn't sure where all this was leading. 'I parked where he did.'

'So, the decision to park there was his?'

'Yes.' I wished he'd get to the point. My head was beginning to ache and I was finding it hard to answer with patience. I didn't understand why we were revisiting all these questions when Verbena was lying dead in the lake just a few yards away.

'Tell me what happened then.'

'I started to cross the bridge and saw there was someone lying on the ramp, so I pointed it out to Luke . . .'

'And you're absolutely certain,' the inspector said, 'you saw the body first and that Luke Rowlands did not draw your attention to it in any way?'

'Yes, I'm certain.' Exasperated, I raked a hand through my hair. 'Look, what is it you're trying to make me say?'

'I'm not trying to make you say anything, Juno,' he said abruptly, 'but there's a murderer out there trying to tie us in knots and what I'm asking you to do is help me tease out a thread.' He sat back. 'We're just exploring an idea, that's all.'

I was tired, slightly hungover and beginning to lose it. I rubbed my aching forehead. 'You think Luke killed Jessie and took me to the Victoria pub and parked by the river deliberately to show me her body?'

'That's not as incredible as it sounds,' he answered steadily.

'And you think he marked the painting?' I asked. 'And then killed Verbena? Well, I certainly didn't see him come into the shop that day.'

'But it was very busy in the shop. You didn't see who marked the painting.'

'No, I didn't,' I admitted in exasperation. 'But Luke couldn't have crept in and out without being noticed. Pat was there, for God's sake!'

There was a knock on the door at that moment and a uniformed officer looked into the room. 'We've picked up Rowlands, sir, and Miss Giddings. They're both at the station.'

The inspector nodded in Dean's direction and he stood up, following the officer out.

'Miss Giddings?' I repeated, my voice rising in astonishment. 'Pat?'

'Miss Giddings' sister is related to Rowlands by marriage. They all live in the same house. He's part of their family,' the inspector answered calmly. 'Pat was involved in a quarrel with Jessie Mole over Rowlands – a fact you neglected to mention . . .'

'I didn't think it was relevant,' I protested. In fact, I'd forgotten about it to be honest. 'How did you find out about it?'

'Miss Sophie Child let it slip when we interviewed her just now. Pat Giddings was alone in the shop when, she claims, the picture sent to you anonymously was delivered by this mystery man. She could have marked that picture as easily as anyone else . . .' He lifted a hand to silence me as I opened my mouth to tell him what garbage he was talking. 'Wait a moment! A dead woman is found here, with, apparently, a reference to that painting tied around her neck – here, in a lake that probably few know exists but where Luke Rowlands has been working – a place you often visit.'

'You're not suggesting that Pat killed Verbena?'

'No, I am not. I just want to ask her and Rowlands a few questions,' he replied. 'That's all.'

I bit my lip, too angry to speak.

'Listen, Juno.' As the inspector stood up, he came closer and laid a hand on my arm. 'Let's assume, for the moment, that Jessie and Ms Clarke were killed by the same person. We don't know if the killer originally put the dummy in the river, but you're the one who found it. The publicity in the paper focussed the killer's attention on you. He's playing games, Juno, with you and with us. Just be careful.'

'And where does the murder of Dave Bryant fit into all this?' I asked him.

He turned at the door and sighed heavily. 'It doesn't,' he said.

The most terrible thought, the one that kept returning to me, was that Verbena had been murdered at the lake while the four of us were sleeping soundly inside the house.

We'd discussed it, over and over. The police left us alone, but they were busy at the lakeside for hours before they took poor Verbena away. We watched them through the French windows, her covered body carried up the grass on a wheeled stretcher as the grey sky wept and tears ran down the glass.

'She's got two teenage girls,' I said. 'What will happen to them now?'

No one spoke. I supposed they would go to live with their father.

'Do you think that's where she was killed?' Sophie's voice was hushed and fearful, her dark eyes fixed on what was happening across the lawn. 'Down there by the water?'

'I think she must have been,' Ricky answered softly. 'It wouldn't have been easy, getting a dead body down there.'

There were no traces of any tyre marks on the lawn. If Verbena's killer had murdered her elsewhere, he must have parked near the house and carried her body across the grass to the water's edge. A strong man could have done it. She couldn't have weighed much. But a dead weight is a dead weight. There was nothing to Amanda Waft, but it still took the efforts of four of us to get her up the stairs, although it was mostly Digby and I who did the carrying. Ricky was right, it wouldn't have been easy.

I went home and crawled into bed early, and although thoughts of Verbena kept me awake for what seemed hours, it wasn't yet midnight when the ringing phone startled me into wakefulness and I realised I must have drifted off to sleep. I dragged myself into the living room, swearing I would commit murder if it was Sandy Thomas from the *Dartmoor Gazette*.

It was Dean. 'Look, I know it's late,' he said, 'but I've got a bit of good news, and after a day like today, I thought you'd want to hear it.'

'Yes, please.' I yawned and rubbed my face, trying to wake myself up.

'Forensics have found traces in Bryant's car and at the crime scene of our two friends—'

'The men in the pub?' I asked, suddenly alert.

'Yes. It places them at the scene of the murder. There's evidence on Bryant's body—'

'But do you know who they are?'

'Oh, yes. After you and the girl behind the bar had identified the photographs we showed you, we knew who we were looking for. They're well known to the force in London as members of a criminal gang. It's likely they recruited Bryant to help smuggle stuff into the prison – phones, drugs, weapons, that kind of thing.'

'Have they caught them?'

'Not yet, but it's only a matter of time.'

'So Bryant's murder isn't linked to Jessie and Verbena?'

'The only connection is the note about Cutty Dyer, which was almost certainly a sick joke, intended to have us running around chasing our tails, thinking that we were after a serial killer. It was also probably a warning to other gang members – this is what happens to you if you step out of line.'

'Does this mean Luke is in the clear now?'

He hesitated a moment. 'Where Bryant's murder is concerned, possibly, yes.'

'But?'

'Well . . . there's been a big spread of the illegal drugs trade out of big cities and into rural areas. I expect you've heard of it – county lines, they call it. Scotland Yard are very excited about establishing this link between Dave Bryant and these criminal gangs in London, because they think a lot of this drug trafficking is being masterminded from prison. Basically, they're reluctant to close the book on Luke Rowlands while there's any possibility he might have been involved.'

'Involved in drugs?'

'He's only recently out of prison. And there must have been some reason why he and Bryant quarrelled.'

'But he told me—' I began.

'I know what he told you, that he complained about Bryant and was beaten up as a result, but you've got to face the fact, Juno, that Rowlands may not have been telling you the truth.'

I bit my tongue. I believed Luke, but I couldn't come up with a reason, just instinct.

'And there's too much coincidence for my liking,' Dean went on. 'There's a connection between Rowlands and each of these killings. He knew Bryant, he found Jessie—'

'We found her together,' I objected.

'True, but then Verbena's body, dumped in the lake at Druid Lodge, the place where he's been working . . .'

'Perhaps someone is trying to frame him.'

Dean was silent a moment, as if he was giving this idea consideration. 'What we have established,' he continued, 'is that Verbena left the ball at around 2 a.m. We talked to Ms Swann and Mr Thorncroft . . . and we'll be speaking to Verbena's ex-husband today.'

'The millionaire has-been rock star?'

'That's the one.'

'That reminds me, when I danced with Daniel Thorncroft at the ball, he said that Verbena was supposed to have been accompanied by some boyfriend who had let her down at the last minute.'

'He mentioned that to us too. He also admitted that he wasn't sure this bloke of Verbena's existed. He didn't think she had a boyfriend at present, and perhaps she invented him to save face. Anyway, he couldn't give us any details about him, and neither could Ms Swann. The three of them were supposed to be spending the night at Meredith's flat to save driving home, but she had a headache – so they took her home first, then Thorncroft dropped Verbena off on his way back to his own place . . .'

I had a sudden peculiar vision of Daniel Thorncroft wandering around that derelict farmhouse in the early hours of the morning, sleeping on a sofa with Lottie while his white tie and tails hung on a hanger from a scaffolding pole.

'He was probably the last person to see her alive,' Dean went on. 'Verbena's place was empty. Both her daughters were at a sleepover with friends. He said he offered to see her safely inside, but she didn't want him to, so he just waited till he saw lights come on in the place and then drove away. He went back to Ms Swann's place, apparently, to check on how she was. He reckons it was three o'clock by then. But as all the lights in her flat were out, he assumed she was in bed and he didn't want to disturb her, so he went home again.'

'So Meredith can't confirm any of what he says?'

'No.'

'And how was Verbena killed?' I asked. 'Did she die at the lake?'

But Dean obviously decided he'd already told me more than he should. There was a moment of silence while the official police shutter came down on our conversation. I heard it click into place. 'Get some sleep, Juno,' he recommended. 'You must be tired.'

CHAPTER TWENTY-ONE

I took the Tribe for a walk across open fields next morning. I didn't want to be in the woods or by the river. I didn't want to be reminded of Verbena lying in the water, her dead eyes staring at the trees. The river was too melancholy, the trees too sad. And although it didn't usually bother me, I didn't want to feel closed in,

At least the rain had stopped. The wide sky was washed, insipid and pale, and a bleary-eyed sun shone weakly through rags of wrung-out cloud. I launched balls for the dogs to chase and they raced around, tumbling over one another in an effort to grab them first. Schnitzel wasn't wearing his raincoat, but EB sported a new jacket with *Emotional Support Dog* embroidered on it. His mum, Val, had begun taking him into Oakdene and other local care homes to be petted and made a fuss of by elderly residents. It cheered them up apparently. I could understand that. As he skipped joyously around my feet, I stooped and hugged him hard, drawing comfort from his warm, furry body until he wriggled away to play, and when Nookie the huskie came close to me, I grabbed her and buried my face in her mane. There's something in the innocence of animals that consoles and reassures, gives solace in a way no human contact can. I thought suddenly of Daniel Thorncroft and little Lottie and understood why he couldn't bear to be parted from her.

I hadn't felt like breakfast when I dragged myself from my bed earlier, still tired after unsatisfying hours of shallow dozing. But by the time I'd walked the dogs and returned them to their homes I realised that if I was going to get through the rest of the day I needed a decent coffee, and not the cheap stuff we keep in the kitchen of *Old Nick's*. I took myself into *Sunflowers*, where I stood at the counter, bringing Kate up to date on all the latest before she gave me a coffee and told me to sit down. She wanted to fix me a veggie breakfast, but I couldn't face it.

There was only one other customer in the cafe. Daniel Thorncroft was white-faced and hollow-eyed, his dark hair tangled. His laptop was open on the table in front of him, but he was staring vacantly, his specs abandoned on the table. At a guess, I'd say he hadn't slept too well either.

'May I join you?' I asked, putting my coffee down as Lottie began wagging her tail and nuzzling her head against my knee.

He looked up, his eyes haunted. Then he saw it was me and his taut features relaxed. 'Oh, Juno, please, sit down!'

It was the first time he had called me by my name without all that *Miss Browne with an 'e'* nonsense.

'This is a bloody awful business,' he sighed, rubbing his face, 'about Verbena.'

'It's terrible,' I agreed, taking a seat while trying to settle Lottie who, blissfully ignorant of any talk of murder, was determined to give me the greeting she felt I deserved.

'I keep wondering if her killer was waiting for her inside her house, in the dark,' he went on. 'If only I'd gone in with her perhaps she might still be alive.' He shook his head in sorrow. 'She wanted me to.'

'She wanted you to?' I repeated. This was not what Dean had told me.

'She wanted me to go in for a nightcap.' He gave a rueful smile. 'I didn't think it was a good idea.'

'No,' I agreed.

'I haven't mentioned it to Meredith.'

Nor the police, it seemed. 'How is Meredith?' I asked.

'She's shattered, obviously. Poor girl, she suffers from these annihilating migraines – they really lay her out. She had one coming on during the ball the other night, which was why we took her home. Verbena and I wanted to stay with her, but she said there was nothing we could do. When she gets these blinders, she's best left lying in a darkened room, usually for a good twenty-four hours. And then with the shock of what happened to Verbena and the police turning up asking questions, well . . .' he shrugged helplessly, 'she's really in a bad way. She's not opening the gallery for a day or two. I want her to go to the doctor, but she says drugs don't help.'

He looked up as Kate, with an air of great determination, deposited a plate of buttered toast and a pot of honey in front of me. 'Eat!' she commanded simply and walked away.

I offered the plate to Mr Thorncroft but he waved it away with a grimace. 'No, thanks. Verbena said that you used to work for her,' he added, watching me drizzle honey onto my toast.

'Until she sacked me.' I licked a sticky finger. 'She offered me my job back later, but I declined. Ever since, relations between us have been . . .' I paused, searching for the right word '. . . strained.'

He smiled. 'I gathered you weren't close.'

'Er . . . no.' I took a sip of coffee. 'I still don't know why anyone would want to kill her, though.' She was a sad soul, really, beautiful but unhappily married to her rock-star husband, unhappily divorced when he dumped her for a newer model, and no one seemed to like her much. She told me once even her own children didn't like her. She might have found a soulmate in Meredith, but frankly I doubted if even a business relationship between them would have lasted long. I suspected they were too much alike.

I finished my coffee and pushed the toast away from me, uneaten. I had clients to get to. I said goodbye to Lottie, thanked Kate and left my companion lost in thoughtful silence – Mr Thorncroft, the last person to see Verbena Clarke alive.

I was booked to clean the Brownlows' kitchen that morning, which at its best is an Augean-stables kind of experience, but this week I had promised to clean inside the cooker as well. In fact, scraping through the accretion of blackened, crusted crud welded to the floor of the oven was just the activity I needed. It required energy and focus, and for just a short while, stopped me thinking about Verbena. But my gloom returned as soon as I called in at the shop, to find a moping Sophie and no Pat.

'She was supposed to take over from me an hour ago,' Sophie complained. 'I'm meant to be somewhere else. I don't mind,' she added hastily, holding up defensive palms, 'but I'm worried about her. I tried phoning Honeysuckle Farm, but no one answered.'

I cursed silently. It was to make sure Pat and Luke had survived their interviews with the police yesterday that I had called in myself. 'Right, I'm going to go up there, see if they're OK.' I told Sophie to ring Elizabeth and ask if she could cover for the afternoon. 'If she can't, just close up,' I said. 'Stick a note on the door, regretting any inconvenience.'

I drove up the hill and turned off along the rutted

track that led to Honeysuckle Farm Animal Sanctuary. As White Van bumped over the potholes, I wondered how many visitors, eager to see and perhaps give a home to a needy animal, had given up the idea and turned back, unwilling to risk their vehicle's suspension. The farm came into sight at last, the brightly painted sign on the gate doing little to dispel the general air of desperate financial need shouting from tumbledown outbuildings and sagging fences. Once through the gate, the view opened up revealing animal enclosures that were clean, secure and well cared for, just like the animals themselves. Unfortunately, not all the visitors got that far.

I parked in the cobbled yard and looked about. I could see the white shapes of portly geese moving about in an orchard, hear their honking cries. A few sheep grazed in a paddock nearby, together with a solitary llama, and two donkeys watched me over a wire fence. But there was no sign of any humans anywhere. As I knocked on the door of the ugly concrete bungalow that had replaced the original farmhouse, I heard dogs barking somewhere. There was no reply, so I walked around the side of the building, passing hutches and low, wire-fenced runs housing an assortment of rabbits and guinea pigs, and a pair of ducks floating contentedly in an old tin bath.

Then a dog appeared. Samdog had been brought in as a rescue in need of a new home, but no one looking for a dog ever wanted him. He always lost out to more appealing-looking canines, to dogs who were handsome or fluffy and cuddly. He was a very plain, very ordinary brown Staffordshire bull terrier and had been at Honeysuckle Farm for years. And despite having the heart of a lion and a soul full of love, was always likely to remain there. When he saw me, he ran towards me, chortling, and I crouched down so we could have a properly rapturous greeting. Pat came around the corner in her overalls and wellington boots, broom and bucket in hand. At the sight of me she dropped the bucket, a hand to her open mouth. 'Oh, I'm sorry, Juno. I forgot all about the shop!'

'Oh, bugger the shop!' I told her, reaching out to give her a hug. 'Are you all right?'

'No, no, we're not!' She put down the bucket and broom, her head moving from side to side in agitation. 'Let's go inside.'

I followed her through the back door into the farmhouse where she scuffed off her wellies and slipped her feet into a pair of old shoes. She shut the door on Samdog's snout, making him stay outside.

'What's the matter?' I asked, but she just shook her head as if she couldn't speak and went to fill the kettle. The kitchen was warm and smelt of an odd mixture of shepherd's pie and wood shavings. A small creature scuffled in a cardboard box on the sideboard and from the next room some kind of caged bird shrieked and whistled.

'It's Luke,' she said, turning to me at last.

'He hasn't been arrested?'

'No, no. Sit down,' she insisted, shifting a plastic

bucket of bird feed from one chair and a pile of newspapers from another, displacing the elderly cat that had been dozing on the top. 'It's worse than that.'

'What?' I breathed. 'Tell me.'

'The police had him in for questioning again yesterday,' she said. 'And me. I was only there an hour or so. That Cruella woman asked me a lot of damn fool questions,' she went on indignantly, 'mostly about that painting. Could I describe the man who delivered it? Were there any witnesses to him bringing it in? Well, there was, as it happened. I was serving a customer . . .'

I nodded. 'I remember you telling me that.'

'It was old Peggy Carter. She bought one o' my knitted toys for her grandson's birthday, a duck it was . . . And then,' she went on, and I could see tears welling up in her pale blue eyes, 'she was asking me about Jessie Mole. When was the last time I talked with her, she wanted to know. Well, I'm not stupid, she must 'ave known I'd quarrelled with her, or she wouldn't have asked, would she?' She fished in the pocket of her cardigan, drew out a crumpled tissue and blew her nose. 'So I told her about it – Jessie telling tales about Luke – "and I smacked her," I said, "and I'd 'ave smacked her a bloody sight harder if I could, and you can make what you want out of that!"' She sniffed, stuffing the tissue back in her pocket. 'She did that nasty thing she does with her mouth – you know, a sort of smirk – then she wrote it all down and let me go.'

'And Luke?' I asked.

She gave a long, shuddering sigh. 'They kept him for hours, asking him the same questions over and over. How did he know Verbena Clarke? Well, he's never even met her! Could he account for how she was found dead at his place of work? Pale as a ghost he was when he came home.'

'Where is he now?'

She bit her lip and I could see she was on the edge of tears again. 'That's just it, we don't know.'

I tried to take her hand across the table, but she turned away to look out of the window, fishing again for the tissue in her pocket. 'He said he'd rather die than go back to prison,' she told me in a shaking voice. 'And then this morning, he'd gone. He left a note, said he'd gone up on the moor, to be by himself, to think. Oh, Juno.' She turned to look at me again, her face wretched. 'We don't know what to do. We're frightened he's going to do something stupid. He didn't take the truck, but his tent and his rucksack are gone . . . He thinks the police are trying to frame him for killing Bryant and those two women.'

'We must call them.'

'No!' Pat cried in a broken voice. 'They told him he mustn't leave Ashburton. If they find out he's disappeared, it'll make it all the worse for him, don't you see?'

'But he's alone on the moor . . .'

She shook her head, subsiding into sobs.

I took her by the shoulders. 'You don't know where he might have gone?'

'Ken and Sue have taken their cars, gone looking for him. They've gone up all around Haytor, round the quarry – places we know he likes – Hound Tor and Burrator, see if they can find him. We've got to talk to him, bring him home before the police find out he's gone.'

No chance, I thought silently, of finding anyone who didn't want to be found. In two hundred square miles of rugged rock and peatbog, abandoned mines and ruins. It would take an army to find him. He couldn't have got far if he was on foot, but if he'd thumbed a lift or bought a ride on the bus and been dropped off, he could be anywhere in that lonely wilderness. I glanced at my watch. If I started out now, I had a few hours of daylight left.

CHAPTER TWENTY-TWO

Before I left Ashburton, I loaded up with supplies: rolling tobacco, cigarette papers, cider, sweets and doggy treats. I also took some cough medicine and first-aid supplies, just in case.

By late afternoon I was driving from Two Bridges towards Princetown, heading for Combeshead Tor, one of Micky's favourite wintering places. If anyone could find Luke it would be Mick, who had spent his life roaming the wilderness and sleeping rough on the moor. Before I left I'd phoned Pat to check if Ken and Sue had reported back. She said they'd searched an area of moor to the north and east of Ashburton but they'd had no luck.

Late in the afternoon I turned off the Princetown road along a track that led to an abandoned tin mine where only the ruined cottages of workers remained. I left the van in the small car park there, changing into my walking boots, and shouldered my rucksack before I set off. It was an easy track for most of the way, popular with hikers in the summer, but deserted now on a late winter afternoon. Despite the recent rains, the ground was dry underfoot. Parched for so long, the moor had sucked up surface water and would take a lot more before its thirst was quenched; the scattered clumps of spiky moorland grass were still dry, bleached white to the tips.

The path led south towards Nun's Cross Farm and more deserted mine workings at Eylesbarrow, but I turned off the track and climbed the hill. From the top I got a view of the winter sun burnishing the water of Burrator Reservoir to the west. It was a fine sight but I didn't have time to linger, the sun already low, and carried on down the hill, splashing my way through the shallows of Narrator Brook before I climbed again, up towards Cuckoo Rock and Combeshead Tor.

At the foot of the tor stood the ruins of Combeshead farm, just a few tumbled walls of blotched granite now and one square aperture that had once been a window. They were melancholy, haunting, these ruins roundabout, the mines, the farms, the cottages, reminders of people who had worked the moor for centuries and whose way of life was now forgotten.

I carried on upward, picking my way through scattered granite boulders that stood out pale against the darker grass. A deep, raw bark echoed around the tor, and I smiled. Duke was giving me fair warning that he knew of my approach. I saw him then, on a bare rock up ahead of me, his huge shape black against a sky smeared with amber. I called his name and his great head swung towards me. He uttered another deep bark, but he had recognised my voice and it was a round-muzzled bark of welcome. He began to bound down the rocks towards me in long, loping strides, landing on pads as big as a lion's. I braced myself. Before now he'd greeted me by leaping up, his paws on my shoulders, and knocked me over beneath his colossal weight. I decided to crouch down, then I wouldn't have far to fall. He came towards me with his head low, his torn ears swinging, nudging me with his grizzled muzzle and panting hot breath as I circled my arms about his neck. The Hound of the Baskervilles let me enfold him in a hug. 'Hello, old friend,' I whispered into his ear, rubbing the fur around his neck. I slipped a dog treat from my pocket and he snuffled it from my hand. 'Where's Mick, eh?' I asked. 'Let's find him.'

Mick had set up camp in an old potato cave, a cavern hollowed out of the rock many years ago for storing vegetables. The cave had been dug deep into the earth, sloping towards the back, and roofed with a massive slab of granite that felt too low over my head, too heavy. I felt as if I was entering an ancient tomb. But it was here that Mick had unrolled his bed, lit his campfire and set up his tea kettle. I was lucky to catch him so near to civilisation. As winter turned to spring, he would move himself away from the hikers and the holidaymakers, deeper into the wilds. He lounged on his bed on one side like a pasha prepared to give visiting dignitaries an audience. I smelt him before I could see him. I usually tried to stay downwind of Mick, but it wasn't possible on this occasion. He nodded his woolly hat in greeting as I sat cross-legged by the fire.

'Maid,' he acknowledged me. That was quite a speech for Mick.

Duke flopped down by my side, leaning his weight against me and I shook out more dog treats for him.

'How are you, Mick?' I asked, gradually unpacking my rucksack. 'Are you keeping well?'

He didn't answer. Very little of his face was visible between the woolly hat rammed low over his shaggy shelf of eyebrow and the bushy beard that reached to his cheekbones. What skin was visible was raw red and weathered as rock, deeply fissured and pitted. But his eyes were bright and alert, and danced as I handed over the tobacco, sweets, cough medicine and cider. He poured me a tin mug of tea straight from the kettle, scalding hot and black as bog-water – hospitality impossible to refuse without giving offence. He sat in silence while I drank it, waiting to learn what I'd come for, what I wanted in trade. I pulled out a photo Pat had given me, and he took it wordlessly, his meaty red fingers wrapped in ragged mittens, his blackened nails thick as horn.

'Have you seen him?' I asked. 'His name is Luke.'

Mick said nothing, just flicked a glance at my face before looking again at the photograph.

'He's in a bit of trouble with the police,' I went on, and Mick gave a grunt that could have been a chuckle.

'But he's not in as much trouble as he thinks. He needs to know that it's safe for him to come home. If you see him, will you tell him? Tell him Juno said. He trusts me.'

Mick nodded to himself as he studied the picture.

'He was in prison once,' I told him, 'but he's just a boy really.'

There was a movement in Mick's beard, a smile. He'd been in prison himself. He cleared his throat of what sounded like the phlegm of centuries. I guess he hadn't needed to speak in a while. 'I haven't seen 'un,' he growled. He took a swig from the cough medicine.

'His family are worried he'll do something stupid.'

'I'll tell 'un, if I see 'un. First light, I'll go look for 'un.'

'Thanks, Mick.'

'Be getting dimmet out there soon.' He nodded towards the open mouth of the cave. 'Stay here the night, maid, with Duke and me. We'll keep 'ee safe.'

'I can't, Mick. Thanks. I'll be all right.' Beyond the mouth of the cave the sun was still staining the sky red. It was not yet full dark. In any case I had a torch. 'I'm parked up by Whiteworks and the walking's easy enough.'

But Mick was shambling to his feet. 'We'll walk 'ee back to the road,' he insisted.

So we strode back together in the gloom, Duke loping along ahead, Mick happily rolling a thin cigarette from a few wisps of tobacco as he trod by my side. He stopped within sight of the car park and I went on alone. As I reached the car, I turned to give him a wave, but he and

Duke had vanished like ghosts. I could see no sign of man or dog on the path we had just walked.

I got back in the van and turned onto the road that would take me back to Ashburton. The sun was almost gone, but there was still some light in the sky, which was clear save for a few strips of dark cloud above the horizon. I was reluctant to go home. I wanted to find Luke, find him and tell him everything I knew, convince him it was safe to come home. Then I saw a fingerpost pointing to a place not far away, a place that I had seen pencilled in stark greyness in Luke's sketchbook: Foggintor.

You can't see Foggintor from the road. That's because it isn't there any more. The Victorians quarried it away to build Dartmoor prison and Nelson's column, amongst other things, and what is left of it now is a deep quarry that over time has filled to become a lake. I left the van at Yellowstone Farm and followed the track for almost a mile, a straight level path patched with giant slabs – the old granite tramway. Ahead of me the sky was red, throwing the ruins of derelict cottages into dark silhouettes of crumbling walls and chimneys and sightless windows.

I had to leave the track so that I could get into the quarry on its southern side, where an entrance between rocks led down to the lake shore. If I took the wrong path, I could find myself on the edge of a sheer cliff, the water way below.

It was uneven ground, a clamber over grassy hummocks and granite boulders in failing light. By now the sun had gone, but the sky was light enough to show me the steep granite walls of the quarry all around, a sheer curtain of rock, rising to a hundred feet on the other side of the lake. I stopped at the water's edge. The surface was still, the water deep enough to tempt swimmers in good weather. But granite boulders lurked in the shallows and there was always a need to be careful. Luke had been drawn to this place, sketched its stark grandeur. There was a chance he might be here now. I yelled his name. My shout sent a ripple of panic across the surface of the lake, waterbirds rising and flapping, their cries piercing the air. I yelled again, my voice echoing around the rocky walls.

I waited, but there was only stillness and silence and the air getting colder. I yelled again, digging my torch from my rucksack. Then I saw him on the high rim of the cliff, his body darker than the dimming sky, striding towards its edge. I yelled again, flashing the torch and waving my arms above my head. He stopped. He saw me.

'Luke!' I yelled, my voice echoing. 'Come down and talk to me!'

'It's no use, Juno!' he cried, his voice raw and cracked in the cold air. 'I'm not going back to prison.'

'You won't. It will all be all right! I promise you!' I ran along the lake edge towards the foot of the rock on which he stood, the torch beam waving wildly as I ran. I stopped, breathless. 'Please!' I called out to him.

'Come down! Come back home with me. We can talk.'

'It's no use!' he yelled back. I stopped. He was poised very still on the edge of the rock wall, gazing down into the water like someone hypnotised. Then he raised his arms. 'Tell them I'm sorry!'

Fear strangled my voice. It came out in a whisper. 'Luke! Don't!'

He stepped off the edge quietly: no noise, no fuss, no cry, a silent fall, then a sound like a gunshot as his body crashed beneath the water.

He didn't come up again. A police diver retrieved his body as soon as it was light. I had stumbled along the lake shore, waving the torch beam wildly, screaming his name, splashing into the shallows, but I knew he had gone, that he was lost, that there was nothing I could do to save him.

I struggled back over the rocks, staggering along the track, choking back sobs, until at last I reached a point where I could get a signal on my phone and call for help. And then I'd waited for it to arrive while a clear sky darkened above and showed me a spangled vault of stars that on any other night would have set my soul singing, but now seemed pitiless and cruel.

CHAPTER TWENTY-THREE

'I've already given my statement to the police.'

Dean was at my front door. I didn't want to talk to him. I didn't want to talk to police ever again. I would have slammed the door in his face if he hadn't already taken the precaution of wedging his foot in it. 'Juno, we need to talk. Let me in.' I let the door go, leaving him to follow me upstairs if he wanted.

'I'm sorry. I really am,' he said as he climbed the stairs behind me.

I'd spent the night before giving my statement at the police station and most of the next day at Honeysuckle Farm. By then, the police had already given Luke's family the bad news, but I told them about his last moments, and then sat with them in their kitchen, feeling like a pariah while Pat and Sue sobbed uncontrollably and Ken sat grim-faced and silent and refused to speak a word.

'We just didn't realise how vulnerable he was,' Dean went on.

I turned to face him when we got inside. 'You could have let Luke off the hook.' My voice was shaking. 'You could have told him that he was no longer a murder suspect.'

'Well, in the case of Bryant, he wasn't, but—'

'And now he's killed himself.'

Dean just stared at me, as if he was slowly turning over in his mind what he should say. 'Unless . . .' he began at last.

'Unless what?'

'His suicide is an admission of guilt.'

I couldn't help it, I laughed. 'Well, that would be mightily convenient for you, wouldn't it?' I couldn't believe that he could seriously think that. 'You think he killed Jessie and Verbena? Why? What was his motive?'

'Well, that we don't know,' he admitted.

'You've got no evidence . . .'

'The evidence is circumstantial,' he agreed loudly, his voice rising to match the level of mine, 'just a lot of coincidence. We don't like coincidence . . .'

'Yes. I've heard you say it before.'

'And we've also got this.' He reached into the briefcase he carried and pulled out something in a plastic evidence bag. 'I think you should see this.'

'That's Luke's sketchbook,' I said numbly.

'We found it in his rucksack.' Dean slid it from the bag and put it on the table. 'You've seen it before?'

I nodded. 'He showed it to me in the pub.'

He was turning the pages, showing me the sketches I had already seen, including the one of myself. He turned to the last page. 'Have you seen this one?'

I was looking at a drawing of a woman lying on the surface of the water, her skirts spread wide, her hair floating, dead eyes staring upward, like Ophelia.

'Verbena Clarke,' I said, turning away. I didn't want to look at it. 'That's not her face. Luke had never met her . . . and there's no ribbon around her neck.'

'No, you're right, it's not her face,' Dean agreed, 'but you're not looking at it properly. Look again, Juno. Look closely.'

Sighing, I turned back to the picture and studied it again. As I stared it was as if a dead numbness settled inside me. I drew in a breath. Dean was right. It wasn't Verbena's face that Luke had drawn on the dead woman. It was mine.

Verbena Clarke didn't drown, so Dean informed me. She was strangled, but not with the red ribbon. This was tied around her neck afterwards, by her killer.

'The same killer?' Elizabeth asked next morning. 'She was killed by whoever killed Jessie?' We were sitting in the shop, nursing cups of coffee. I had already received the Juno-you-look-dreadful-you-should-be-at-home-in-bed lecture. But I couldn't stay at home. I couldn't sleep. Questions reeling in my brain were driving me to the edge of madness. I'd never been so grateful to get up and walk the Tribe.

'The police think so,' I responded miserably. 'She was killed in her house, apparently. They found signs of a struggle.'

'And they think Luke is their man?' Elizabeth was quiet for a moment, thoughtful. 'The picture of you as Ophelia that he drew,' she asked gently, 'it doesn't disturb you?'

'Of course it disturbs me.' I'd been able to think of little else in the hours since Dean had shown it to me. But I refused to believe that Luke was ever a threat to me or that his drawing meant that he'd killed Verbena.

I could sense before she spoke that Elizabeth didn't agree. 'You don't think, perhaps your friendship with Luke is blinding you to what some people might consider pretty damning evidence?'

'No, I don't.' Luke was distressed, confused after hours of police questioning. He'd taken refuge in the isolation of the moor and in his art. He had drawn from his imagination, from memory, that was all. I was sure of it. Certainly, it was strange he'd drawn my face on the drowned Ophelia, but he had never seen Verbena. 'I can't believe Luke was a murderer.'

'Perhaps you don't want to believe it,' Elizabeth suggested, 'for Pat's sake.'

I let out a sigh and pushed a hand through curls that felt matted. I didn't remember going anywhere near a hairbrush since I'd crawled out of bed that morning, or anywhere near a mirror. God knows what I looked like. 'The whole family is in pieces.' It was bad enough that poor Luke was dead, unthinkable that they should have to face the thought that he was a killer. 'We won't be seeing Pat in here for a while.'

'What about this man, Bryant?' Elizabeth asked.

'The police have arrested some criminals in London for his murder. They don't seem to think there's a connection between his death and the murders of Jessie and Verbena. The only tenuous link is Luke.'

'You said he didn't know Verbena. What about Jessie, did Luke know her?'

'I wouldn't have thought so. He hadn't been staying in Ashburton long. He might have known that she'd been telling tales about his being in prison, if Pat had told him.'

Elizabeth tapped her fingers thoughtfully. 'It's hardly a motive for murder, is it? The fact that he was tried in a court and sent to prison is information in the public domain. It's not something you can keep secret. So, setting the murder of Bryant aside as being unconnected,' she went on, drawing a notepad towards her, 'what have we got?' She picked up a pen. 'I think we need to go right back to the beginning, make a list.'

I smiled in spite of myself. She might have been discussing organising a birthday party or dealing with some minor administrative problem. 'So,' she added, her pen poised, 'where do we begin, with finding Jessie's body?'

'No,' I said, 'with finding the effigy in the river.'

After a great deal of discussion, this is what we wrote:

Who made the effigy and put it into the water?
Who killed Jessie Mole and why?
Who sent me the picture of the drowning Ophelia?
Who cut her throat with a red marker?
Who killed Verbena and why?
Are all these 'who's the same person?

I don't know that it helped much. We could have added another hundred questions, but Elizabeth was determined to keep it simple. She refused to be discouraged. 'I think we should begin with the picture, with finding out who sent it to you. How many antique shops are there in Ashburton?'

I pulled a face. Too many. 'Last count, I think about sixteen.'

'So, it is possible that whoever sent it to you might have bought it locally. You don't sell a picture like that every day. I'm sure if someone had sold it in the last few weeks they would remember. They might even remember who they sold it to.'

'I suppose it would be worth asking around,' I conceded.

'You don't need to lug the thing around, just take a picture of it on your phone, but make sure you include the frame. You could get around all of the antique shops in a couple of hours.' She put down her pen. 'Why not do it now?'

'Now?'

'It would give you something to focus on, my dear.'

Stop me brooding about Luke is what she meant. 'I can't go this afternoon. I'm helping Chloe Berkeley-Smythe with her packing.'

Elizabeth laughed. 'She's off again, is she?'

'Oh, it's only Cyprus!' I mimicked Chloe's fruity tones. 'Then she's transferring to a different boat for a trip around the Croatian islands. She won't be back for weeks.'

'Has she got shares in the cruise line?'

'I wouldn't be surprised. They gave her a medal once for being their most loyal customer for the last ten years. Anyway, I can't let her down, so that's my afternoon taken care of.'

I left Elizabeth in charge of the shop. It was a good idea to ask around the other antique traders. I don't know why I hadn't thought of it before, but it would have to wait until another day. She was right, I needed to focus. But for the moment I took refuge in work. I called on Tom Carter, cleaned his kitchen and picked up his prescriptions, then went around to Maisie, changed her bed, did her washing, walked Jacko and got back to her with her shopping before lunchtime. I couldn't be bothered to go home, grabbed a wrap from the deli in town and then climbed up Stapledon Lane to Chloe's cottage.

She was just completing the demolition of a large schooner of sherry and a prawn sandwich and after insisting on making us both a cup of coffee, let me get started on her packing. The only items Chloe always packs herself are her make-up, her medication and her jewellery.

I have a method. It begins with carting all the empty suitcases downstairs into the hall to pack as they'll be too heavy to lug down once they're full. Chloe usually needs to lie down after she's watched me struggle with this and so I get on by myself. I have a very good idea now of what her 'can't manage without' clothes and shoes are, and so I pack those, including nightclothes and underwear. Then I pack all her new stuff, garments she's bought specially since the last cruise she went on. Then it's simply a question of asking her what else she wants. She doesn't always know, and if she does, she doesn't always describe it very coherently, so there's a lot of holding things up on hangers to get her nod, or not, of approval as she lies on the sofa. This can take hours.

We were halfway through this procedure when the doorbell rang. I offered to answer it as I was in the hall and tiptoed my way carefully around the open suitcases.

I opened the door to Meredith Swann. I don't know which of us was the more taken aback. For a moment we just stared at each other. I thought she looked tired and pale, her dark eyes huge and bruised with shadows. 'How's your head?' I asked.

She seemed surprised that I knew about it. 'Oh . . . better, thanks.'

Again, we hesitated, as if neither of us wanted to be the first to speak Verbena's name.

'Is Mrs Berkeley-Smythe at home?' she asked suddenly, and the tension was broken.

I stood back to let her in. 'Watch your step. It's a bit of an obstacle course in here, I'm afraid.'

'My goodness!' Meredith whispered. 'What a lot of luggage!'

'This is just for a short trip,' I murmured. 'You should see it when she's going around the world.'

I led her into the sitting room where Chloe was reclining. 'I'm sorry to interrupt,' Meredith said pleasantly, 'I can see you're busy.'

'I'm off the day after tomorrow,' Chloe told her. 'I'm exhausted with all this horrible murder,' she sighed, as if it were happening to her personally. 'I can't wait to get away. Anyway, nice to see you, my dear, what can I do for you?'

'Well, I was bringing you one of these,' she said, handing Chloe a gilt-edged card, 'seeing that you've shown an interest in Anthony's work . . .'

Chloe frowned, puzzled and slightly suspicious. Her polished fingertips hovered near the card nervously as if she thought it might bite her. Meredith pointed to the ceramic otter she had bought in her gallery, which now had pride of place in her inglenook fireplace. 'Anthony is the sculptor.'

'Ah!' she cried, enlightened.

'I'm holding an exhibition of his work soon at the gallery. I've brought you an invitation to the opening.'

'What a shame I'm going away!' Chloe responded in a voice that indicated it wasn't a shame at all. She took the invitation and looked at the date. 'I'm afraid I won't be here.'

Meredith smiled. 'It doesn't matter.'

'It's still on, then, the exhibition?' I thought as Verbena had been helping to organise it, Meredith might have decided to call it off.

'I thought about cancelling it, obviously,' she responded, meeting my gaze, 'but that didn't really seem fair to Anthony and . . .' she shook her head sadly, 'it wouldn't help Verbena.'

'No, of course not,' Chloe agreed briskly. 'Well, I think you're jolly brave – both of you girls,' she added, glancing at me. She knew nothing about Luke's death and neither, I imagined, did Meredith. I hadn't mentioned it to anyone except Elizabeth. The news would get out soon enough without my help.

Chloe then offered Meredith sherry, which she declined, saying she must be on her way and I showed her out.

'I suppose it seems strange,' she admitted to me, hovering at the door, 'going around with these invitations so soon after . . .' She cast me a sudden despairing look. 'I couldn't bear sitting in the gallery waiting for customers to come in. To be honest, I needed something to do.'

'Something to focus on,' I said.

She smiled. 'You understand.' There was a rare moment of empathy between us and she surprised me by giving me a hug.

Oh, I understood exactly.

As it turned out, I didn't need to go around Ashburton's antique shops enquiring if they'd recently sold a print of

Millais' Ophelia. That part of the mystery was solved without any effort from me by a phone call from Vicky Smithson, a fellow antiques dealer based near Exeter. She'd heard about what she called 'the dreadful goings-on in Ashburton', and phoned to ask how I was. She and her husband Tom knew Verbena professionally and were shocked to learn of her murder. I didn't really want to go into detail and Vicky is too polite to ask a lot of probing questions, so after assuring her I was fine, it looked as if our conversation might be at an end, and then she said, 'Has Ian delivered the picture yet?'

'Picture?' I repeated, my antennae suddenly bristling. 'What picture?'

'The Pre-Raphaelite print.'

'A Millais?'

'Yes, *Ophelia*,' she responded cheerfully. 'One of the dealers at our place, Ian, promised to drop it into you next time he was calling in to Ashburton to see a dealer friend of his. That was weeks ago. Don't tell me he's forgotten and it's still riding around in his van!'

'Um . . . no, I did get it,' I told her cautiously. 'I didn't realise it had come from you.'

'Don't you remember? We were at that auction in Exeter before Christmas and you'd bid for that very pretty Victorian print. And when we were packing away, Tom managed to step back on it . . .'

'Oh, yes, he broke the glass!' I remembered. I'd just been thankful he hadn't cut himself.

'He put his great foot right through it,' Vicky

continued, 'and made a huge hole getting it out. The print was completely ruined.'

I'd forgotten all about it. Tom was mortified and promised to send me another picture in exchange. I told him not to worry. It had only been worth a few pounds. I certainly didn't expect him to replace it.

'We couldn't find anything similar,' Vicky explained. 'But we thought you'd like the Millais. Didn't Ian explain it to you?'

'I wasn't in the shop at the time,' I responded. 'Ophelia's arrival has been a bit of a mystery.'

After laughing about how silly it all was, we said our goodbyes. At least there was one thing I could cross off Elizabeth's list.

CHAPTER TWENTY-FOUR

I phoned Inspector Ford first thing, to give him the information about where the picture had come from. I also phoned Pat. She tried bravely to pretend she was bearing up, but her voice was broken. She sounded worn out with weariness and grief. She promised to be back in the shop soon. I told her to take her time.

Unfortunately, finding out where the picture had come from didn't shed any light on any of the other questions on the list. If the killer didn't send it, then the person who marked it with the red marker must have done so spontaneously on seeing it hanging on the shop wall, probably as a tasteless joke. But whoever had made the mark on the painting, Verbena's killer must have seen it, must have known it was there. I couldn't get away from the unpleasant fact that her killer was one of the people who came into the shop that Saturday. I told all this to Sally the Labrador as I walked the Tribe that morning. She plodded along beside me while the younger dogs raced on. She was a very attentive listener, and although she looked incredibly wise, the fur around her dark brown eyes flecked with owlish grey, she could offer no help on the situation.

There was one item Elizabeth and I had deliberately left off the list, probably because we only knew one answer and didn't like it. The question was: who had the opportunity to kill Verbena and to dump her body in the lake? The only answer was Daniel Thorncroft, the man who drove her home alone, the last person to see her alive. Elizabeth didn't like the idea that he might be a killer, and despite the fact I found the man profoundly annoying, neither did I. He didn't seem the violent type.

And if he did kill her, what was his motive? Perhaps he was the one who wanted to go inside for a nightcap and Verbena the one who had refused. This could have led to an argument, a fight, a fatal accident. But if he'd killed her accidentally, why dump her body in the lake, why not just leave her in her house where it might be days before she was found? No, I was sure the killing must have been premeditated and putting her body in the lake was all part of the plan. And if Daniel Thorncroft had killed Verbena, did that mean he had also killed Jessie? Questions raced in my brain like trapped rats hunting for a way out. It was difficult to concentrate on anything.

Chloe's packing took me most of the day to get finished, ready to hand her over to Charles and his limousine on Friday morning.

Ricky rang later, when I was back at the flat, to ask if I could give him and Morris a hand next day. He told me that the police had been searching the field on the far side of the lake. He inherited the field from his aunt along with Druid Lodge, but he has no use for it so he rents it out to a farmer who grazes sheep. The only separation between the field and the water is an old wire fence. It seems that the police found a strange track leading across the field from a gate in the lane to the fence at the water's edge, as if something had been dragged over the grass. They also found tyre marks in the muddy lane by the gate. It seemed the killer must have parked there and dragged Verbena's body across the field, somehow.

They had taken casts of the tyre marks. I rang Dean Collins later, who told me the marks didn't match the tyres on Luke's pickup or any of the other vehicles at Honeysuckle Farm.

I could have told you that, I thought, as I put the phone down on him.

Much as I love her, I was relieved to see the back of Chloe Berkeley-Smythe. She had become increasingly agitated following Verbena's death, convinced that for the last two nights someone had been prowling around her cottage, trying to get in. I think she's been having nightmares.

'Someone rang my doorbell last night at nine o'clock,' she told me indignantly. 'But as you know, I never open my door after dark.'

'Didn't you look out of your window to see who it was?' I asked, as chauffeur Charles and I began manoeuvring her luggage out of her front door.

'Oh, no!' she shuddered. 'Just think! I might find myself staring into the eyes of a killer! I kept my curtains tight shut.'

When the last of her luggage was loaded into the limousine, she turned to give me a farewell hug. 'Now, you will be careful, won't you, Juno, dear? I wouldn't like to come back from my trip and find something dreadful has happened to you.'

I promised I'd take care and stood in the lane waving her goodbye until the limousine was out of sight and I could let out a sigh of relief. Dear Chloe, for whom peril on the sea in the form of storms, sickness, modern-day pirates, collisions with container ships, icebergs, incidents in international waters, predatory con men cruising on the hunt for a rich widow, held no fears at all compared to the terror of staying in Ashburton.

CHAPTER TWENTY-FIVE

'I don't wish to sound callous,' Morris began solemnly as he poured tea, later that afternoon, 'but it is a great relief to me that poor Verbena wasn't actually drowned in our lake. I've barely been able to look at that water since all this happened.'

'You and me both,' agreed Ricky, sucking pensively on his vaping device.

We'd stopped for a break from hunting for costumes for *Teahouse of the August Moon*, a play with a large cast of Japanese villagers. It was taking a while to find costumes to fit them all. 'It's bad enough her body being deliberately put there. I've been thinking about getting the bleeding thing filled in.'

'Oh, you mustn't!' I protested, 'Not after all Luke's hard work. It looks so beautiful now. You can see the original planting.' It was a sad irony: the blossom was a pale mist of pink amongst the bare branches, early primroses and daffodils were in flower. Winter was turning into spring and Luke was not there to see it.

'I don't want it filled in,' Morris added, shaking his head. 'I'd hate that. But I don't want it to be a sad place, either.'

We sat in thoughtful silence for a minute or two. Then Ricky asked, 'So, where are the police now, with their enquiries?'

'God knows!' I answered bitterly. 'They seemed to think Luke fitted the profile of a killer, but so far they haven't found any evidence to link him to Jessie's death or Verbena's. I think they got distracted by the murder of Dave Bryant. Arresting his killers was a major coup, apparently, and will help them break up a prison smuggling ring. But when it comes to Jessie and Verbena, I think they're back to square one, frankly.' Not, I had to admit, that they were talking to me. Other than the little information I had managed to squeeze out of Dean Collins, I was as much in the dark as Ricky and Morris.

I told them about the phone call from Vicky clearing up the mystery of where *Ophelia* had come from – not that it helped much – and also about the questions on Elizabeth's list.

'It's strange that none of us noticed somebody marking that picture.' Ricky puffed out a cloud of vanilla-smelling smoke, obliging Morris and me to cough ostentatiously and wave our arms about. He ignored us and rolled his eyes. 'There were enough of us there.'

'But the shop was very busy,' I added, 'busiest day we've ever had.'

Morris gave an agitated sigh and began polishing his specs on his jumper. 'I can't remember everyone who came in.'

'Well, there was Digby of course,' Ricky mused, 'and Amanda.' He grinned. 'The only crime she committed was quoting all that Shakespeare – and waltzing out with our feather boa, which she still hasn't paid for yet.'

'That young idiot from the *Dartmoor Gazette* came in,' I added, 'trying to pretend he was a customer.'

'And Meredith,' Morris remembered, 'with that man you danced with at the ball.'

'Daniel Thorncroft,' I told him. I hadn't forgotten him either.

Ricky shrugged. 'There were dozens of people in and out. That's the problem with these old shops that have got so many rooms, you can't keep an eye on everyone all of the time. It's a pity you don't have security cameras installed. Some of the other antique shops do.'

I made a face. 'I'd hate that.'

'Then it's just a pity you didn't notice the mark on the picture, my love, before you closed up.'

Yes, I agreed, it was a pity.

After all the trouble and strife it was a relief to enjoy a couple of days when nothing exciting or dreadful happened. I just got on with my Domestic Goddess duties while Sophie manned the shop. There was still no sign of Pat and she was being a real star, covering Pat's shifts on top of her own so that I could catch up. I popped into *Old Nick's* at the end of the day on Wednesday so that I could let her off early. The spring-like weather must have brought out the customers. In the last two days she'd sold an expensive Imari bowl for me and a solid-silver jam spoon, circa 1830, one of the lonely valuable items that I kept locked in my glass cabinet. Another customer had donated several boxes of paperback books they didn't want. I was trying to build up a second-hand book department to fill empty shelves at the back of the shop and good-quality paperbacks were just what I needed, especially if they were free. Sophie had also made sales for Pat and sold two paintings herself, so all in all, we'd had a good couple of days. After she had gone, I closed up and sat for a while, actually counting cash. I could afford to pay one of the bills. *Please God*, I entreated, *can we have another good day tomorrow?*

Of course, I should have gone home then. But I couldn't help myself; I was longing to look through the donated books. They were all quite new and in good condition, as if they'd only been read once. I unpacked them, gave the covers a wipe over and then arranged them on the shelves in alphabetical order of author. I'm a stickler for alphabetical order. I think charity shops that fail to arrange their books in this way make it difficult for customers and don't deserve to sell any. It's probably just the pernickety Capricorn in me.

I heard bell-ringing practice start up in St Andrew's Church. It's one of those things that, like the evening ritual of the circling rooks, makes me feel glad that Ashburton is my home. But the start of bell-ringing, which takes place every Wednesday, signalled that it must be seven o'clock. It was dark outside. In a few weeks the clocks would go forward an hour and it would be light at this time, but for now, night had descended on Shadow Lane.

I took one last satisfying look at my gradually filling bookshelves, was about to turn out the lights, when I realised I'd left my bag in the storeroom. I nipped back, picked it up and flipped off the lights. Something strange happened then. There's a small window high up in the storeroom that overlooks the alley that runs down the side of the shop. During the day it's a convenient nip-through connecting Shadow Lane to Sun Street, but few people use it at night unless they're prepared to risk blundering into wheelie bins in the dark. Just after I had plunged the room into blackness a light outside passed slowly over this window, a white glaring beam that shone across the glass from below. It could only be from someone standing in the alley with a torch. I watched, fascinated, as the beam went back and forth across the glass, and then around the frame, as if someone was searching to find out how the window opened. Unfortunately, from a burglar's point of view, it was nailed shut. The only way in would be to make a noise and break the glass.

The beam of light moved away, leaving the window a dim rectangle barely lighter than the surrounding walls. I slid across the hallway and flicked off the lights in the shop, just leaving the spotlights on in the windows. I was grateful I'd had the presence of mind to lock the shop door after Sophie had gone. As I slipped back into the hallway, barely able to make out the motionless figure of Mavis the shop mannequin in the darkness, there was a sudden rattling of the door that opened into the alley. It was kept bolted. We never came in that way, preferring to use the shop door. I crept up to the door, my heart thumping fast. The rattling came a second time. I took a deep breath and yelled, 'Who is it? Who's out there? What do you want?' There was a moment's silence then I heard footsteps hurrying away up the alley towards Sun Street, a bottle rolling across cobbles kicked by a hastily departing foot. I rammed back the bolts, my fingers fumbling for them in the dark, and rushed out into the alley.

No sign of anyone. I ran up the alleyway, forced to weave my way between the bins. There was a pulse beating in my throat and my heart was racing. But by the time I reached the corner of Sun Street, my would-be intruder had gone. I looked up and down the street, but there were too many little lanes and ginnels leading off it for me to search. Whoever it was had slipped away. I walked slowly back to the shop, my heartbeat gradually returning to normal, bolted the alley door, then nervously checked all around the shop and flat above to make sure no one had slipped inside in my absence. Satisfied that everything was secure, I grabbed my bag and rooted for the keys, preparing to let myself out of the shop door. I crossed the shop in semi-darkness and stopped. A tall figure on the other side of the glass was staring in at the spotlit windows. I let out a shriek.

The figure stepped back, waving his arms at me. It was Daniel Thorncroft.

'Sorry! Sorry!' he was yelling. 'I didn't mean to frighten you!'

'What are you doing here?' I shouted back, furious that he'd startled me.

He pointed to a white carrier bag dangling from his wrist. 'I was just fetching a takeaway for Lottie and me,' he explained, giving a lopsided grin.

I wrenched open the door. 'That wasn't you, was it?' I demanded loudly. 'Messing about in the alley just now with a torch?'

His grin disappeared and he frowned, looking mystified. 'Why would I be doing that?'

'I think someone was trying to break in.'

'Do you want me to go and check?'

I shook my head. 'I've already done that. Whoever it was has gone.'

'You should tell the police,' he said seriously.

Reluctantly I agreed with him, although the last thing I wanted to do was talk to them right now. 'I'll phone them when I get home . . . so, why were you were staring in the windows?' I asked.

'Uh . . . because it's a shop?' he ventured uncertainly.

'Isn't that why you leave shop windows lit at night, because you want people to look in?'

I realised how hostile I had sounded and I should have apologised. But the man was so bloody infuriating. I was still cross with him for scaring me like that.

'I'm sorry I frightened you.' He seemed genuinely apologetic and I nodded an ungracious acceptance. 'Listen,' he went on, his tone more serious, 'I was very sorry to hear about your friend, Luke. In the paper it said that his death was . . .'

'Suicide,' I snapped. 'But in my opinion the police killed him.' I felt my eyes fill with tears and blinked them away rapidly. I didn't want to give way to tears in front of this man.

Daniel Thorncroft studied me gravely, his eyes sympathetic. In the light of the street lamp his thin features looked gaunt, accentuated by heavy shadows. 'You know, Miss B, it's none of my business,' he began carefully, 'but I think the person really responsible for Luke's death is whoever committed these dreadful killings.'

I didn't answer.

'And you know,' he went on, a slight huskiness in his voice, 'it's a tragic thing, but there are some people you just can't save.'

I realised he wasn't only talking about Luke, he was talking about his wife. I couldn't think of anything to say. For a moment we just stared at each other. Then he smiled. 'I'm not happy about you walking home alone, Miss Browne with an "e",' he said lightly, 'may I walk with you?'

I gestured towards White Van parked on the opposite kerb. 'I'm not walking,' I told him. 'This is mine, just here.'

'Ah! Well, goodnight, then, Miss B,' he said, and strode off down the lane, his bag of takeaway goodies hanging from one hand.

It was curry. I could smell it. It literally made my mouth water. I thought, as I unlocked the van and slid into the driver's seat, that I could murder a curry right now.

I resisted the temptation to go to the Indian takeaway and settled for toast and Marmite when I got home. I was too lazy to cook and anyway, there wasn't much in the fridge. You can't do a lot with one onion, a pear and a tomato. I promised myself I would find time to shop for groceries next day. Actually, I had the tomato and the pear for dessert. I didn't fancy the onion.

I lay on the sofa with Bill purring on my stomach, brooding over Daniel Thorncroft and wondering if it could have been him in the alley looking for a way to break in. It couldn't, I decided. For one thing, the intruder hurried away heading for Sun Street, and there was no way he could have made it back to Shadow Lane in the time it took me to lock the shop. Actually, yes, he could, I realised, while I was busy checking the flat upstairs. But why would he? And somehow, I doubted if even Daniel Thorncroft would attempt breaking and entering hampered by a bag full of Indian takeaway.

The phone rang, disturbing my musings. It was Chloe Berkeley-Smythe, ship-to-shore.

'Are you all right?' I couldn't imagine why she was phoning. She'd only been gone a few days.

'Oh, I'm perfectly all right,' she assured me, 'but I've lost my thingy – you know, the thing I keep my photos on.'

'Your tablet?'

'That's it! Well, it's not amongst my luggage, which means it's either been stolen or I've lost it, which makes me wonder if we ever packed it in the first place. I don't suppose you can remember?'

'No, I can't,' I admitted frankly. 'You think it might still be in the cottage?'

'Juno, my dear, would you mind having a look for me?'

'I'll take a look in the morning.'

'Oh, you are an angel,' she cooed. 'It would set my mind at rest. I'd hate to lose all my photographs, so if you wouldn't mind taking a peek? Don't try and call me, dear. I'll phone again.'

We wished each other goodnight and I put the phone down. But it was bugging me, not being able to remember whether I'd packed the tablet. I decided I wouldn't wait until next day, I'd drive to Stapledon Lane and check it out right now. If it was in the cottage, I might bring it home for safekeeping. Chloe had been burgled before when she was away on a cruise and there was always the possibility it might happen again.

I found the tablet almost as soon as I'd got in through the front door and keyed in the code that switched off the burglar alarm. It was sitting on a table in the hall, still plugged in and fully charged. Everything else seemed to be in order. I was in and out in five minutes.

Of course I switched it on. Back in the flat, accompanied by Bill and a mug of tea, I nosed through hundreds of Chloe's photos. She was really quite a good photographer. I found the photos she had shown me before, of the Ashburton river festival with the procession that included the water sprite and the monstrous figure of Cutty Dyer with Jessie Mole standing in the way.

Jessie featured in quite a few of Chloe's photographs. I picked her out in the crowd watching the procession go by on the day of the Ale-Tasting and Bread-Weighing Ceremony in July. It's an Ashburton tradition that goes back to the Middle Ages. Everyone in the procession dresses in a rough approximation of medieval costume, usually accompanied by strolling musicians playing a rough approximation of medieval music. Chloe had taken a picture of Jessie with the Portreeve, Ashburton's equivalent of a mayor, just the two of them standing together, smiling for the camera.

Bored with the local stuff, I skimmed with my finger, sending the photos whizzing across the screen until I came to her cruise boat pictures. There were hundreds of photos taken on these floating palaces: in port, at sea, with people on deck looking sunburned and sporty in shorts and deck shoes, in the state dining room with buffet tables groaning under dishes of pineapple and lobster and ice sculptures shaped like swans, or at the captain's table with men in dinner jackets and women in long dresses. I began to yawn, and then came across some pictures of Digby Jerkin and Amanda Waft.

Digby and Amanda, who had come to settle in Ashburton after seeing Chloe's charming pictures of the town and surrounding countryside. Digby and Amanda, who had seen the same photographs I had just been looking at: photographs of the town, of the processions, of the carnival, of Jessie Mole.

Way past bedtime I found what I was looking for. I'd been trawling the Internet, researching the careers of Digby Jerkin and Amanda Waft. Most of the information came in the form of reviews of the various shows they had been in, dating back fifty years, and stories about the television series they had starred in. But then I came across a twenty-year-old article from a Bath newspaper. The headline read *Popular Television Actress Arrested in Bath Store.* Digby and Amanda had been appearing in a farce at the Theatre Royal at the time and the article reported that Amanda had been apprehended by a store detective for shoplifting. He was quoted as saying that he had Ms Waft under observation for twenty minutes and had followed her out of the shop. When stopped, she was found to be carrying several items of clothing in her bag, which she had not paid for, and the police had been called. It went on to say that Ms Waft denied shoplifting and put the incident down to forgetfulness and stress. The store did not press charges as the items were returned but Ms Waft was banned from the store in future.

I sat back in my chair and sighed. Poor Amanda! How humiliating for her. It was shortly after this incident, I worked out, that she and Digby had started entertaining on the cruise ships. Perhaps they were trying to get away from the negative publicity, trying to put the embarrassing incident in Bath behind them. I wondered if this little scandal had ended their television careers.

And was it enough? I asked myself. I'd been searching for some connection with Jessie, something in the couple's past that might have led her to blackmail them, to start sending them her poisonous letters, something so incriminating that on recognising Jessie from Chloe's photos, they would actually come to Ashburton so they could get rid of her. The shoplifting incident was certainly the kind of thing she would latch on to – something she would love to have tormented Amanda with – supposing she'd ever found out about it, which she could have done from the local paper if she had been living in Bath at the time. But was Bath the place Jessie had spent those missing years?

As a theory it was all a bit thin, frankly. I admitted as much to Bill as he wandered across the keyboard. I closed the laptop, he sat on the lid and I fondled his ears as I brooded. If someone had been blackmailing me, and years later I found out where that person was living, I'd probably want to run as far away from them as possible, not go and live in the same place. And could I really see either Amanda or Digby as a murderer? Perhaps Digby might kill in order to protect his beloved Amanda. But could he hold Jessie's head under the water until she drowned and afterwards cut her throat? I shuddered at the thought but decided it was not a convincing image. No, it was impossible. And neither he or Amanda could have had anything to do with the murder of Verbena because I was with them when it happened. All I had done was nose around in their past and dig up an unfortunate incident from long ago that was best forgotten. I felt like some snooping paparazzi, like Sandy Thomas from the *Dartmoor Gazette*. I felt mean.

When I could find the time, I decided, I would pop around to their cottage and say hello. After all, they didn't know many people in Ashburton. I'd find out how the house-hunting was going, and maybe I could discover a bit more about what had made them decide to come and live here. Because the idea that they had come on the strength of Chloe's photographs was something that still bothered me, just a bit.

CHAPTER TWENTY-SIX

I didn't get an opportunity to do this for several days. I got stuck in the shop. We were still short-handed with Pat not coming in, Sophie was offered waitressing shifts at a hotel that she couldn't afford to turn down – not if she was going to stay friends with her mum – and Elizabeth wasn't able to help out because she was struck down by an appalling stomach bug that it seemed Olly had brought home from school. I didn't get around to see Maisie until the following Monday.

'They sent a new one from the agency this morning,' she told me ominously as soon as I walked in her cottage door.

'Oh?' I asked, hauling Jacko off by his collar as he tried to hump my leg. Unabashed he trotted off into the kitchen and I heard him loudly gulping water from his bowl. 'What's happened to Maria?' She was the carer usually sent by the agency to help Maisie get bathed and dressed in the mornings, a service paid for by Our Janet up north.

Maisie sniffed in disgust. 'God knows!'

'Well, was she OK, this carer?' I asked, suspecting I already knew the answer.

'She was all right,' she conceded grudgingly. 'She was only a young thing. But she had that skinny hair, d'you know what I mean? A lot of the young girls have got it.'

'They straighten it with tongs.' I laughed. They'd have a job on straightening mine.

'I said to her,' Maisie went on, '"What d'you want to do that for? When I was a girl, no one wanted hair straight as pump-water."'

'Things have changed a bit since then, Maisie.'

She rolled her eyes. 'I said to her, "What d'you want to paint them big black eyebrows on for? They look ridiculous!"'

'It's the fashion.'

'You don't do it.'

'No, I don't.'

'Well, there you are then!' she responded, as if this settled the matter. 'It's not natural, is it?' she asked, shaking her apricot perm, 'I told her, "No one with hair as yellow as yours is going to have great blocky black eyebrows like that."'

'Um . . . you actually said that to her?' I asked, trying to sound casual.

'Course! They looked like caterpillars. And another thing,' she went on, 'she told me she'd bought this puppy. Doodle, she calls it. I said, "Why d'you call it Doodle?" She said it was a Labradoodle. I said, "What the hell is that?" It's a cross between a Labrador and a poodle, she tells me. She paid three hundred and fifty pounds for it. "Getaway!" I said. "Years ago, we'd have called that a mongrel and you couldn't have given it away."'

'Mm. What was her name, this carer?'

She tutted. 'Ashleigh.'

'Well, I wouldn't worry about it, Maisie, I don't expect Ashleigh will be back.'

She scowled suspiciously. 'Why not?'

'Well, let's just hope Maria's back tomorrow, eh? Now, what can I do for you?'

We put together a shopping list and I went forth, minus the rumbustious Jacko. I had a lot of shopping to get and could manage him better without shopping bags in both hands. I'd take him out later.

It was as well I decided not to take him, as on my way into town I bumped into Daniel Thorncroft with Lottie. Jacko is an aggressive little bully with other dogs and he'd have tried to show Lottie who was boss, straight off. I wouldn't have wanted him pitching into her. She greeted me with her usual rapturous enthusiasm, but Mr Thorncroft seemed not to notice me. He seemed abstracted, miles away. He almost fell over me.

'Ah! I'm glad I've seen you,' he began without preamble, once he'd actually focussed on who I was. 'The other evening, when I nearly frightened you to death in your shop, it was a Wednesday, wasn't it?'

'Hello,' I said pointedly, stooping to pet Lottie. 'Yes, it was Wednesday.'

'You're sure?' he asked, his grey eyes narrowed.

'Yes, I remember the bells.'

He frowned. 'Bells?'

'Bell-ringing practice,' I explained, 'in St Andrew's. It's always on a Wednesday evening.'

'Ah!' He nodded to himself. 'I thought it was . . . Wednesday, I mean.'

And with that he went striding off. I gaped after him. *Was that it?* I asked myself.

'Bye!' I called out. But I got no reply. He'd already disappeared back into whatever parallel universe he'd been living in when I encountered him. He was odd. He'd make a good Doctor Who.

I did Maisie's shopping, walked Jacko, and then walked down to the other end of town to Station Cottages, to collect a prescription for Tom Carter. As I came out of the pharmacy someone hailed me in a jolly fashion from outside Taylor's tea room. It was Digby Jerkin. I crossed over the road to him. I hadn't seen him since the night of the ball and he thanked me for my help with Amanda. It was nothing, I assured him, feeling horribly guilty about the snooping into their lives I'd recently done. Of course, we both shook our heads over what had happened to Verbena.

'Ghastly business altogether,' he said. 'Are the police any nearer to finding her killer, do you think?'

I had to admit I didn't know. 'Is Amanda well?' I ventured.

'Yes, yes! She's just taking a little nap . . . She always

does, after lunch,' he explained, seeing my querying look. 'I usually go for a walk so that I don't disturb her. I was just looking at that building over there,' he said, pointing across the road to a shop. It was an old building, its frontage hung with grey tiles. 'It's rather interesting. Some of the tiles are shaped like hearts and spades, and diamonds . . . and look, yes, there's clubs!'

'It used to be the gaming house,' I explained.

He laughed in surprise. 'Gaming house?'

'Ashburton had quite a reputation for bad behaviour back in the day,' I told him. 'People who couldn't pay their gambling debts would sell off odd bits of land. That's why so many properties here have weirdly shaped gardens.'

'Good Lord!' Digby exclaimed. 'That explains it! The garden of the cottage we're renting looks as if it's had a great bite taken out of it. It's almost chopped in two by a wall.'

I nodded. 'I expect that's it.' The gaming house was long gone, but the way people in Ashburton paid their gambling debts in the past led to disputes over boundaries and access to property even now.

Digby and I nattered on for a little longer. 'I bumped into Meredith before I saw you. Are you coming to the opening of the exhibition at her gallery?' he asked me.

'I haven't been invited.'

He raised his eyebrows in surprise. 'Really? Meredith and that boyfriend of hers popped around with an invitation the other day.'

'They only invite the rich and famous.'

He laughed. 'Well, never mind, my dear, I expect it'll be a bore.'

I couldn't help feeling sorry for him. He was so resolutely cheerful, so adoring of his Amanda, and yet I was sure he had a lot to put up with. Living with her couldn't be easy, and it was possible that her actions long ago had cost them their careers. I told him I thought I might pop into the cottage one day and see them both. He seemed delighted. 'Come today,' he insisted. 'This afternoon, come to tea.'

I promised I would, when I had finished my various jobs. Elizabeth was manning the shop that afternoon and once I'd done all I had to do for Tom Carter I should have an hour before I needed to go around and help her close up.

I didn't get my tea as it turned out, or get to the shop. When I arrived at Digby and Amanda's rented cottage there was an ambulance parked outside, blue lights flashing. I hurried through the open doorway, calling out as I entered the hall. I was confronted by a white and shaken Digby slumped in a chair in the living room while a team of paramedics worked on Amanda who lay prostrate on a chaise longue.

'Digby, whatever's happened?'

He could barely speak. I dropped to my knees by the side of his chair and took his hand.

'Someone tried to kill Amanda,' he managed in a trembling voice.

'Kill her?' I glanced across at the figure lying on the

chaise longue, an oxygen mask over her pale face, her half-closed eyelids fluttering.

'If I hadn't come back when I did . . .' Digby shook his head, thrusting his hands through his thick hair.

'Tell me what happened.'

'Someone must have got in through the back door. I came back here not long after I had left you, and I heard this fearful crash, you see. That's what alerted me. Whoever it was heard me come in and slammed out through the back door. And my poor darling was lying here . . .' his voice began to shake and he pressed his fist to his mouth, biting down on his knuckle '. . . fighting for breath . . .'

I glanced again towards her. The paramedics had fixed her up to some kind of heart monitor.

'She's asthmatic, you see,' he told me pathetically, 'and she has a weak heart.'

I wouldn't like to think what state her liver was in, either. 'I'm sure she'll be all right,' I told him, although she was as pallid as a corpse already. 'Was she able to speak, to tell you anything?'

'Only that she'd woken up with someone pressing a cushion down over her face. Of course, she tried to fight him off but . . . if I hadn't come back when I did . . .'

'And she didn't manage to get a look at him?'

He shook his head. 'Even if she could have got the cushion off her face, she always wears a sleep mask.' He pointed to a black velvet eye mask lying on the carpet.

At that moment heavy footsteps sounded in the hallway, and a uniformed policeman came in followed by the much smaller figure of Detective Sergeant Cruella DeVille. She took in the scene at a glance, although she did a double take when she saw me.

'What are you doing here?' was her first question.

'I was visiting.' I stood up. 'Do you want me to leave?'

The violet eyes considered me for a moment.

'Oh, don't go, Juno!' Digby entreated, grabbing my hand as if he were a little boy.

'You can stay,' Cruella agreed. 'Just sit down and keep quiet.'

I squeezed Digby's hand for a moment, then did as I was told.

'She will be all right, won't she?' he asked the paramedics in an agonised voice.

'She's in shock,' one of them told him gently. 'We're going to take her in to hospital, get her stable and run some checks.'

Digby hurried to Amanda's side while the paramedic went to fetch a wheelchair, and sat clasping her hand, murmuring, 'Oh, my darling,' over and over again.

Cruella turned to me. 'Do you know anything about what's happened here?'

I repeated what Digby had told me.

'And you just happened to be passing?' she demanded with obvious scepticism.

'No, I was planning to drop in. I saw the ambulance and that the cottage door was open. I was concerned . . .'

'You know Mr and Mrs Jerkin then?' She obviously wasn't prepared to indulge Amanda by referring to her by her professional name.

'We shared a table at the ball together.' I could have added that I'd helped Digby to cart a drunken Mandy up the stairs but didn't.

'Mr Jerkin,' Cruella addressed him, 'you didn't see whoever it was who attacked your wife?'

'I heard a crash. Whoever it was must have escaped through the garden.'

'Do you know if anything is missing?'

He shook his head. That was scarcely important to him now.

I stood up and wandered to the window. The garden was as Digby had described it, almost cut in half by a high stone wall that marked out next door's garden plot. There was just a narrow path down the side of it, which presumably led to the rest, but the wall effectively blocked the view of anyone escaping.

'Where do you think you're going?' Cruella demanded as I headed towards the kitchen.

'I thought I'd look in the garden.'

'You stay where you are.' She murmured to her colleague in uniform. 'Get a dog handler sent over. See if we can pick up a trail.' She glanced at the chaise longue and the scene of activity. 'Obviously, Mr Jerkin will wish to accompany his wife to the hospital,' she said to me. 'We can take his statement there later. In the meantime, Juno,' she gave that little tug of her mouth that passes for her smile, 'I'd like you to accompany me to the station.'

* * *

I swear the bitch only did it to wind me up. She sat me down at a table in an interview room saying she wanted to take my statement, and then went off and left me there kicking my heels for fifty-five minutes. Eventually, a police constable came in and took my statement. When she'd written it all down and I'd signed it, I asked if I could go.

'If you don't mind sitting here a little longer, Sergeant DeVille would like to speak to you.' She offered me a cup of tea, which I'm glad I accepted, because it was another forty-five minutes before Cruella eventually strolled into the room. She was holding my statement in her hand and sat down at the table making a great performance of carefully reading every word.

I sat back and folded my arms. 'Was there something you wanted to ask me?'

She favoured me with a long stare before she spoke, a trick she'd learnt from Inspector Ford. 'It's always you, isn't it, Juno?' She gave her little tug of a smile.

I frowned. 'What do you mean?'

'Inspector Ford might think you can do no wrong . . .' she began.

You could have fooled me, I thought. He threatened to arrest me only a little while ago.

'—but I see you rather differently.'

'I bet you do.'

She fixed me with her glacial stare. 'You found the effigy in the Ashburn. You found the body of Jessie Mole. It was you who discovered Verbena Clarke's body, you who found Luke Rowlands on the moor, and this morning when Amanda Waft was nearly murdered, you're there on the scene almost immediately.'

'I told you, I was just—'

'Yes, yes!' She silenced me with a wave of her hand. 'You were just visiting.'

'I was invited. You can ask Digby.'

'Oh, we will.'

I took a very deep breath. 'Exactly what are you trying to say?'

'I'm saying it's a lot of coincidence.'

I could feel my temper rising inside like a steadily ascending skyrocket. I struggled to keep my tone level. Cruella had never liked me and I could sense that she was enjoying herself. 'Well, for a start,' I said, 'it wasn't me who discovered the effigy, it was Hayley.'

'Hayley?' Her dark brows drew together. 'Who's Hayley?'

'She's about four years old. She and her sister were playing in the Ashburn and got frightened when they saw the dummy under the bridge. You can ask her mother,' I added, 'that is, if you can find the feckless young hag.'

'None of this was in your statement,' Cruella objected, 'at the time.'

'I didn't make a formal statement *at the time*,' I responded with heavy emphasis, 'because, at the time, no one seemed to think it was important. Your desk sergeant thought it was such a joke he nearly wet himself. It was only considered of any importance when Jessie's body was found with the same postcard attached.'

'Jessie's body,' Cruella leant forward intently, 'which you found, with your friend Rowlands.'

'She was lying there in plain view,' I protested. 'Anyone could have found the poor woman.'

Again, Cruella smiled. 'But it just happened to be you, just as it was you found Verbena's body.' She studied me reflectively for a moment. 'When did you last see Verbena alive?'

'At the ball,' I retorted. 'You should know, you were there!'

She ignored this. 'And you didn't see her afterwards?'

'No, I was too busy helping Digby Jerkin carry his drunken wife out of the ballroom and home into her bed. And I've got three witnesses to that, not counting Digby himself.'

'And afterwards you returned to Druid Lodge, is that correct?'

'Yes.'

'And you found Ms Clarke's body floating in the lake.'

I sighed. She knew all this. 'Yes.'

'The lake where Luke Rowlands had been working,' she went on. 'How many people do you suppose know of that lake's existence?'

'Hundreds, I should think. Ricky and Morris have thrown an awful lot of garden parties.'

Cruella's little mouth was working, as if she'd suddenly discovered a lump of gristle in something she was eating. She leant forward, intently holding my gaze. 'Who got him the job working on their property?'

She must know the answer or she wouldn't be asking. I leant forward too. 'I did. Now, do you want to tell me what the hell you're getting at?'

'Funny, isn't it, that you could find Luke Rowlands up on the moor when no one else – not even his own family – knew where to look.'

'The clue was in his sketchbook.'

'Ah yes,' she smiled. 'The sketchbook.' She leant back, looking smug. 'Containing his drawings of you. There's one common factor in all of this, Juno. It's you.'

'Aren't you forgetting the murder of Dave Bryant?' I asked, folding my arms.

She shrugged. 'That's a separate investigation.'

'So, you think I killed Verbena?'

'No,' she answered quietly. 'I think Luke Rowlands killed her while you were with your friends at Druid Lodge. I think you told him to do it, and how, and where to dump her body.'

I gave a laugh of contempt that sounded perilously like a snort. 'And do I have a motive for all this?'

'She sacked you last year. She accused you of theft.'

'And afterwards she was forced to admit she'd been wrong, to offer me my job back. It's hardly a motive for murder.'

'Oh, you'd be surprised.'

'Yes, I would,' I admitted frankly. 'And why would Luke Rowlands agree to kill her?'

'He was already a killer,' she answered, holding my gaze, 'and he was fixated on you, as evidenced by his drawings of you in his sketchbook. I reckon he would have done anything you asked him to.'

I have to admit, that made me pause for a moment. 'What about Jessie?' I asked. 'Did I tell Luke to kill her too?'

'Did you?' she asked softly.

I laughed, shaking my head in disbelief. I'd had enough of this farce. 'Right, you've had your fun,' I said, kicking back my chair and standing up. 'Can I go now?'

She hunched a shoulder in the tiniest of shrugs. 'You've been free to leave at any time, you know that.'

'Fine!' I headed for the door.

'Unless there's anything else you'd like to tell me, Juno,' she added smoothly.

'No, there isn't,' I told her, my teeth gritted as I grabbed the handle and wrenched the door open. 'And it's Miss Browne to you,' I flung at her as I departed, 'with an "e"!'

I stomped out into the corridor just in time to see Dean Collins walking towards me. Before I could open my mouth to tell him what I thought about his superior officer, he opened the door to another interview room and stood back to show someone else inside. It was Daniel Thorncroft, looking pale and troubled. He glanced in my direction but he didn't have time to speak. Inspector Ford followed him into the room and quickly shut the door.

CHAPTER TWENTY-SEVEN

Possibly Dean Collins could tell that Godmother wasn't happy. I had bent and possibly burnt his ear with what I thought of Detective Sergeant DeVille. It was a wonder the phone didn't burst into flames. He was quick to distance himself. She had been pursuing her own line of enquiry, he told me.

'Well, she was out of order,' I told him frankly. 'I hope Inspector Ford is going to rein her in.'

He muttered something inaudible. I decided not to pursue it. I had more important questions to ask. 'What was Daniel Thorncroft doing at the station?'

'He came in voluntarily.'

'To assist you with your enquiries?' I asked acidly.

'To volunteer a sample of his DNA.'

'Shit!' I was shocked. 'Is he really a suspect?' Somehow, I still didn't like that idea.

Dean sighed heavily. 'We've got no evidence against

him and no motive, but he's the only person of interest who had opportunity.'

'What about Verbena's ex?'

'The has-been rock singer?' Dean gave a grunt of laughter. 'He might have a sound motive for bumping Verbena off, but he also has a splendid alibi – performing a concert in front of thousands of adoring fans.'

'Blimey! I wonder what the average age was.'

Dean laughed again. 'There might have been a few Zimmer frames amongst the crowd.'

'He could have put out a contract on her.'

This frivolous suggestion was actually given a moment's consideration.

'D'you know, Juno,' Dean said slowly, 'Verbena's murder is almost like the work of a hitman. I mean, there were signs of a struggle at her place – a table knocked over, a few things scattered on the floor – but no forensic evidence. No fibres from clothing, not a hair, things you might expect to find after a fight.'

'And nothing on Verbena's body, I suppose?'

'It had been in the water too long,' he responded gloomily. 'There were just a few blades of grass stuck in her skirts, which must have happened when she was dragged across that field.'

'Have you worked out on what yet?' I asked.

'No, trouble was that the marks across the field disappeared from the grass as soon as the sun dried off the dew. We think it might have been something like a waterboard, you know, or a surfboard.'

'Not a lot of help,' I said. We were only a half-hour drive from the coast. 'An awful lot of people round here would own one of those.'

'True,' he sighed.

'But I don't,' I added firmly.

'How is Amanda now?' Morris asked, blinking at me anxiously. 'Do we know?'

I was kneeling on the hall floor, surrounded by hampers full of costumes returned from *School for Scandal*, trying to match up shoes that apparently had been tossed in from a great height, with no attempt to keep the pairs together. This was not the way they had been sent and the theatre company in question would be receiving a complaint. I tried not to be overwhelmed by the smell of old shoe leather and sweaty feet.

'She's OK. I called Digby this morning. She spent last night in hospital but he was going to fetch her home. No real damage done except for nearly being frightened to death.'

'We must go round and see them,' Morris said.

Ricky looked up from the hamper of wigs he was unpacking. 'Do the police think she was a target?'

I sat back on my heels. 'No. They think an opportunist burglar broke in and panicked when he saw her lying on the chaise longue. Perhaps she'd started to wake up.'

I couldn't have sounded convinced. He raised an eyebrow. 'But you don't think so?'

'I don't know.' I rubbed a hand through the tangle of my hair. 'Digby says nothing was taken except for a silver photograph frame.' I smiled. 'The police found it later in the garden, broken. They think the thief just grabbed the first thing he could carry but discarded it as he fled.'

'No fingerprints, I suppose?'

I pulled a face. 'Nothing so useful, I'm afraid. Sadly, the photograph was nowhere to be seen. It probably blew away.'

I passed a matched pair of shoes up to Morris. He put a thick elastic band around them to keep them together and placed them on the stairs. 'Didn't the police dog find anything?' he asked.

I'd got my information from Dean. The dog had followed a scent until he reached the wall at the far end of the garden. The culprit had obviously climbed over the wall into the neighbouring garden, and then over into another, probably then escaping down an adjacent lane. Whoever he was, he must have been fit. The boundaries of several gardens come together in a knot at this point. The handler couldn't haul the dog over all the walls and had to find different ways into the gardens, which meant knocking up each of the householders. By which time the culprit was long gone and the trail had become muddled and confused.

I handed Morris another pair of shoes and he placed them on the next step up. This was part of his system. Different sizes were placed on different steps. Then, when we'd got them all sorted, they would be carried up to the storeroom.

Ricky was inspecting an elaborate wig for damage. He blew on it and white powder came off in a cloud.

'What about your friend, Mr Thorncroft?' he asked.

'He's not my friend,' I objected, and getting information about him had proved a lot more difficult. I'd only managed to prise it out of Dean because I threatened to try to get it directly from Inspector Ford. 'They've no evidence against him. Forensics went over his car but all they found was a hair of Verbena's on the passenger head rest, which they couldn't count as suspicious because Thorncroft had admitted to giving her a lift home. There was nothing on the back seat or in the boot – no hairs or fibres from her clothing, which was what they would have liked to have found – or blood, which they would have liked even better.'

I'd just started telling them all this when the phone rang and Ricky wandered off into the living room to answer it. He came back quickly.

'That was the police station,' he told me. 'The burglar alarm is going off in Chloe Berkeley-Smythe's place, and they say you're listed as the keyholder. They tried the shop and Sophie told them you were here. Can you go down to her cottage? There's a copper waiting there apparently.'

'Hell's teeth!' I grunted, struggling up off my knees. I glanced at my watch. It was only three o'clock. What a time to go burgling. 'I might see you later. With any luck it'll only be a false alarm and I won't be long.'

Unfortunately, my luck was out. I unlocked the front door, letting in the uniformed officer who was waiting on the doorstep, and switched off the flashing alarm. It was a silent alarm linked directly to a monitoring service who would contact the police if an intruder was detected. By the time I arrived it had been going off too long for me to reset it by keying the code in the box in the hall and I had to phone the monitoring company and quote a long string of obscure digits before they agreed to reset it remotely. While all this was going on, the uniformed officer was enjoying himself poking around Chloe's house. He came back to tell me that a window in the kitchen had been forced and the lock broken. He seemed as pleased as Punch.

I walked around the house with him to see if anything had been taken. Chloe always took most of her jewellery away with her in a secure case. What she left behind was locked in a small safe in the spare bedroom. It seemed the intruder hadn't tried to tamper with it. In fact, apart from opening her wardrobes and pulling out a few boxes, he hadn't done much. Most of her clothes were still hanging tidily on hangers. The drawers of her chest and dressing table had been pulled open and the contents rifled, but at least they hadn't been tipped out onto the floor.

Downstairs there was very little sign of a search, but perhaps the intruder had been interrupted. The only signal that the silent alarm would have been triggered was a tiny red light on the box in the hall, which would begin to flash. If the intruder had caught sight of it he wouldn't have hung around. I doubt he would have gone back out through the window. He might have just sneaked out of the front door and closed it behind him.

'Anything missing?' the police constable asked me.

'Not that I can tell,' I admitted, 'but Mrs Berkeley-Smythe will be the only person who'll know for sure.'

'And when does she come home?'

'Not for several weeks.'

He sucked in his breath and shook his head. With that he prepared to leave, to file his report at the station. Was that it? I asked. No forensics? No dusting of the window frame for fingerprints? He pulled the kind of face that tells you you're asking for the impossible. As nothing appeared to have been taken, there was no injury to persons and only minimal damage to property, he doubted if the force would spare the resources. If they did, he warned me with a slow shake of his head, it might take a few days. Did I not know, he asked me reproachfully, how much crime was currently committed in Ashburton? I did have a fair idea but I didn't comment. And of course, he went on, I wouldn't be able to get the lock mended in the meantime. Wouldn't I rather make the place secure? Well, of course I would. As the keyholder, I was responsible. I wouldn't be able to leave the cottage until I was sure it was safe.

As soon as the useless git had gone, I phoned around locksmiths until I found one who promised to come at once. I tidied up while I waited for him to arrive.

I was puzzled by this intruder. There were bits and pieces of silver and fine ornaments around that he hadn't touched. It was as if he was searching for something specific, something he could see at a glance wasn't in view, but which might have been contained in a drawer or cardboard box. Perhaps he was only interested in smartphones, or expensive technical things he could easily sell on. I was glad I'd taken Chloe's tablet to my place.

The locksmith's idea of at once wasn't the same as mine. It was an hour and three-quarters before he turned up, by which time I'd tidied up the bedroom and phoned Ricky and Morris to tell them I wouldn't be coming back today. Getting through to Chloe was a bit more complicated and I'd leave it until later.

When the locksmith had finished, I had to pay him. His charge was extortionate, but I didn't really have a choice. I'd recoup the money later from Chloe but that didn't make me feel happy about having to fork out there and then. On the whole, I decided when I got back home, I would not class this as the best of days. I managed to get through to Chloe later, on board ship, and told her the tale, reassuring her that nothing seemed to have been taken. She promised to arrange an electronic transfer of money into my account as soon as she could. I didn't mention what had happened to Amanda. It would only frighten her and it was a story that could keep until her return.

I'd not long been tucking into a curried vegetable pie, provided by Kate, and a particularly ghastly romantic novel I'd forgotten to return to the library for Maisie, when the phone rang. It was Digby. I enquired after Amanda and he told me all was well.

'She was more upset about losing the photograph than anything else,' he said. 'It was taken on our wedding anniversary a few years ago, on board ship. Dear old Chloe took it, you know.'

'In which case,' I said, 'she might still have it on her tablet and we could get a copy printed.'

'That's exactly what I was thinking,' he chortled. 'I don't suppose there's any possibility of getting in touch . . . ?'

'No need. She left her tablet behind. I've got it here in the flat for safekeeping. Why don't I bring it over and you can look through it together, see if you can find it?'

'If you don't think Chloe would mind?' he asked doubtfully. 'I'd hate to upset the old girl.'

'We'll only be looking through her cruise pictures and I'm sure she'd be glad to help.'

'What about tomorrow evening, then? Come over and have a drink.'

'That would be wonderful,' I lied bravely.

'Right, then, Juno,' Digby said happily. 'It's a date.'

I put the phone down and got back into my pie and book. Outside the wind was getting up, roaring down from the moor and buffeting against the chimney pots. Rain began to spot the windowpanes, to patter on the roof of the conservatory. Inside I was cosy, happily oblivious of what was to come. I didn't know it but my date with Digby and Amanda would not be kept tomorrow. It would not be kept for a very long time.

CHAPTER TWENTY-EIGHT

It must have rained heavily all night long. In the early morning the lanes were thick with mud, every little rut and hollow shining with its own puddle. In the woods the first shoots of wild garlic were thrusting through the dead leaves, turning the floor green, and wild daffodils and the tiny yellow flowers of dog's mercury sparkled in the shadows. The weak morning sunshine made every bough shine with wetness, diamond raindrops dripping from the branches and scattered in the moss. The dogs raced ahead of me, heads down, tails up, sniffing damp bark and toadstools, excited as children in the blustering wind. I breathed in deep. The air was fresh, not cold, the wet wood smelt of spring. And still we'd had no snow, no frost, no winter.

There would be more rain to come, though, judging by the clouds piling up in the west. I walked the Tribe in a brisk circuit through the woods, along the lanes and back into the shelter of town. After I'd taken them all home, I checked in at the shop – Sophie was in charge, still no sign of Pat – and went off to tackle two blisteringly boring hours of ironing for Simon, the accountant.

When I'd steamed his shirts and pressed all his collars and cuffs, I called in on Maisie. Maria, her agency carer, had returned after only one day off sick, which was just as well. After being insulted about her hair, her eyebrows and her dog, I didn't put much faith in Ashleigh reappearing. I sorted Maisie's recycling, hung up her washing, did her shopping, walked Jacko, picked up her prescriptions and took her novel back to the library. I hadn't bothered to finish it. I could stand no more of the insipid blonde heroine or the arrogant black-browed hero into whose arms she was undoubtedly destined to fall. I selected another for her by the same author, as requested. This time, the heroine on the cover was a brunette but the plot looked pretty much the same.

By mid-afternoon I realised I had had no lunch. There was not much going on at the shop, so I strolled along to *Sunflowers* to see if I could bag anything past its sell-by date. I was pleased to see that the cafe was quite busy.

Kate was behind the counter. 'Your friend was here earlier,' she told me, smiling.

I frowned. 'Friend?'

'The tall one . . . um . . . Daniel?'

'Why does everyone keep calling him my friend?' I asked, feeling cross. 'He's not my friend.'

'Oh, sorry!' Kate shrugged. 'I've seen you chatting to him in here a couple of times, so I thought . . .' She tilted her head on one side, making the end of her plait slide down over her shoulder. 'Don't you like him? I think he's nice.' She laughed. 'He's a funny one, though. He's always leaving things behind him.' She picked up a large envelope from beneath the counter. 'Today it was this. He was sitting at his usual table, typing away on his laptop, when suddenly he went rushing off as if he was late for something. He took the laptop but left this behind. He even forgot the dog. The poor little thing had to go scurrying off after him.'

'I'll take it,' I said, stretching out my arm for the envelope.

Kate looked doubtful. 'Are you likely to be seeing him, then?'

I shrugged airily. 'I don't mind driving up that way after the shop's closed.' I realised I'd like an excuse to talk to Mr Thorncroft. We hadn't spoken since I'd seen him at the police station – before that, since the day he stopped me to ask what day it was when we had talked outside *Old Nick's*. Why that was important, I didn't know. Perhaps it wasn't. But I wouldn't mind knowing more about what had taken place between him and the police.

'He'll probably come back here for it,' she objected.

'If he's not at home, I'll post it through his letter box,' I promised, and still a little unsure if she was doing the right thing, she handed me the envelope.

I wasn't sure I was doing the right thing, either. If Daniel Thorncroft had murdered Verbena Clarke, then it wasn't the most sensible thing to be visiting him alone in his isolated farmhouse on Halsanger Common. But someone who is constantly leaving a trail of his belongings behind him doesn't strike me as a man who could commit murder without leaving any evidence, unless his persona of absent-minded professor was all an act. Somehow, I sensed it was horribly real. In any case, I might not get the chance to speak to him. He probably wasn't at home. He was most likely to be at Meredith's place, I thought with a sneer, spooning.

The rain had started again in the afternoon and by the time I'd closed the shop and was driving up the hill towards the common, water was glazing the tarmac and trickling past me in a river down the side of the road. In theory, there should still have been some light in the sky, but the gloom was so deep I had to switch on my headlights to see the way ahead, my windscreen wipers swishing wildly. As I reached the brow of the hill and the common opened up around me, White Van was punched in the side by a giant fistful of wind. Clouds as dark as bruises hung over the hills. Thunder rumbled, lightning split the sky, the clouds glowed with it and for a moment the moor before me pulsed with light. Then all was dark again. In the dimness the farmhouse loomed as a black shape up the track to my right. I slowed down as I approached the gate and peered through the rain.

No smoke came from the chimney. The place seemed to be in darkness. Thunder rumbled again, echoing around the moor. I decided not to risk driving up that muddy track, I could too easily get bogged down and I didn't want to park White Van in the open. I crawled on past the house, out of sight, bounced up over the bumpy grass and tucked the van behind the shelter of a stone barn.

I kicked off my shoes, pulled on my wellies, stuffed keys, phone and torch into my pockets and shrugged on my rainproof jacket, tucking as much hair as I could under the hood. I put the envelope into a deep inside pocket. Then I braced myself and clambered out into the wind and rain.

As I turned towards the farmhouse the wind pummelled me in the face, sprayed rain like shrapnel and blew the hood back off my head. I tried to grab the edge of it, hauling it back up over my hair, keeping a grip on it with wet fingers, the torch clutched in my other hand. It lit the ground as I trudged over soggy turf, squinting against the needles of rain, my boots squelching in puddles, and picked my way carefully amongst a scattering of boulders from a collapsed garden wall. From there the path to the front door was a series of granite stepping stones that shone wet in the light of the torch. I slithered on the surface of one, the toes of my boot getting hitched on the edge of the next one and almost pitching me forward. I dropped the torch. Whose stupid idea was this? I asked myself as I bent to pick it up. As I straightened, thunder growled and lightning flashed, lighting up the sky, turning a nearby twisted thorn tree to a crouching silhouette. It was not safe here out in the open. I ran for the shelter of the front door and banged on it hard. 'Anyone at home?' I yelled.

But there was no answer, no welcoming bark or comforting light, just the shrill whistle of the wind as it sneaked under doors and through cracks in window frames, as it rattled doorknobs, boomed under corrugated iron sheeting and loosened the corner of the tarpaulin over the upstairs window, making it flap like a flag.

Well, I wasn't hanging around. I'd deliver the envelope and head back to the safety of White Van. I pointed the torch towards the place where I thought the letter box should be and discovered that there wasn't one. Cursing, I bent lower with the idea of shoving the thing under the door. There was a space that was certainly wide enough, but the flagstone doorstep was wet. Rain had blown in under the door. I didn't want the envelope and its contents to get ruined. I should have listened to Kate and left the wretched thing at *Sunflowers*. Nothing for it, I'd have to take it back.

I hunched my shoulders against the rain and set out across the grass. I didn't bother with the hood this time; it was clearly not going to stay up. I just lowered my head and met the rain full on, the wind pushing me from behind now, forcing me into a run, blowing my hair in front of me to obscure my vision, strands clinging like seaweed to my wet face. My hands were numb with cold, the pitiless rain golden in the bouncing light of the torch as I ran. Thunder echoed. A blinding light cracked open the blackness of the sky. Sparks flew as lightning struck the twisted thorn tree, splitting it in two. I watched transfixed as a branch crashed to earth, leaving the torn and splintered trunk still standing. The air smelt scorched, pulsated with a strange energy that thrummed in the ground beneath my feet. My hair crackled.

I ran for the shelter of the stone barn, pushing its wide wooden door open enough to slide myself in. For a moment I stood in the darkness, getting my breath. I slid a hand through the dripping ringlets of my hair, pulling strands away that clung to my face. It was pitch-black inside the building and I shone the torch around, hoping to find a light switch. There was an antiquated one near the door frame and I flicked it on. A single bulb hanging from a rafter on an old twisted brown flex cast a dull yellow glow not much brighter than a candle, but it was enough to show me my surroundings, enough to stop me bumping into the elderly tractor that took up most of the space. I put away the torch and checked in my coat to make sure the envelope hadn't fallen from my pocket. It was still there, and still dry, although the flap had become ungummed. In fact, I couldn't remember whether it had been sealed in the first place.

I drew it from my pocket, unable to resist the temptation to peek inside. There was some legal-looking stuff on headed paper, and a postcard. I drew it from the envelope between my thumb and forefinger. On the front was a picture of a Dartmoor pony and the words *From Devon With Love*. A nervous pulse began to beat in my throat. I turned the card over and read the words in stark, black, childish writing: *Everyone knows you murdered your wife*.

This was from Jessie. Whether or not her terrible accusation was true, had this postcard provoked Daniel Thorncroft into killing her? Did he act out of a sense of guilt, or rage? I took a deep breath, steadying myself, my hand against the wall. I felt sick. Either way, I didn't want it to be true.

There was a noise of an engine outside and I flipped off the light, pushing the door closed, leaving just a narrow slit to look through. Headlights shone in the gloom, a car turned in the gate, its driver prepared to risk the muddy track that led up to the farmhouse. His wheels spun as they tried to find traction. The car struggled. It stopped halfway and there was a crash of gears before it shuddered onward. It drew to a halt at the end of the path, the driver's door opened and its driver backed out, carrying something in his arms, something that wriggled. 'It's only rain, Lottie,' I heard him tell her as his dark figure stomped up the path. 'I'll have to put you down now.' He stooped as they reached the front door. 'I've got to find the key.'

He deposited her on the doorstep. I could see her slender, pale form against the dark wood of the door. She turned her head, nose pointing towards the barn as if she could sense my presence. She barked. The tip of her tail began to wag.

I cursed softly. 'Lottie, don't come over here,' I willed her silently. 'Stay where you are.'

'Don't be silly,' her master admonished her, swinging the front door open. He nudged her with his leg. 'Go inside.'

The door shut behind them and I could breathe again. A dim light began to shine through the kitchen window as lanterns were lit inside. Now what? I asked myself.

I slid the postcard back into the envelope. I had only to slip out of the door, around the corner of the barn, get in the van and go. But would the occupant of the farmhouse hear the van start up? What if my wheels stuck in the mud and I couldn't get away?

Suddenly the door opened again and Daniel Thorncroft ran out to his car, his shoulders hunched against the rain, arms crossed over his chest. I stepped back hastily, bumping into something hanging in the dark, something that swung slightly. Lottie had come to the open door of the farmhouse and watched her master as he retrieved something from the boot. But she was still bothered by me, staring at the barn and whining.

'It's probably just a fox,' he called to her. 'Go on, good girl, go inside.' As he slammed the boot shut a flash of lightning showed him the stricken tree. I heard him exclaim and mutter something, but the wind took his voice away. Thunder grumbled, more distant now.

He hurried back to the house and the door slammed a second time. Now was the time to go. Right now. Except when I rooted in my pocket I couldn't find the envelope. I must have let it drop. I crouched, feeling around the floor of the barn, my fingers finding nothing but tiny stones in the earth and stiff stalks of straw. I dug out my torch and shone the beam over the ground, praying that at that moment Daniel Thorncroft wasn't looking out of his window to see the thin beam of light shining through the gap under the barn door. I found it inches from where my fumbling fingers had been searching, grabbed it and stood up, bumping my head a second time against the thing that was hanging from the beam.

I ran the torchlight over it. It was a sledge, Edwardian, just like the one in *Keepsakes* antique shop, perhaps the very one that Ron had told me he'd sold to a man at Christmas, warning him there would be no snow. Some tiny fragment sparkled in the light, just like a snowflake, some tiny wisp of something trapped between two pieces of wood. I teased it out with my fingers and held it up in the light. A scrap of cloth, a filmy fabric that wasn't quite white, wasn't quite silver and wasn't quite blue. I gazed at the scrap of Verbena's dress lying in my palm and my hand began to tremble. I ran the torchlight over the sledge once more, searching for more of it. There was nothing but odd blades of grass clinging to the runners, as if they had been pulled across a field. My trembling hand covered my mouth to stifle the cry that rose to my lips. I knew now how Verbena's body had been dragged to the lake and who had dragged her there.

CHAPTER TWENTY-NINE

I dared not switch on the torch until I had turned the corner of the barn and was out of sight of the farmhouse windows. I fumbled in the dark and rain, feeling my way, inching my way forward, desperate not to slip in mud or trip over stones, keeping one hand on the rough wall of the barn until I came to the corner and changed direction. Then I felt I could flip the torch on without being seen, although I kept it in my left hand, between me and the wall, pointing directly at the ground, lighting the scattered stones and puddles in my path.

I eased around the back of the barn and got some respite from the wind. I could see dear old White Van waiting where I had parked it. As I drew out my keys and pressed unlock it gave a little chirrup of welcome, a sound I sincerely hoped wouldn't carry through the storm to the occupant of the farmhouse.

I slid inside, locking the doors after me, thankful at last

to be out of the storm. I was breathing heavily. I wiped away the rain that ran down into my eyes. There was no time to brood about what I'd just discovered. I mustn't think about anything except getting away. But I couldn't drive like this. My boots were caked, the soles slippery, thick with mud. I eased them off into the footwell of the passenger seat and slipped into my shoes. My jeans were sodden with the run-off from my waterproof jacket and my hair was dripping. All that would have to wait. I had a terror that Daniel Thorncroft would suddenly appear, banging on the windscreen, rattling the doors, trying to get at me. I turned the ignition, praying the van would start, put it in reverse, let off the handbrake and began to back, very slowly over the bumpy turf. I didn't put my lights on. I could see almost nothing as I turned to look out of the rear windscreen except for a narrow strip of pale sky on the distant horizon where the storm was clearing. I was relying on the fact I'd parked straight, and going back for a hundred yards should bring me safely onto the road. I felt my wheels crunch on gravel as it crossed the verge and then the smoothness of tarmac. I hit the lights, slammed into first gear and turned onto the road, just as the farmhouse door opened and I saw the tall figure of Daniel Thorncroft, a dark silhouette against the light behind him, standing in the doorway and watching as the van sped away.

To this day I don't know why I didn't drive straight to the police station or ring Dean Collins and tell him what I'd found. Sometimes instinct holds us back and we never know why. The message from Jessie and the sledge were evidence enough to bring Daniel Thorncroft in for questioning, maybe to arrest him, to get a warrant to search his house and barn. But I didn't. I felt as if I was clutching the handbrake of a juggernaut, and once I released it, sent it rolling down the hill, it would crush someone, just as it had crushed Luke. I had to be sure it wasn't the wrong someone. And despite what I had found in the barn there was still a tiny voice inside me crying that Daniel Thorncroft couldn't be a murderer. Perhaps, I realised, acknowledging the ache I felt inside, I just didn't want him to be. In spite of myself I couldn't help liking him. But Dean had said it: I had liked murderers before.

I brooded on this as I soaked in a hot bath, my sodden clothing stripped off in a heap on the bathroom floor. Daniel Thorncroft must have known that the note accusing him of murdering his wife came from Jessie. Had she taunted him about it? He told me Jessie used to work for his aunt, Selena Harrington. Jessie must have found out about Claire's death from her. And perhaps from his aunt, Daniel had learnt of Jessie's history of writing poison-pen letters. Grief or guilt might have tipped him over the edge, rage at her terrible accusation. Verbena had found out somehow, and was that why he'd murdered her too? Then there was Meredith, who swam every day in the river, alone, vulnerable. I must talk to her. If Daniel suspected she knew anything she could be his next intended victim. I must warn her to be careful.

I hauled myself out of the bath, wrapped my towelling robe around me and headed into the living room to grab the phone. I tried Meredith's number, letting it ring for a long time, whispering repeatedly for her to pick up. Eventually, an answering machine kicked in; Meredith's voice, low and charming, invited me to leave a message. 'Meredith, it's Juno. If you're there, pick up, it's really important . . .' I waited, just in case, but there was no response. I hesitated, wondered if I should say more. What if she was listening to the message and she wasn't alone? What if Daniel Thorncroft had left the farmhouse and was with her in the flat now, listening too? If I said too much, revealed that I knew who'd killed Verbena I could be putting her in more danger. 'Just ring me, please, as soon as you can,' I said and put the receiver down.

It was only then that I saw the red light flashing on my own answering machine. I pressed play and heard Digby's voice, jovially enquiring if I had forgotten our date for that evening. I was supposed to have gone around with Chloe's tablet so that he and Amanda could hunt for their photograph. It could wait for another occasion, he went on politely. They just hoped I was all right.

I must be thick, I suppose. It was only then that I put it together. Someone had tried to kill Amanda, someone who broke in and stole the photograph, possibly the same person who had broken into Chloe's place to steal her tablet. Perhaps I'd been right after all about the killer seeing Jessie in those photos. I had thought the killer might be Digby or Amanda, but what if someone else had been on that cruise, someone who was a victim of her blackmail?

I grabbed the tablet and began hunting through Chloe's photos, my fingers skimming each one, flicking one after another aside until I came to pictures of Amanda and Digby. Chloe had taken several photos of the two of them, smiling happily into the camera. Then there were some group shots: the happy couple in the foreground, other people grouped behind, all smiling, all with glasses raised in their hands. I scrutinised each face in the crowd, but saw no one I knew. I kept on skimming through. Then I felt a jolt of recognition. Someone had taken a picture of Chloe. She was standing on deck, smiling, her face shaded by a large sun hat. In the background, leaning against the ship's railing, was someone I had seen before. I stroked my fingers over the screen to enlarge the picture, to be sure, to focus on the face. I took in a sharp breath. It wasn't the face I had been expecting to find.

Next morning I came to the place early, the mist hanging over the river, the leaves underfoot turning to mulch, every branch and stone slick from last night's rain. I hadn't collected the dogs. They would have to wait. This was the time I knew I'd find the person I was looking for. Here, in this place by the river, where the water ran deep. I had walked along a muddy bridle path to get here. I was a long way from the road.

Swollen by the rain, the river swept down under the tiny bridge, its ancient stones green with moss. Water foamed white between boulders in its path before it fell over a ledge in a curtain, forming a deep pool beneath, and filtered through the branches of a tree the storm had torn down. It lay like a fallen giant across the stream, its stout trunk wedged between rocks, the crooked fingers of its roots still holding the soil torn away in its fall. The purling of the water was the only noise. The dripping trees were silent. A footstep, quiet as a falling leaf, made me turn. A tall, dark figure stood behind me: someone I was willing to bet had never had a migraine in her life.

'Clever, Juno.' Meredith smiled. 'I knew you'd work it out eventually. When I heard your message on the phone last night, I could tell you'd done it at last. I've been waiting for you. I knew you would come.'

'Your favourite spot,' I said. She was wearing her wetsuit, the hood tight around her pale face, as she must have worn it when she'd killed Verbena – no fibres from any clothing, Dean had said, not a hair.

'Why Jessie?' I asked.

'Because of my mother,' she answered simply. 'She was involved in a road accident, years ago, a crash with a motorbike. It wasn't her fault. There were witnesses – they all said that she couldn't have avoided him, she was completely exonerated.' Her usually low voice had risen high, like a child's, and she took in a deep breath to control it, clenching her hands into fists. 'But after the inquest, the letters started. We knew it was Jessie. The police warned her, but she didn't stop. My mother was blameless, but she was tormented by guilt because the stupid bike rider died. After months of Jessie taunting her, she killed herself. And then Jessie disappeared, just slipped quietly away. I was fourteen. I vowed if I ever found her I would kill her.' She took a deep breath, struggling to master her emotions. 'And then, two years ago . . .'

'You went on a cruise,' I said.

She laughed. 'It wasn't my idea. I went to keep a friend company. One evening I found myself next to your Mrs Berkeley-Smythe, subjected to her boring photographs . . .'

'And you recognised Jessie?'

She nodded, a strange half-smile twisting her lips.

'And came to live here,' I went on, 'so that you could kill her.'

'I'd sworn I would.' She laughed. Her eyes, burning like dark furnaces, never left my face. 'I'd have killed that fat old bitch too! I came to her house to do it, that day when you were there packing for her cruise. I'd have killed her if you hadn't been there. I went back the next night, but I couldn't get in.' She smiled again. 'I'll get her one day.'

I thanked God Chloe was safely on the high seas. 'But why? She hasn't even recognised you. She thinks you remind her of a film star.'

'But if she keeps looking at those photographs, one day, she may. The other woman did.'

I frowned. 'You mean Amanda?'

'She came into the gallery. I don't know where dear Digby was, but for once she was sober enough to walk upright on her own. Just as she was leaving, she realised she knew where she'd seen me before. I told her she was mistaken and some customers came in then, wanting my attention, so she had to cut the conversation short.'

'So you broke into her cottage.'

'I knew she'd be there alone, sleeping. Digby had told me she sleeps every day after lunch while he takes a walk.' She bit her lip. 'I nearly got caught, though. I thought I'd better steal something to make it look like a burglary.' She gave a low laugh as if she'd enjoyed it all, got a kick out of flirting with danger. 'The photograph was the first thing that came to hand, ironic it should have been taken on the cruise.'

'So, you'd been on the cruise,' I said, shrugging. 'On its own that doesn't make you a murder suspect.'

'You worked it out.' She smiled. 'I'm just rubbing out the links in the chain, eliminating the risks. Besides, if you want to hide a tree, the best place is in a forest.' She laughed, amused by her own wit.

'A forest of dead bodies,' I said. 'It was you who tried to break into my shop. Were you planning to murder me too?'

She didn't answer. Just smiled. I wanted to keep her talking. I knew what would happen when she thought she'd said enough. 'Didn't Jessie recognise you?'

'She hadn't seen me since I was fourteen.' She laughed. 'It was all so easy! She thought I wanted to be her friend. She would come into the gallery and talk, even tell me about the poisonous little notes she was sending. I encouraged her, persuaded her I wanted to join in. Then she showed me a dummy some children must have made, she found it by the river . . . just a pair of overalls stuffed with plastic.'

'And you made the mask.'

She nodded. 'I told Jessie we could have some fun. She was obsessed with that stupid legend . . .'

'*Cutty Dyer Dun This*.' I smiled back at her, although I felt sick inside. 'I bet the postcards were your idea.'

She nodded. 'I made her practise writing them.'

Poor Jessie, she never knew that one day one of them would be pinned to her own corpse. 'So you got your revenge.'

'Do you know what the sweetest moment was?' she asked softly. 'Telling her why I was killing her.' She sucked in a breath at the memory of it, a frisson of pleasure shuddering through her body. I've faced men who wanted to kill me before, violent characters, far more powerful adversaries than Meredith, but no one had made me as afraid as she did in that moment.

'Of course, I couldn't know that *you* would be the one to find her, but it was so perfect that you did – Ashburton's very own amateur sleuth!' Her laughter was mocking, her smile one of genuine amusement.

'You held Jessie's head under the water,' I accused her, trying to keep my own voice level. 'Didn't you feel any pity for her?'

'She had none for my mother.'

'She must have struggled.'

'I am very strong,' she flashed back at me. I realised that despite her arrogant calm, her assured laughter, inside she was coiled tight as a snake. I resisted the urge to step back.

'What about Dave Bryant?' I asked.

'His death was nothing to do with me.' Her dark eyes blazed with sudden fury. 'How dare they? The lowlifes who murdered him, how dare they steal my idea and use it for their clumsy, ugly slaughter?' Her voice rose high, shrill, once again like a child's. 'It ruined everything!'

Madness, if the word meant anything, was what flamed in her eyes now.

'And Verbena?' I asked.

She smiled again, once more composed. 'Didn't she make the perfect Ophelia? I couldn't bear to cut her pretty white throat, that's why I tied the red ribbon. I got the idea from the painting in your shop . . . Oh, not straight away, of course! I only marked it with that red pen for a joke – that day when we came in and bought the watercolour by your friend Sophie. Not even Daniel saw me do it. I didn't think about killing Verbena until a few days before the ball, when she came around to show me that ridiculous dress she'd had made . . .'

My anger rose like bile. Because of her, because she had murdered Jessie and Verbena, Luke had thrown his life away. I struggled to stay calm, to keep her talking. My voice came out in a savage whisper. 'What had she ever done to you?'

She bit her lip, her answer almost defensive. 'She was trying to take what was mine.'

'Daniel?'

'Not that I want him,' she added petulantly, 'but that's not the point. After the ball I sent the two of them away, pretending I had a migraine. I changed into my wetsuit and drove to her house. I had the sledge ready, in position—'

'—which you stole from Daniel's barn.'

'He didn't even notice it had gone.' Her voice was laden with contempt. 'I knew Verbena would answer when I knocked. I could hear her laughing. She thought I was Daniel. "I knew you'd come back" she was saying when she opened the door.' She looked at me slyly. 'I was right about her, you see.'

'Does Daniel know any of this?' I asked.

'Daniel?' She laughed as if the idea was ridiculous. 'He doesn't even know what day of the week it is!'

Actually, I thought to myself, *I think he does*.

'And you've put the sledge back in his barn.'

'With a few clues for when the police find it,' she added smiling. 'I shall call them myself, you see, to tell them of my terrible suspicions about him. And I've planted Verbena's scarf in his house,' she added proudly. 'It won't be difficult for them to find.'

'You don't love him, then?'

She hesitated. 'I could have done,' she admitted, and for once there was no hint of mocking pride in her voice, 'if he wasn't so pathetic about his beloved Claire . . .'

'You sent him that terrible postcard.'

She shrugged. 'Of course.'

'You're a cruel bitch,' I told her softly.

She scowled. 'She is all he thinks about, apart from that damn dog. Although I think . . .' her words faded, she tipped her head on one side, as if considering something for the first time.

'What?' I asked.

'I think he's a little in love with you,' she answered, eyes widening with wonder. 'Poor Daniel!'

She sprang at me like a cat. I thought I was ready for her, but she took me by surprise, knocking me backwards. I staggered, trying to place my foot flat amongst a knotted network of gnarled roots. My ankle turned. I felt a sharp needle of pain and I fell, hitting the ground hard, the breath punched out of me. She was quick and fierce, on me at once, straddling my body, her hands around my throat.

I bent my knees up behind her, dug in with my feet and thrust upward hard with my hips, dislodging her body. She was tipped forward by her own momentum and rolled away over my shoulder. I turned and scrabbled to my knees, tried to get to my feet but was knifed by the pain in my ankle. My leg wouldn't support me. I tottered like a drunk, and before I could draw myself upright, Meredith charged. We went flying, rolling down the shallow bank together, kicking and scratching. Meredith's hands were in my hair, but my clawing fingers could not reach her face and I could get no purchase on the slick arms of her wetsuit.

We crashed into the river. Cold shock stole my breath. Suddenly I was underwater, seeing the world through a brown-tinted lens as it rushed before my eyes, Meredith's hand hard on top of my head, pushing me down. I reached up and grabbed her wrist, lashing out with my good leg and kicking her in the knee. She staggered, releasing her hold and my head broke the surface. I rose out of the water, gasping, my wet clothes dragging me down. I grabbed a loop of root breaking through the earthen bank and hauled myself up. I managed to stand on the river bed, clinging on. The cold of the rushing water had numbed the pain in my ankle, but I could put no weight on it. I turned to face Meredith, but she had disappeared. I stared down at the water's rippling mirror, trying to see her through constantly shifting fragments of light and shadow. She was down there somewhere, swimming around me. She might pull my legs from under me, or rise up from the depths like Cutty Dyer.

Suddenly she broke the surface, sleek and sinuous as an eel. She came at me, a rock clenched in her hand. I punched her hard, my fist making crushing contact with the delicate bone of her nose. She reeled back, floundering, splashing into the water. But the force of the blow I delivered unbalanced me. I staggered, unable to keep my footing, and was once again lost beneath the swirling brown water. As I broke the surface, gasping, Meredith was waiting and smashed the rock into my head.

In that moment I knew she had done for me. My strength slid from my body like a shadow melting in the sun. It floated away. My legs buckled, my body sinking back, my feet came up in the water and I was floating. Warm blood was trickling through my hair, mingling with the cold water. Only my hold on the tree root remained. Meredith was staring, still clutching the rock. She took a step back away from me towards the middle of the river and raised her arm to come in for the final blow.

A sudden surge beneath my back seemed to lift my body. I couldn't raise my head; it was heavy as stone. There was a roaring in my ears that was not just the rush of my blood. Something groaned, crashed as it came tearing through the water. I saw Meredith turn, the oval of her face drained white, her lips parted in shock. Something huge rolled like a leviathan in the water, brushed past me, its stiff fingers whipping against my face, scraping against the stony river bed as it passed. The tree trunk under the bridge, dislodged by the sudden surge, crashed down over the boulders midstream and swept Meredith away. I heard her scream. Then nothing.

I was drifting. The rush of water had dragged me from my hold on the bank. I was looking at the sky. Bare branches of trees slid by above me and everything was going away, fading. I couldn't think. Cold water was creeping towards the corners of my mouth and strange words filled my heavy head. *There is a willow grows aslant a brook that shows his hoar leaves in the glassy stream . . . There is a willow grows . . . there is a willow . . .* the water was singing to me, over and over, purling quieter and ever quieter in my ear . . . *dragged her from her melodious lay . . . to muddy death . . . There is a willow . . .*

Sudden pain in my chest and agonising drawing in of breath, choking, water running out of my nose, burning, and sour vomit scorching my throat and my mouth. Terrible pain in my head. I coughed, retched, drew in shuddering breath, desperate to heave air into my lungs. Hard ground was beneath me, someone yelling in my ear, someone repeatedly hitting me on my back. It hurt. I wanted them to stop. I coughed, spluttered, breathed. 'Good girl!' a voice close by my ear shouted. 'And again. Once more! Come on!' Someone had hauled me out onto the bank and I lay gasping like a fish. I threw up, water and vomit. 'That's it!' The voice belonged to someone rubbing me on my back, more gently now. I breathed. I breathed. I breathed. 'You're going to be all right,' the voice behind me told me, 'Miss Browne with an "e".'

CHAPTER THIRTY

I very nearly wasn't all right. I was very nearly all wrong. I died on that riverbank. Like Sleeping Beauty I was awakened with a kiss; the kiss of life from Daniel Thorncroft, information I still find hard to process. Giving the kiss of life is not romantic. You have to be prepared to brave snot and vomit. Also, dragging my inanimate body, my wet weight out of the river and up onto the bank was no mean feat. I'm glad I didn't know anything about it at the time. I had a depressed fracture of the skull, they told me later. They'd had to operate to relieve the pressure on my brain. I also had a broken ankle and several cracked ribs.

There's a lot about the next few days I don't remember. I would drift in and out of deep, dark sleep into a softly lit room. It was very quiet. Screens with coloured lights beeped gently, tubes connecting me to drips, and there was a nurse who'd come and look at me and smile. There was always someone in the room with me, sat on a chair by the door. Sometimes it was Dean Collins. I wanted to tell him something, but my head was so heavy, thick with bandages, and around the bandages I could feel no hair, just prickles. My chest hurt and one leg felt much heavier than the other and I couldn't work out why.

Sometimes it wasn't Dean. Once it was Elizabeth, and one time it was Morris, chair drawn up to the bed, staring at me anxiously, holding my hand. And sometimes someone else but I didn't know who. And then it was Dean again. And I was properly awake for the first time.

'The detective's been waiting to ask you some questions,' the nurse told me softly, and I nodded.

My head felt heavy, my mouth was dry, but I got my question in first. 'Meredith?' My voice came out in a rasp, barely more than a whisper.

He shook his head. 'Gone.'

He wanted to know what had happened at the riverbank. I told him, painfully, slowly, what Meredith had told me, that she had killed Jessie and why, and that she had killed Verbena and how. And that was all I could say because the nurse came up with a drink in a big cup with a straw and told him to go away.

I came out of intensive care after a few days and it was only then, as they wheeled my bed through endless, brightly lit corridors, that I realised I wasn't in Ashburton's little hospital, but in the vast sprawling complex of Derriford in Plymouth. I'd been flown there, apparently. Didn't I remember being winched up in the helicopter? the laughing orderly asked me. No, I didn't, I told him, and I'm glad because I don't think I'd have liked it. Then I started to cry and said I wanted to go home. And he told me not to worry, I'd only be in the ward there overnight, that there was a bed waiting for me in Ashburton. I might be in hospital there a few weeks. Weeks? I couldn't stay in hospital weeks, I'd told him. I had a business to run, I had clients to look after, I had dogs to walk – and I started to cry all over again.

They found Meredith half a mile downstream, her drowned body tangled in the tree's gnarled embrace. Despite everything, I couldn't help feeling sorry for her.

It was Inspector Ford who told me, back in Ashburton, the first person to come and see me there. I had to repeat what I had told Dean. He told me other things I didn't know: that they had found a rucksack in Meredith's car with a knife and a note saying *Cutty Dyer Dun This*. So I was to have been Cutty's next victim. 'Meredith Swann chose her own road,' the inspector reminded me when I expressed my sadness. 'No one forced her to come here, to kill Jessie Mole.'

'No,' I admitted, sighing.

He got up to leave. 'You know, Mr Thorncroft had a terrible choice to make down by the river. He could try to rescue Meredith or he could save you.' He smiled and patted my hand. 'I'm glad he made the right decision.'

I had a succession of visitors after that, though they were carefully vetted by the ward sister after the

Dartmoor Gazette had been caught creeping into the ward to try and get my story. Elizabeth came first, complete with clipboard. 'I don't want you to worry about anything,' she told me as she sat by my bed. 'We've been through your diary and we've got it all in hand.' She popped her specs on the end of her nose and consulted her clipboard. 'Sophie is running the shop, with help from Pat and me . . . oh, Pat came back as soon as she heard about you,' she added, before I could ask. 'She's fine. She and Olly are walking the dogs between them, that's before Olly goes to school. Pat is calling in on Maisie, I'm looking after Tom Carter – I know him slightly from church choir,' she added, 'and your lady in Woodland . . . and we decided everyone else could wait until you're back on your feet. Although Morris will take on the ironing if your accountant turns nasty.' She smiled at me over the clipboard. Then her expression changed to one of horror. 'Oh, Juno! Don't cry!'

'I can't help it,' I sobbed helplessly. 'I keep doing it. You're all so good to me.'

'Nonsense!' Elizabeth responded crisply. 'Dry your eyes.'

'Elizabeth,' I gulped, when I'd mopped myself up, 'you know those useful moves you taught Olly when he was being bullied at school? Do you think, when I'm better, you could teach me some?'

'I think it's high time I did,' she agreed, 'especially if you're going to keep on getting yourself into trouble.'

'I probably am,' I admitted dolefully. 'I don't seem able to avoid it.'

Over the next few days everyone came: Kate, Adam and Sophie, Pat, Olly, Morris and Ricky, Dean and Gemma with baby Alice, Digby and Amanda – even Maisie came tottering in on Pat's arm, all dressed up in her black coat and dusty velvet beret, bringing me a bag of Maltesers and an orange. But there was no sign of Daniel Thorncroft, the man who had saved my life. Where was he?

'Well, the bruising on your face has gone down anyway, Princess,' Ricky informed me brightly, 'you're only yellow and green now, not black and blue.'

'Take no notice of him, Juno.' Morris patted my hand. 'You're looking better every day.'

'I look grotesque.' I put my hand up to the bristly scalp that surrounded my surgical dressing. 'They've shaved off half my hair.'

'Nonsense! It's only a little patch.' Ricky dismissed it with a wave of his hand. 'We can arrange the rest to hide it. I'll give you a comb-over. It won't show. Just leave it to me!'

'Thank you,' I said meekly.

'Now then, darlin', we've had a council of war,' he began. 'Haven't we, *Maurice*?'

Morris nodded enthusiastically.

I wasn't sure I liked the sound of that. 'Council of war?'

'All of us – well, Sophie and her mum, Kate and Adam,' he ticked them off on his fingers, 'Pat, Elizabeth and Olly– we got together to decide who's going to look after you when you come out of hospital. Only now that you can pee all right – I had a word with the nurse,' he explained as I gaped at him dumbfounded, 'they'll let you out of here in a day or two . . .'

'But with you being on crutches,' Morris put in, looking very serious, 'they won't let you out unless there's someone to look after you. You're not ready to look after yourself.'

'No. Quite,' Ricky went on. 'So, we had an argument—'

'—because everyone wanted to do it,' Morris added.

'But Elizabeth and Olly's place is no good because they haven't got a downstairs bedroom and you couldn't make it up the stairs to their loo on crutches, same with Sophie's place and anyway, her mum's at work all day and she's running the shop. Kate and Adam have got a bedroom downstairs but—'

'I'm not expecting anyone to look after me,' I protested, trying to headbutt my way through Ricky's unstoppable flow, 'and anyway, Kate and Adam are much too busy.'

'Exactly. Likewise Pat, Ken and Sue looking after all those animals . . . which leaves us!' he finished triumphantly.

'Do I get any say in the matter?' I asked.

'Course not! You're only the invalid.'

'You're coming home with us!' Morris beamed, blinking through his spectacles, as if this were a grand treat. 'We're going to look after you!'

'We're putting you in the guest bedroom downstairs,' Ricky informed me. 'It's en suite,' he added, just in case I'd forgotten.

'That's very sweet of you,' I began, 'but I really don't want to be a—'

'No buts about it!' he said flatly.

'You can't manage on your own, my love, not yet,' Morris said solemnly, 'not after a head injury. You might get dizzy spells. And you'll be on crutches for a while. If you've no one to look after you, the doctors will make you stay here.'

I suppose I had no choice. I thanked them for their kindness and prepared myself to be cossetted into insanity. It's a pity, when they were growing up, that neither Ricky nor Morris had been given a dolly to play with. That sounds ungrateful, and I don't mean to. I was grateful, really.

'You've lost so much weight,' Morris added, shaking his head. 'We'll soon feed you up.'

'That's one of the things I'm afraid of,' I said.

But there was only one thing that was really bugging me: it was over six feet tall, had dark hair, sometimes wore glasses and was often accompanied by a whippet. Mr Daniel Thorncroft, who had dragged me from the river and saved my life, and for whom I had carefully rehearsed a very pretty thank you speech, had so far not put in an appearance.

'He really is the most exasperating man,' I complained

to Elizabeth when she came to see me next. 'I mean, really! He saves my life and then completely ignores me. Not even a "how are you?". . . Not that I care,' I added, just to make that clear. 'I wanted to thank him, that's all.'

Elizabeth shot me one of her shrewd looks. 'Actually, he's in Scotland.'

'Scotland?' I repeated dumbly. 'You mean the damn man's buggered off? What's he doing in Scotland?'

'He's gone back to work. He stayed until he knew you were out of danger and then he went back to his job.'

'Oh.' I felt crushed, suddenly. 'I see.'

She opened her handbag and took out an envelope. 'He asked me to give you this.'

I took it from her. It had *Miss Browne with an 'e'* written in bold, black handwriting.

Elizabeth smiled. 'I'll leave you to read it in peace.' She kissed me on the forehead and left.

I opened the letter with a sinking feeling inside me. There were several pages of it:

My dear Miss B, it began.

I am so sorry I had to leave Ashburton without saying goodbye. The firm I work for have been very generous in allowing me a long period of compassionate leave following the death of my wife, and then more leave to sort out the affairs of my aunt, but a crisis arose and I felt I must answer the call and make an overdue return to work. I am currently managing a re-wilding project up in the Highlands, mostly reforestation, but I'm also involved in a more sensitive experiment in returning wolves to an island where the size of the deer population has become unmanageable. It's not an idea that's popular with everyone, as I am sure you can imagine, and many of the local landowners take a lot of persuading. They have to be convinced of the economic as well as the environmental benefits. I'm likely to be involved with this for several more months. Then I am planning to relocate to Devon to manage new projects there. I hope to make some flying visits to the West Country in the meantime. I think I may have a buyer for my aunt's Torquay property, which would allow me to get repairs started on the farmhouse.

My good friend Elizabeth tells me that you are doing well. She says your recovery may take some weeks, but I hope that by the time you read this you are feeling better.

I was so afraid that I had arrived at that riverbank too late. Meredith had sent me on a wild goose chase that morning, texting me to meet her at Staverton, an attempt, I now realise, to keep me out of the way. By then, of course, I knew about Meredith. I had been out searching for her all the previous night, looking in all her usual haunts. I should explain that shortly before you fled from Moorview Farm in your van, I had discovered a scarf that Verbena had worn on the night of the ball. In fact, Lottie found it. It had been stuffed down the back of her armchair and she pulled it out. Verbena had never been to my house. I knew there was only one person who could have put it there, and I could guess why. I had already discovered the sledge earlier in the day, returned after it had strangely disappeared some time before.

I blame myself entirely for what happened to you, that I had not sufficiently gained your trust. If you had felt you could talk to me about what you had discovered, it might have saved you so much suffering.

Perhaps I should explain more about Meredith. I was dazzled by her at first. She looked so much like my wife, Claire, I suppose I couldn't help but be drawn to her. But the two of them could not have been more different. Claire was a light, loving soul and I began to sense the darkness in Meredith almost at once and realised we had no future together. She would lie all the time, needlessly, about trivial things: where she was, and when. I began to wonder if she was secretly seeing someone else.

That dreadful morning by the river I went looking for her in all her favourite haunts. I was determined to confront her about Verbena, persuade her to come with me to the police. Then I found her car parked by the road and I knew where she would be. Lottie usually stays close by me, but she went racing ahead off down the bridle path. It was she who found you both. Afterwards, when you had started breathing again, I had to leave you. There was no phone signal by the river. I had to run back to the road to get help. I left Lottie on guard. When I got back to you, you were still breathing but unconscious. Lottie had snuggled up next to you. I think she was trying to keep you warm. The rescue services seemed to take so long. I didn't know if I should wait for them or if I should try to carry you to my car, try to get you to hospital sooner. You had a head injury and probably shouldn't be moved, and I didn't know if I'd already done you terrible damage in dragging you onto the bank. And all the time I could see Meredith out in the river. I could see she was dead – at least, to my shame, I hoped she was.

I still talk to my wife, to Claire, tell her things, a fact that enraged Meredith. I cannot pretend that it is easy to forget her, or that I would wish to do so. I told her all about you, told her I had met an extraordinary young woman with red hair, that I wasn't sure that she liked me, but she seemed to like Lottie, and that Lottie adored her. And Claire agreed with me that anyone whom Lottie adored must be worth getting to know. So that's really the reason why I am writing to you, Miss B, to ask if, when I come down to Ashburton again, you think you could put up with my getting to know you better. I hope you feel you can. I very much look forward to seeing you again. Please take care in the meantime.

Yours,

Daniel Thorncroft

I reached the end of the letter and let out a breath. For some reason my eyes had gone blurry and I had to blink. It's typical, I told myself, struggling to master conflicting emotions. The man is infuriating. He saves my life, gets me feeling warm and fluffy towards him, and then buggers off to Scotland, for an unspecified number of months. Bloody Scotland! I mean, I ask you.

CHAPTER THIRTY-ONE

I was determined to make it down to the lake on my crutches and not be wheeled down the sloping lawn in Ricky and Morris's old bath chair, which was how they wanted me to travel.

It was Sunday March 21st – officially the first day of spring – and although there was a stiff breeze, the sun was shining.

A small crowd had gathered at the lake: Sophie, Digby and Amanda, Pat, who'd come with Ken and Sue, Elizabeth and Olly, Adam and Kate, Ricky, Morris and me – and the vicar, who'd come to give the lake a blessing. We stood on the path at the water's edge while he made a speech about how we must not think of the lake as a sad place, but a place where we should come to remember, to celebrate the lives of our friends. To remember Luke, who had worked so hard to recreate its beauty, and Verbena, who had rested here a while.

Amanda read a poem in her beautiful voice, and then the vicar led us in a prayer. The sun was slanting through the trees and shone on the mirror of the water, barely ruffled by the breeze. We each cast a flower on the surface. And then the vicar said that we must not think of death, but of the spring, of new life, and he talked about the green plants already shooting up in the clearings Luke had made. From the corner of my eye I saw Kate smile at Adam as he put his arm around her shoulders, and I realised at last why she was looking so very beautiful just now. She was pregnant. And at that moment, two ducks flew from beyond the trees and landed on the water in a flurry of splashing and quacking and began swimming about happily. 'Wouldn't it be lovely if they stayed,' Morris sighed, 'if they made their home here on the lake.'

'They will if you encourage 'em.' Pat sniffed, putting away her handkerchief. 'I'll bring you some duck pellets.'

We turned and began to trek up the lawn towards the house where an extravagant afternoon tea was waiting in the dining room. I knew, I'd buttered the bread for all the neat little sandwiches and piped cream into the delicate golden meringues that Morris had baked in the oven.

'Can you manage, Juno?' Adam asked. 'Or do you need a piggyback?'

'I'll be fine,' I assured him. 'I'll just take it slowly. You look after your wife,' I added, and he grinned.

The others went on ahead, Morris scuttling to get the kettle on. Digby steered Amanda up the sloping lawn, their progress not much faster than mine. Ricky strolled along at my pace, ready to lend me a hand as I began my long trek back up the lawn. I'm hoping to throw away these wretched crutches soon, before baby Alice's christening next month. Ricky paused to light a cigarette and winked at me. He's given up vaping as a bad job; he's back on the fags.

Olly suddenly dropped back behind the others, turned to me and said loudly, 'Guess what? Lizzie's got a boyfriend.'

'Boyfriend?' I repeated.

Elizabeth turned around, stifling a sigh. 'Olly, you are a wretch!' she told him severely. 'Just because I expressed an interest in fly-fishing . . .'

Fly-fishing? Elizabeth and Tom Carter? Well, well! That could work; I thought about it as I crawled along on my crutches and Elizabeth shooed a gleefully grinning Olly on ahead of her. If I was to be displaced in Tom's affections, I couldn't help feeling slightly jealous.

At the top of the lawn I stopped for a breather.

'You all right, Princess?' Ricky asked, slyly from the corner of his mouth. 'Pity your swain couldn't be here.' He nudged Digby with his elbow. 'There's been letters flying back and forth between here and Scotland,' he told him, 'addressed to "Miss Browne with an 'e'". It's like something out of a bleedin' *Pride and Prejudice*. I keep asking Juno to read 'em out at the breakfast table, but she won't. She's not sporting, that girl!'

I laughed. 'Miss Browne with an "e".' It used to annoy me so much. Now I liked it. Daniel had also sent me pictures on his phone, mostly of Lottie racing about in the heather, but also of some wolf cubs. He'd phoned to say that he had definitely sold his aunt's Torquay flat. He would be flying down to Exeter in a few weeks, for a short visit, to get work started on the farmhouse. He was looking forward to seeing me, he said. And I'm looking forward to seeing him. I think. He suggested that we carry out an experiment, purely in the interests of science, to see if he could kiss me without my throwing up and I agreed that we owed it to science to find out.

'Teatime,' Ricky said, taking my arm. 'Come inside. This wind's a bit chilly.'

But I wanted to linger a moment longer. I could hear the ducks down on the lake. I looked around me at the wide blue sky, the water shining between the budding trees. It was the first long afternoon of the year. It seemed we had escaped the winter after all.

ACKNOWLEDGEMENTS

As always my thanks go to the team at Allison & Busby and my agent, Teresa Chris, to Martin for his unfailing support and to my 'book buddy' Di.

Thanks also to Tim Sandles for his wonderful Legendary Dartmoor website and to Francis Pilkington's book *Ashburton the Dartmoor Town* for information about Cutty Dyer.

Stephanie Austin graduated from Bristol University with a degree in English and Education and has enjoyed a varied career as an artist, astrologer, and trader in antiques and crafts. More respectable professions include teaching and working for Devon Schools Library Service. When not writing, she is involved in local amateur theatre as an actor and director. She lives on the English Riviera in Devon where she attempts to be a competent gardener and cook.

stephanieaustin.co.uk